MARA
TRAINS RANDY

WORKBOOK PRESS LLC
187 E Warm Springs Rd,
Suite B285, Las Vegas, NV 89119, USA

Website: https://workbookpress.com/
Hotline: 1-888-818-4856
Email: admin@workbookpress.com

Ordering Information:
Quantity sales. Special discounts are available on quantity purchases by corporations, associations, and others.
For details, contact the publisher at the address above.

Library of Congress Control Number:

ISBN-13:   978-1-958176-43-6 (Paperback Version)
              978-1-958176-44-3 (Digital Version)

REV. DATE: 22/05/2022

Chapter 1

Breaking in their Doctor

Dr. Meranda Riser was called Randy by her friends, and the N-Sign family picked up on it rather quickly to do the same. Gary, Jerry, and Granda (Shelly) were all on the mend due to her surgical skills.

Pat and Mara, the A twins, had a conference with the Doctor to find out the status of Granda, the latest to have surgery in the family. The patients would return home on Friday of that week.

Next on the agenda was a meeting with their Hospital Administrator Katrina Price. She was young to be placed in such a position, according to others, from whom she had requested a job. However, Mara felt she would do the job, and more important, so did Thunder.

"Hello, Katrina, how is the job going?" asked Mara with a smile once they were seated in a private, unmonitored conference room.

"I would like to inform you about a few changes here and there. We are seeing specialists apply for offices at the clinic. Now have them in ENT, eyes, Ortho, pediatrics, podiatrist, children, and women's issues. They also work at the hospital if they have patients there. The hospital has been quite busy. Drea wanted me to tell you that she put two doctors in charge of patients' everyday medical needs. Two more covers the emergency part of the clinic. The demand and support income is there, so both facilities are well in the black. I received word from the business office a short time ago that Dr. Meranda Riser is leaving us; however, another woman is taking her place. The new woman is a sports and health promoter, and we have heard good things about her. Believe she started yesterday if the last report is in."

"Yes, we have the report. Dr. Riser will be going into private practice. Yes, we are aware of the switch as we asked it to happen. You will have three of our family here until Friday when we bring everyone home. We have to be out of town for a time, and this way, patients get the care necessary until our return," said Mara.

Afterward, the Alpha Twins went to locate lunch for Mara said they had a mission.

Shandra, the Bravo Twins leader, was always the driver if those two were on the move while her twin took a second seat. Charlie Twins, Michelle, and Gretch were to remain at the house. Since they were all four fully trained now, they could do whatever tasks were asked of them and became known as A Quad.

When they reached the restaurant, the A-B Twins and Kennet moved inside. The pairs were identical, and the four were related was the thought of those who saw them together. The boy looked much like Mara. The women moved to a table out of the flow of traffic and quiet to talk.

"I don't want to ask G for aid, so bear with me while I see if this will work for me," said Mara meaning Granda.

"This is Thunder Press, need silence bubble for us once our food comes," directed Mara in a whisper.

They waited for the waitress and spoke of general things until then. They discussed the food, the weather, and the people in the hospital, plus their need for tutors: Gwen, Dan, Eva, Joy, Kennet, James & Peter (Delta Twins), Tracee & Nancee (Echo Twins). Once the orders came, they felt the bubble form. The kids would need testing to see which instructors would teach and what subjects were needed.

"Since some read lips, you all need to listen, and if you don't understand, let me know, and I will try something else," directed Mara in a deadly serious tone, which was unusual for her when with family.

"Use the communicator," suggested Pat.

Mara smiled and nodded her head. She had forgotten they had it though all four of Pat's girls had a communicator, for they found they needed the device, and none of them compromised any of the Thunder group. Kennet was sitting next to Mara though he was watching around them in case of any problems. He also wore a communicator though Mara could open or close channels by directing it. In an emergency, any of them could request a made available track, and the AI would comply.

"When we get home, I will have a meeting with Star. Try to keep the rest occupied. We will be leaving in the morning to take Star home. Her kids are not going with her. While we are here, there will be some folks coming to the table to speak with me. Just let them talk, and I will handle what is required. Randy is going with us tomorrow. She, too, will have a double ID when we depart. There is a possibility that Granda's injury was not an accident. From here on, the Doctor will be traveling with us. Do any of you have any objections or questions?" asked Mara.

"I have one; what took you so long?" asked Pat.

"Other things had priority though now it has to be done. Anyone else?" Mara never played around when answering questions, for that could be the one answer that saved lives.

"Who is going, and who is staying?" Shandra asked for it would be her duty to see that everything got done.

Pat and Mara had a great deal to keep track of, especially with Granda out of commission.

"You five go. Joy will take care of the home. Dan and Gwen have agreed to care for the stock while we are gone, for we discussed it while they were at the hospital to see Granda. Joy will take care of the four new ones, plus Joey though the new ones, will live in my unit. Never will I leave without Kennet. There will be eight going and seven of us coming back. When you four have the time, would you please get Randy on pace with the sword drill? Don't expect her to fight; however, she needs to know how if she is the only one standing. Now we have some folks waiting to speak with me. Enjoy your dessert while I get things started," Mara advised.

The silence bubble dissolved. Mara rose from her seat, and as she moved, a couple of folks moved to their table. Kennet was immediately by his Mom.

"We are advised that you need some employees. The agency sent us to test your group of children. The oldest daughters need to take the exams you have already passed. Do you understand the message? If not, I am speaking to the wrong person," said the man before them.

"You have the right group. Need your resume as well as the ones for the rest of your group. Do you know one another? Do you speak languages other than the one spoken here?"

"I have twelve languages with native fluency. The others have as many though we don't all know the same ones. Now that you have received the message, we will need to back up and start over, for I will not recall the message once I turn around. Thank you for your trust," said the man who left with the message delivered.

"Okay, everyone, sit down. The man has identified us, and a few tutors are about to be hired. The B and C Twins need to take the tests Granda, Pat, and I have already taken. All kids need schooling. They need regular classes plus whatever they have an interest in and the physical training we all have to maintain. Also, everyone will learn to ride properly. These folks will be traveling with us in the coming days. They speak at least twelve languages, so we have interpreters if needed. Since we in the Thunder group speak those languages, there shouldn't be any problems in understanding," advised Mara.

When the tutors made their presence known, I requested that they hold their questions and follow them to the ranch. There were six teachers in the group of applicants, of which only one was male. That meant that both Star's kids and Mara's would have no more than two kids under any one tutor. Mara would also see that one was sent to her Mother's place so that Eva could get her education as well, although the person assigned would have regular hours for Eva, although that tutor would live at the complex. Grace, Mara's Mom, could teach her; however, that would take time from her sewing and designing business; therefore, a tutor would be available. She wanted them caught up with their grade level as soon as possible though they might continue on computers with the instructors to aid with any help needed. If Mara's Mother didn't object, Eva could go with them out of the country and train at the kids' ongoing training.

The tutors selected suites on the second floor of one wing of the complex at the house, where there was a classroom with smaller rooms off it for individual instruction on the first floor. There were exercise areas for days when the weather did not allow them outside much. Mara explained the morning schedule, for the soon to be students had training before breakfast then had to clean up their rooms after breakfast though a shower came after working the horses. Some of the lessons the family would be giving were open to the new instructors, like riding for pleasure. The band was a family thing and not mentioned. The study schedule with the tutors was from 9 AM to 3 PM with a lunch break. As soon as a Chef materialized, they would have meals regularly though they would take care of that request upon their return.

Next on her to-do list was the conversation with Star. Mara went to the kitchen, where she felt it would be most likely to find the woman.

"Star, do you have a few minutes? I have some things to discuss with you if you don't mind," Mara advised in her

Thunder role.

"Sure, would you like to use my suite?" the woman asked.

"That would be fine."

They walked to the back of the kitchen and a different hallway, where Star had picked out a room for herself.

Once inside the unit, they sat in the kitchen to talk.

"Why do you want to go home?" Mara asked for she wanted this resolved.

"Because I hate it here, I lost my value in coming here. My kids won't go back, and I refuse to remain where I am not needed," the woman honestly replied.

"Then you need to pack because you go back tomorrow morning. Not the kids, which I adopted, for they have asked to remain here. You are old enough to make your own decision. Did you have anything to do with Granda's injury?" Mara asked for she had to know and had her hand on the sword as she asked.

"She brought us here, was the one in charge, and didn't want me here. You now have control of what she oversees. The team you have assembled will work well for you. I'm glad my kids can find a worth here, for I only wish the best for them," replied Star, who did not answer what Mara asked.

"No, she did not bring you here, nor did she request that I do so. I decided to do that. Now I see it was not a good decision. As it happens, I am the owner of this property, the horses, all of it. Granda never had anything against you or any of the others. Her own family abandoned her as they moved on in their lives after she raised them. I asked her to be part of my family, and it was allowed. It was my asking that made me Thunder Press. True Granda aided me in those endeavors, although not until I first asked. If you must hate someone, then please know the truth. Granda had done nothing except give and aid in all that has transpired. I had finished my regular schooling and was accepted to enter college. Now I will never take that route, for the courses I would have taken have all been passed with the degree of Master. That turns out to be a good thing because we have many kids, including yours, to get educated and make a life for themselves. For your health, I ask that you not hate me either, though if you feel such emotion is necessary, you need to know I am the one who should feel that anger. None of us intended anything except good for any of you. It was not my intent to bring you here until your kids mentioned their dreams and asked me to remove them. They would never have realized their dreams if they remained where they were. Nothing chained them there as your memory of your husband had chained you. Due to legal actions, the property behind the river is indeed in my name. I paid for it in full. The ranch is no longer accessible by you, for you have forgotten where and how to enter. Though we may need to be in that area again, you will not see any of us or know us if called. I'm sorry you could not see the good in this venture, only the hate. I will take everyone out to dinner, including you, and Michelle will bring Eva for the meal with us. Tomorrow morning at six, the Thunder team will depart, and you will be going with us. Once you set foot on the Inn property, we will no longer be part of your memory," said Mara sadly.

"Thank you; it is what I requested. Thank you also for explaining. Please tell Granda that I apologize for taking out my frustration on her. The money she paid me will remain, for I did not use any. My kids, while they are still mine, will know of my love then we part ways. Take care of them please, as I'm sure you will, or you would not have my consent for them to remain," said Star, and Mara had tears in her eyes as did the woman before her.

"Try to make this a good evening for your kids. They will not be going with you. Eva is enjoying her training with Mom and will be soon adding schooling to her lessons. Dan and Gwen will one day be well educated, and they want to be in professions of their choice. What they learn here will make it impossible for them to return to your time and life. The men who came here for surgery have asked to remain as well though you will not recall them either."

"I will always remain on the side of the law and recall that I made some very critical decisions that nearly killed one who could have been a good friend. My sins are my own, and the sentence is not as severe as it should have been," replied Star, who got up and gave Mara a heartfelt hug before departing the room.

The walk to Mara's quarters was a long one for Thunder, yet she held her head up and didn't let others see her tears. Once inside her suite, she went to her bedroom and closed the door. Then she could cry the hurt she felt yet dare not show. She heard the door open and knew only two people who would enter her bedroom without knocking. One was in the hospital, so it had to be Kennet.

"Mom, I'm sorry she hurt you. Dan was never the problem; she was. Thank you for bringing me here and letting me stay. I will one day be a son you can be proud of," said Kennet.

His Mother held open her arms, and he ran into them, where they both shed a few tears as they dealt with the disappointment and hurt of the meeting. What hurts his Mom also hurt Kennet though he knew he could not keep her from the pain, only help her deal with it.

"Son, I will always be proud of you. Since the day we first met, you should know that you will always be my natural son. You are much loved, and because of you, we have succeeded. Thank you, and please continue to watch my back," said Mara with more tears.

When they finally stood to rejoin the family, Kennet led Mara to the restroom and told her to wash her face though he said it with love, not condemnation. She understood and did as he directed, only to notice he had grabbed another washrag and was doing the same.

Mara realized that the boy (D) and girl (E) sets of twins were too isolated for their age; therefore, she moved them to her quarters. The younger boy twins had one bedroom and the girls another. She was thankful that she had four bedrooms in her quarters, for Kennet had his own space, though not a whole suite.

When Mara's space received a makeover, she asked that those needing space, such as Joy, be given what they needed. She asked for a private bedroom for Dan with extra bedrooms in case of more influx. She ended up with seven bedrooms, including her own. Each of the kids would have a suite of their own in time. For now, a bedroom was enough space for them with school and playing areas there.

Mara asked Kennet if he would allow Dan to share if Star remained in the book. He agreed as the two had become friends once Dan accepted them all as family. However, once the additional space was available, they each had a room of their own, for Dan was sixteen going on seventeen and Kennet eleven going on twelve.

Joy's room had always been across from Mara if she needed help with Joey while her body was healing. Though Joy was a teenager in years, she was a grown woman with a son to care for and would aid any clan member she saw with a need. Joy asked if Gwen would be alright in one of the bedrooms in her suite since she would be alone otherwise. It was allowed as an excellent solution to the kids' isolation though Joy's unit was only four bedrooms until or unless she needed some more space for some reason.

Pat had the suite next to Mara, who was next to Granda. Shelly N-Sign, aka Granda, had a personal area at the very end of the building, giving her as much space as Mara. Simultaneously, the remainder of the group would have at least two-bedroom suites unless they needed more room. The complex's main floor was a kitchen, Chef's quarters, assembly room, front room, and general use areas. The second floor was women-only and would hold at least fifty suites. The top floor was set up for fifty more and was where men would live.

Pat's four were in the suites next to Joy and across the hall from their Mom. It was the second story of that wing of the main building and for family members only, with its AI security.

Star had maintained her suite on the same floor as the kitchen, claiming it allowed her to clean the house or cook if everyone else was sleeping. The cleaning and cooking were things she felt she knew how to do, and therefore she kept the kitchen and everything on the first floor in immaculate condition. There were suites for a hundred people in the main complex, so no one was crowded. In the school and Tutor wing were also fifty suites. The tutors, and older students, lived there, and the AI was in control of security.

There were people to patrol the grounds and make sure that no one entered them when the leaders were away. Mara wanted to locate a cook. She needed someone to look after the stock while they were out of the country. And an auditorium where the band could play. It had all been put on hold when Granda was injured.

Pat knocked lightly on the door and then entered when Mara called. However, Pat could enter Mara's suite, never her personal space, unless she knocked at the door, which she did out of courtesy.

"I was afraid that might be the case. Sister Dear, you didn't do a thing for which you need to apologize. Star came only to be sure someone took care of her kids. She was scared that they could die in that backwater town. She hated it here, yet she did it for her kids, or so she told herself. Now she is at peace and is glad that she has no memory of her contact with us. With that is the memory of her soon to be forgotten, children. She can resume her interrupted life and live with the memories that remain in her life."

"Thank you, Pat, I needed that. It is hard to feel that Thunder would misjudge another that badly; therefore, only Mara messed up, not Thunder Press. For that, I am thankful since it is a duty that must always receive our best. It has made me wiser, and hopefully, I will remember to be very cautious in my decisions so that the ones made by Mara get looked at before being given the go-ahead by Thunder," Mara explained.

"Now we have a dinner to attend, a family to get settled, some folks to find and hire plus get with the new teachers and give them the schedule for the kids starting tomorrow. That way, the kids can be tested and put on a schedule to train them in all knowledge as soon as possible. My girls will be going to the University when we return to take their exams, as you and I did. That way, we will be as ready as we can be for the flight out of the country. Our group is growing. Where will we put them all?" asked Pat.

"They have assigned seating, and places to study that do not interfere with the rest of what is going on. We have enough pilots to fly as long as we need to in taking care of business. Only Pi and Shira will be going with us animal wise. The reason being we may need to bring some back with us. I cannot go as Thunder without them, nor can any of us. Another subject that you and I need to discuss. I made a trip to the vault. Here is a sack that you need to keep on your person someplace to keep you from becoming as tired as you have been. All of us need to have them, so got enough for all that are going. You can sew it in a sleeve, pants leg, or whatever is comfortable; however, you need to keep it on your person."

"She never told you what happened, did she?" Pat asked, for if Granda explained anything, it would be to Mara.

"No, and it is doubtful she ever will. It is not in her makeup to condemn anyone. She forgave and moved on. We need to protect her better. It would have been a significant loss if they had not been able to repair her hip. We will remove the braces and casts when we get them home on Friday, for they need their freedom for the flight. You and I both know that, as with Joy and Joey, the three are good as new. All this will require an explanation to our new Doctor, I suppose, though unless she sees something wrong, it is doubtful she will even ask. Another 'find' that I am so grateful to have with us. Pat, this duty is beyond me without you and your four. Thank you for being here and for being willing to follow my directions without question. Shandra was right when she said her family needed them all. We have a lot to accomplish and only three days to get it done. The pack horses are going back with us. They agreed to help, and we need to bring out as much dust as we can for this trip out of the country could be very expensive. I'll get the gold that we don't need to the Goldsmith so it can be processed. We also might want to allow room for the Guard that asked to come back with us and was one of Kennet's Friends. See no reason they can't remain here and have their business or employment in the commuting distance if that is what they want. Wait a minute. Kennet, how about finding that rider guard that helped you and ask him if he still wants to come with us. He could be in charge of the guard group here, watch over the horses while we are gone, and get paid," commented Mara.

"He is waiting. I told him we would pick him up next time," smiled Kennet.

"Anyone else we need to fi nd a slot for?"

"Not if the Goldsmith can have a place. The rest can remain where they are. We did what was needed. Now we can learn new things, go to diff erent places, learn to fly, grow as a family, and know where we all came from, which is here," said Kennet with a smile.

"Okay, let's call everyone and head for town to eat. Kennet, would you make sure that Gwen and Dan have fed? Pat, get your four on their way to gather up the new folks and ask Michelle to get Eva. I called Mom, and she said she needed the time. I'll round up my brood, then all we have to do is figure out how to get everyone in a vehicle," laughed Mara.

As it turned out, the two largest vans could accommodate them all, for they were sixteen passenger vans, and there were twenty-five going on the flight, which meant twenty-one were going out to eat. Mike took Pat's van to get Eva. Pat called and made a reservation at a restaurant that had room for the large group yet was not one they frequented. She asked for twenty-five seats.

No sooner did they sit down than someone else approached their table. It was Randy.

"May I crash your party? I need a place for tonight. Granda said this is where you were," the Doctor told Mara with a pleading look.

"Of course, have a seat. Don't worry about names, for you will learn them over time. You know Pat and me, that is enough for now. Folks, this is Randy, and she will be going with us on some business. Sit you down," directed Mara after checking with her Thunder side.

Everyone seemed to be having a good time though Mara noticed the hurt in Randy's eyes and Star's pain. The A Twins made sure everyone had a good meal and that there was no sadness.

The Tutors were dropped off at their wing of the building when they returned home. The horses were cared for, so the rest drove into the central portion of the complex and parked. All departed to their various dwellings while Mara took Randy to introduce her to her new abode.

Once inside and the door shut, Mara waited.

"Divorce papers were served on me today. My husband is leaving me. He says he has fallen out of love with me. I've been so happy I did not see it coming. Please can I stay here while my thoughts settle?" Randy asked.

"No, you can stay here as long as any of us live, for you are part of us. Your husband will find out tomorrow: the court is serving him papers, and he will no longer have a job at the hospital, nor will she. All he owned has now become yours. He won't need it where he is going, nor will she. Their replacements will be on duty at eight tomorrow morning, and those two will be gone. If you wish it, your marriage will get annulled, and you can become part of our family. In time you will understand how I knew ahead of time. Now is not the time for the hurt is too fresh," explained Mara.

"How can you be so young seeming, yet have such a wellspring of knowledge?" asked Randy with shock.

"In truth, I have yet to see my eighteenth birthday. I graduated from regular school at fifteen and college at sixteen. My twin and I have over a dozen master's degrees. Being Doctors is only a couple of those. We know, however, not the hands-on practice; therefore, we need you. I am the one in charge of all we have, while Granda is my Grandmother and mentor. All of us are rescues of one kind or another. Tomorrow you will see something you will never be able to tell anyone about, except those of us who make the trip with you. Watch and learn while your heart heals. Jack gave himself away when he allowed you to take a lessor position so he could show how much smarter he was than you, yet you are the better surgeon. Now he will pay the piper, and you are not involved in his judgment. Know we all love you and unanimously agreed you should join us. However, I have the final say; try to get everyone's opinion on such a decision, for my desire is to keep this a family or Clan and have some unity," said Mara with a smile.

Randy had a stunned expression on her face as she tried to understand.

"Don't try, accept a hug, and let's go talk to the horses who have to know who you are, or you won't get back onto the place," said Mara.

The two women headed to the stables arm in arm, and soon five, then six more joined them. It was Pat and her four, plus Kennet.

"Ladies, let's go for a ride," Mara said, and the horses immediately came to be saddled.

After an hour of riding, the group was relaxed and ready for some sleep. The horses were thanked, grained, and brushed down.

"Do any of you want a snack before bed?" asked Mara.

"All I want is a pillow, for we have to be up at an early hour," responded Shandra.

"I agree. It has been a day of many things, and we have much to do ahead of us. We will be taking pack animals and extra mounts with us though we usually bring back more than we take," Mara advised.

"Then let's go to bed," said Pat.

As each went to their suite, Mara asked Randy to come to the suite where Mara lived. They moved to each bedroom to check on the kids already asleep there. Kennet remained in his room to prepare for bed.

The two women sat at the table in the little kitchenette that each suite had.

"Randy, tomorrow might be a bit of a shock for you. All I ask is your faith and trust. Don't doubt anything asked of you and follow the rest of us. Also, the Quad will be training you in some sword drills. A time will come when you may need those skills, and if not, you will better understand why the rest of us use them daily. For tonight why don't you sleep here with us? This bedroom here by me is open. The suite will remain yours though I doubt you want to be alone tonight. In the morning, you will be up at four. Breakfast will be ready soon after. On a duty day, we do not train with the horses, for we will be in the saddle a good portion of the day. Also, music lessons get skipped before a trip. We can work that in when we get home at the end of the day. Wear the type of clothing you see us in. Now comes some things that may concern you. Trust your mount, for they have made this trip many times and know the way. Kennet will lead with me while Pat will bring up the rear. All in between us will just hang on," laughed Mara.

"Thank you for the wonderful meal and for having one of the Quad drive my car to my new home. I am at peace here. Thank you for the offer of a bedroom is accepted for tonight. When we return, I will pick up my belongings and move into the new suite," said Randy.

"Not necessary, you see you moved while we were at dinner. Everything you have ever owned is in your suite if something you wished to keep."

"In that case, best I get a nightgown and tomorrow's clothes, then it is to bed," Randy responded. She ran to get the necessary gear and noted a backpack by a chair that she grabbed though not sure. In time, Randy found it was her 'hurry sack' for those trips out of time. Never again would she be without one near her.

The complex was soon dark, though the hour was not entirely dark. Everyone was asleep and didn't hear the disturbance outside, for the Rangers took care of those who entered the area. Rangers would guard the felons until Thunder could deal with them in the morning.

Mara got up, took her shower, and dressed, then headed to the kitchen to get food ready for everyone. She knew what nearly everyone in her family wanted. The tutors knew to be in the main building dining room at seven and direct all questions to Joy, who would be in charge with the rest gone. When the meal was over, dishes went in the dishwasher, set in the cupboards, and everything cleaned up, then the Quad, T Twins, Kennet, and Randy departed for the stable. There was work to deal with before their departure.

Randy received the instruction about where to be, and Mara called for Shira to bring the prisoners. The studs opened the doors of their stalls and joined the group. It was time to train the new stud. When he passed Mara, Pi was there with teeth bared. She nipped the stud and pushed him back where he needed to be. He never had to be reminded again.

When Mara called Thunder Court to order, the Doctor was stunned; two of those in the group were her husband and his mistress. He never looked her way, for all he saw around him were Thunder riders and knew that they were in trouble.

When the court was over, all confessions signed, recorded, and prepared for the district to verify before those charged would be put in prison by a local authority, it was time for Pat to send for the local law. The vehicles came with flashers on though no sirens.

Kennet and Shira met the drivers and led them to the prisoners' location.

As quickly as they were loaded in the vehicles the force brought with them, the group departed.

Chapter 2

One lesson at a time

"Okay folks, time to mount up," directed T1.

Saddles were placed on the mounts going, pack animals had pack boards placed on their backs, and as this was Randy's first trip, she was 'tied in' for they didn't want to lose her.

Randy's mind was on the confession of her husband. Yes, she would get that annulment and move on. She looked up and realized they were disappearing into a book lying on the floor of the stable. Before she could react, they were in a stable elsewhere. She didn't know where she was; however, the rest did. It was the horse stable for the Wren's Nest. The women dismounted, and some of the horses left as well.

Star took the underground passage to the lower Inn and never looked back.

"We need to check with Jennie then return home. There is a lot to accomplish before we can return home. Randy, you have now become a Thunder Guard."

The mounts that the women arrived on were waiting while the rest went to the stable at Thunder's hidden ranch. They walked their horses to the main gate, and once outside, they mounted. Once again in the saddle, they departed for Jennie's Farm. The women saw a lone rider riding their way. It was a man, and he had full saddlebags, carried weapons, and moved with a horseman's Grace.

"Hello Kennet, thought I would save everyone a trip to the mines. May I ride along?" asked the man.

"Remember the rules," Kennet told him, and he joined

the group by riding behind the leaders.

When they reached the farm, they found Jennie waiting for them.

"Hello sisters, what brings you out this way?" asked Jennie with a smile, for she genuinely felt related to those before her.

"We have some information for you and a suggestion to offer," responded T1.

"Go ahead," replied the woman, who was instantly alert for the information.

"There is a female guard that works the gate in town. Her name is Sandrea Chicks. She would like to work with you if you allow. The woman is a Warrior and will only need to learn the sword drill to be a good second if you agree. Then there is the owner of Wren's Nest. Try not to interact with her. If someone threatens her life, then, by all means, rescue her, otherwise give her plenty of room. Since you have the information we came to deliver, is there anything we can do for you?" asked Mara.

"Yes, a few things. I have ended up with some good-looking horses, yet this is a farm, not a ranch. I have no idea what to do with them, have you some suggestions? I need to pick up some decent weapons fitted to my kid's hands so they can begin learning how to use them. Who do you suggest I see about making them?"

"Send word to Maggie the blacksmith. She makes excellent weapons and made some for myself and my son. She lives at the Wren's Inn. A message left there will reach her, I'm sure."

"Would it work to send a message to that Chick's person on how to find me?" asked Jennie.

"Yes, only that one should be directed to the guard shack. She has a guard dog that travels with her. Have you found someone to keep an eye on your place when you are working in town or the general area?" T1 asked.

"Took in a woman that needed a place to stay, turns out she is arms qualified and willing to look after the place. I checked her out with the sword, and she can stay Can even trust her to work with the girls if I'm busy," replied the woman.

"Glad to hear that. If you run into problems, call for T1, and I will try to answer whatever the issue is. If you truly don't want the stock you have acquired, you can send them with me, and they will get new homes. For now, we have to get some other problems settled. Thank you for your time and safe traveling," said Mara.

Jennie called, and the horses came on the run.

"You are to go with Thunder and do as she directs. I am sorry. However, I don't have the time at the moment to take proper care of you. My daughters are too small to help, and you need help now. She has agreed if you do," Jennie advised.

The Thunder group then turned their mounts and departed for Pi filled in the new ones.

Upon reaching the town, Mara took her group to the side opposite the Inn's stables, where she led her team into the caves. When they reached the end, a push of a panel opened the exit putting them at her ranch. Once inside, Mara said to make themselves at home. They would be there for a couple of hours at least.

Randy followed Michelle toward the ranch home at her request.

"Randy, you have some lessons you need to take. Now is the time so I will start. When one of my sisters is free, that person will relieve me, and on it will go until you have learned the drill. You have yet to see it in operation yet need to know how to use the tools we have before we go out of the country," Michelle explained.

They moved behind the house and out of any chance of being seen from the Inn's back. There the drill began.

"My goodness, and you do this all the time?" asked Randy as she tried to keep up.

"It took me a while to get the hang of it; however, now it is easy. Just go with the flow," replied Michelle, who made a move to her right, and her sister Gretchen moved into her place to continue the drill.

Meantime Pat was rounding up the horses and giving them a rubdown plus taking the saddles off. They were given a bit of grain, for the transfer that affected people could also be a problem for the animals, so all received care. Shandra and Cherry helped her with the task.

Mara was loading the mined ore onto the animals' pack boards that would take the gold home. Their packs looked like wooden boxes yet were silk-lined sealed containers in the shape of rectangular boxes. The animals patiently stood while Mara finished, for they knew their share of the grain would be waiting when the loading was complete.

The Guard they picked up was kept in one area by Kennetso that they did not give out any secrets too soon.

Within an hour, everything was in place. The mounts were again ready, and everyone got aboard. It was time to return to the real world.

Instead of moving to the Inn stable, they rode into a wall made of stone, and when they felt a change, they knew they were near where their family lived.

When they set foot in the home stable, they knew something was amiss. There was a tension in the air that was palpable. The horses were quick to run as soon as their saddles were off without looking at the stalls. The new horses they returned with were to remain in one of the stables until their return. The stud and Pi kept watching with Shira, so the second stud did the same. The gold went to the basement vault by Pat and Mara. Then it was time to find out what was going on.

"Secure stables," directed Mara as they departed the building.

They heard the click of the doors locking as the resident horses ran in the pasture. The mares and their new off spring needed to be secure regardless of what was happening. Also, the new horses required protection until whatever was wrong could be resolved. Suddenly, the two studs ran to Mara and Pat, who mounted on the run and followed the field's running horses. The Quad and Kennet were mounted and riding right behind them with the new male guard keeping pace. Randy was not as fast as the rest; however, she asked her mount to catch up with the rest once mounted. Much to her surprise, they did a racehorse pace. Pi was her mount.

They saw several big stock trucks loading their horses out of sight of the house, and to one side, sat Dan and Gwen. Two men watched over them. The new male Guard moved out immediately and took care of those with the two children. He swung Gwen up behind him, and Kennet stopped long enough for Dan to mount with him.

The lead stud trumpeted, and the horses were suddenly on the run. Those already loaded broke their way out of the trucks, and soon the horses were pushing the ones trying to steal them, making the rustlers now prisoners. Every time someone reached for a weapon, a horse hit them. Weapons got dropped, and the herd continued to push the men until they reached the home corral.

Mara remained mounted and looked out over the group of men.

"Quad, get those trucks here but make sure you wear gloves. Pick up any weapons you see on the way. They will be needed as evidence when we hold court," directed Mara, who then dismounted and pulled her sword, for the men had fired many times, though the shots went into the ground.

Pat did the same, and the two of them matched steps as they moved into the corral. Once they entered, the horses moved behind them and waited.

Randy fell into the row that the Quad was in though she was at one end. It was her intent not to move unless the entire row did. However, when Mara commanded the Quad to move, Randy was left standing alone at one end of the lead group and moved closer to Thunder One while trying to keep the same distance from her as was between Mara and her twins. Kennet stood between the Thunder Twins though behind them. Shira was at one end of the formation and Pi at the other while the two studs stood next to them.

There were over forty men in the corral. Thunder Press stood looking them over. One of the men thought he was out of her sight and pulled a weapon. It was the signal for those with swords to remove them. Randy did the drill as she had been shown and was glad she was to one side, for the shells she was returning were aimed carefully back at the sender and no place near the leaders.

The Quad returned as soon as the shots stopped. By then, they had made relays to get the trucks close to the stables. Four of the horses volunteered to move with them, so once a stock truck stopped, the women mounted and returned for the next ones. The trucks sat on the driveway parking pad, out of the way of those Pat would call to pick up the felons.

They returned to their places in the formation, and Randy again moved. Her new place to stand was between the middle two in the Quad group. She had never felt so alive or dreamed that she would be in her current position. Nothing in her life had prepared her for the new set of duties, yet it all had.

The trial proved that this was part of the group that

owned the original horses. Now they had lost all that they owned and contributed a few more ranches along the way. This time the questions were more explicit: Mara asked who was their contact in the other world; How did they get there; Who was in charge; how much had been taken from that different world in the form of cash, precious metals, and personnel? When done, she knew what had to happen. All those incarcerated at the 'other book' were sent for and added to those waiting at the ranch. Though the information related to the Book World when heard, it was on the recording as if on Mara's homeworld.

"Sis, warn those coming that they will be taking about five hundred to a thousand back with them. They can walk them if that is the best way. Only need enough guards to get them there without anyone on the legal side getting injured," directed Mara.

"Why not load them on the stock trucks and send them back that way? You have the power to freeze them until they are at the prison for unloading. No doubt they can make sure no one leaves on the trip to town. I hope the jail has room for them all. On second thought, erase that the state prison is there and has space for five thousand. I doubt there will be any problems. None of them will ever see the sky again once they reach the prison. I heard that there is an isolated spot that takes certain prisoners, and I understand it is those sent there by a team called Thunder," Pat told her sister. It was information she didn't recall until she gave it to Mara.

When the law enforcement officers arrived, they loaded the prisoners one at a time after doing a complete search of them for any weapons. The stock trucks were crammed full. The patrol cars led and followed the trucks into town.

Mara was greatly relieved that the prisoners were no longer her problem.

Once Thunder Court duties were over, the family moved

to the main house, where they found Joy was pacing the front step with Joey in her arms.

"Joy, what's wrong?" asked Mara as she ran to the woman.

"Thank goodness you got here in time. I knew once the patrol cars got here that all was okay yet hadn't seen any of you, and it worried me," replied the young woman.

"We are fine and no scratches even," responded Mara in relief.

"This will be your last alone duty. Please meet Chester, and he will be the Guard when we are not here as well as will take care of the horses while we are out of the country," Kennet told his sister.

The ones who had been to the book world headed for their showers, for they didn't want to bring the horse smell into the home complex. Once cleaned up, Mara called a meeting.

Mara told them that when everyone was in place, they needed to listen to what she wanted them to know as it was necessary.

"This is Wednesday, and it is ten AM. Quads, you need to go to the University where they are holding slots open for you to take the exams. Tell the person in charge that you need to be tested in the same fields that the N-Sign twins were. Kennet, I know this is a stretch; however, would you go with them, please? Pat, you and I have to take care of business in town. Joy, if you would like to join us, you are welcome. Gwen and Dan, you may come as well. The four youngest are in classes, and we will leave them there for now. Chester, we need to take you to meet the horses in charge. Meet my twin, Pat. She will show you how to take over the outside home security. Do not work alone. If you find someone you feel will work with you, let me know, and they will get a background check. Now those of you who have assignments, go to it," said Mara with a smile.

Pat took Chester to meet the horses and introduced the lead guard, who knew he was in charge only until their leader got there. The Quad and Kennet left for the University. Dan and Gwen asked if they could check on the horses to be sure none received an injury during the attempt at their capture.

Joy went to get Joey ready to travel.

Mara asked Randy to follow.

Mara's suite sounded empty without the shouts of children, although they had not been there very long. Since the kids were in classes, it was a good time to bring Randy up to speed.

"Question time is here. What did you think of your first visit to the Book World?" asked Mara with a smile.

"Is that where we were? I find this all very interesting. It seems to me it would be like if one stepped back in time. The people there obviously knew and trusted you. I quickly realized that the horses were on a familiar trail, for they knew where to go and what to do for the duties required. The drills that the Quad group did with me were very timely. I never imagined I would be using a sword in my life, yet it is familiar and welcome," Randy responded.

"No questions in that; surely you have some," laughed Mara.

"I told you I'm amazed at your wisdom for one so young. There is shock at being part of your wonderful family with no recriminations due to Jack's departure. I am very appreciative of the way you handled his case. Not everyone in your family uses a sword, I understand, yet you allowed me to learn. May I ask why? We have known each other only a short time, although this is home, and I will follow any orders you give without question. The next adventures with this wonderful family are looked forward to with great anticipation. Yes, there will be bumps in the road, for we each have to learn and earn our way in life. We will support one another in learning and in dealing with those bumps. You didn't assign me a duty which makes me wonder what you wish of me at this time," replied Randy.

"On the upcoming trip or trips, Granda needs a guard. You are to be her Guard. Pat and I have to take care of a lot of property we inherited. Also, some things you need to handle. Gary and Jerry will be going with us, and both are arms qualified. All of us have concealed weapons permits issued by the National Department of Defense in this nation and the countries we will need to enter. When on our airplane, we will be just us with no camouflage. Once we prepare to depart the aircraft, our persona has to change in some cases. For instance, we have to enter a couple of countries where women cannot own property. In that case, we become men with ID to match. I intend to dispose of some of those properties if we can get a fair market value if we get some of the stock shipped to us and think we have a use for them. On the new properties are many ranches. I will be looking for managers, foremen, or women, if in a nation that allows such."

"In some cases, we may need to bring a breeding pair back with us. Each time you take on an additional duty, you will receive additional pay. Example being: you are a physician, a surgeon, and now a guard. By the time we return, you will be a linguist, a pilot, and anything else you think you want to become. The Quads and Kennet are currently getting tested. If my guess is correct, they will pass with flying colors, and all end up with Master's degrees, making Kennet the youngest graduate of that prestigious University. When we return, you will do the same. We all have that information: if one of the leaders is injured, someone must take up the slack. To do that, we all need the same information. In Granda's case, it was me. If I go down, so does Pat due to our being twins in both realms. That means the Quad would have had to do it. Now you will be the one to take control above them, and they become your guards. They will also take care of all other duties such as horses, ranch, planes, and the like. You will take care of medical and the family in its entirety," Mara advised.

"You trained for this, and I did not; why would you do that?" asked the woman in shock.

"First off, believe, and have faith. If you think you can do it, you will. We need you. At present, you will be Granda's Guard. When Pat and I have to take duty in town, you will remain or go depending on Granda's activity. During times like today, when Granda is not here, you will go when we do. You did a good job taking over the Quad duties when I sent them to get the trucks. Now we all know you can handle the job. Yes, we need you as a medic and surgeon. However, you can't sit around the rest of the time and would leave us quickly if that were to happen. Therefore you will have duties that you are responsible for and that there isn't anyone filling at the moment."

"When time is available, you will be tested at the University in all areas the same as the rest of us. You may need that knowledge to oversee what is in our care. If the time becomes available for some strange reason, you might even get tested before we depart. The three who had surgery will be home on Friday and hopefully early. We have to pack a plane and load up what we need for the trip. That means health and shot records for all on-board. We need to secure those medical kits on-board where no one will find them except us. Remember, some of the nations we will be visiting have a ban on drugs getting imported. Rather than hassle with them, we will not acknowledge that we have any aboard. Everyone has to have at least one Passport. You will need two, as do the Quads, the adult twins, and Granda because each is a Thunder as well as an N-Sign. My kids and grandkids will also carry two, so I can claim them. If I am in Thunder mode, then it would be difficult to say the kids are mine when no one named Mara is even aboard the plane," Mara advised.

"That makes sense to me though I doubt I would have followed the thought as far as you have," laughed Randy.

"Best learn, my friend since that duty could one day become yours. Pat is just coming in the front door. Those of us left here will go into town where we have to look at a stadium that is for sale. As normal, we will eat out for some people who still need hiring though not sure if we will hire them here or where we are going. We can't leave Chester here by himself. That means two teams of outside guards, one for day and one for the night. I have asked the Tutors to look after the four small ones until we return. They are not aware we are here," Mara told her.

"I watch and learn," said Randy, and she seriously meant it.

"Pat, please tell Joy we are ready," directed Mara.

"One question I have is the hurry sack. Do we keep it with us all the time or only when going to the book?"

"Always with you since we never what will happen next. Now that there is a resident Thunder at Star's location, we probably won't be called there very often though it is necessary to make trips to my ranch to check on things. When we return from town, we need to make sure that Chester and Kemper have suites in the men's hall. For now, Chester is learning the parameters of the property and some of the misadventures we have had here. Price, will be picked up in town when our duties in town finish. He has work to do here, plus his residence is changing," commented Mara.

"How do you know what to pack in that sack?" asked Randy.

"We take jeans, shirts, underclothes, gloves, socks, and a jacket. When Granda is again in control, she can send us whatever we need," Mara said as she stood up for she heard Pat and Joy in the hall.

"I look forward to getting to know her. Thank you for the information. Now I will listen and learn again," Randy told her new Mom, for that is where she joined the family, Mara advised.

Since she had her marriage to Jack annulled, she could never return to her birth family. Now she had a new identity and new family. Granda had rewritten her entire history, though Granda would be the one to advise her of that.

Pat was waiting in the hall, for she knew of their conversation. With her were Joy and Joey.

Eva had been returned to Grace the following evening. They would have taken Grace along; only she had a rush order she needed to get done and begged off.

Since most of the family was busy, Mara, Pat, Randy, Joy, and Joey would be going. Gwen and Dan wanted to learn so badly that they took off for the instructors as soon as they finished chores, and Kennet went with the Quad.

With the numbers they had, they could get by with a smaller van.

Mara checked a map she picked up and found that the stadium they wanted to look at was near the University. She had asked Pat to drive so she could be the navigator. When they reached the location, it looked like it was huge. Mara asked her AI to place a call to the number on the door of the building. The AI at home would do so for her.

"Hello, this is Priceman Enterprises," said a voice.

"I wish to see the stadium you are selling," responded Mara.

"Which one?"

"The one I was aware of is the one by the University, which is where we are at the moment."

"Oh yeah, the Georginshire one, let me get the agent

to meet you there. I answer the phone," the young male voice told her.

The phone was quiet for a couple of minutes; then the man was again on the phone.

"She says she will be there in ten minutes. She has to come from across town."

"Thank you, we will wait," replied Mara. "Now, let's get out and look around. Shira, would you please keep an eye on the van?"

Shira got out and looked to the top of the van. Mara moved to brace her hands on her knees and waited as the wolf ran up her back and onto the unit's roof where she could watch the area.

They looked at many windows to see inside; however, paint covered the glass to keep snoops out, it appeared. Finally, they gave up and returned to their vehicles.

"You each have a degree in real estate. I need to know the building's condition, access, and rated building codes, how many people it holds, how sound is wiring, plumbing, you know the drill. When done, give me the info, for I would prefer not to be here all night," laughed Mara.

They looked at a car coming up the road the same way they entered. Each group member moved slightly to have easy access to something if this was not the person they were to meet.

An exhausted woman departed the vehicle.

"Are you the folks asking about the Georginshire Stadium?" asked the woman as she tried to put on a smile, which also looked tired.

"Yes, may we see inside? What can you tell us about it?" asked Mara.

"I can tell you that they remodeled it extensively a year

ago. The former owners died in a plane crash. The estate is getting settled, and my directions are to sell it to the first person who shows interest. Come this way, please. There isn't any problem with theft here unless it happens during an event. The place has some surprises," she handed Pat and Mara the information sheets.

"We need to get this done," Mara directed her group.

Joy had already taken out the stroller, and as soon as the door was open, everyone went inside.

"Oh, thank you, I have been on my feet for twenty-four hours with a sick child and trying to work. I'm about exhausted," said the woman in a whisper to Mara.

"What is your normal profession? Somehow I don't think this is it," commented Mara.

"No, I was a makeup artist; however, when Sean died, and the baby got sick, I had to look for a better paying job," the woman replied.

"I want you to stand right here. Now stand there, Randy check with T," directed Mara.

Randy started to pull the sword but saw the frown and just let her hand sit on it as she looked at the exhausted woman.

"Needs rescued," said Randy, who then removed her hand from above her head and walked to where the woman stood with a frown.

"It is alright; when we finish, we might be able to be of some assistance. For now, show us all you know about this place. Look at it as if you were purchasing and tell us all you know positive, yet we need to know any negatives. Be honest," directed Randy, for the woman was so tired she was shaking, and the Doc knew that was not a good thing.

"The folks who owned it came about a year ago and purchased the old stadium. It had been rather small by today's standards, so they enlarged it, making it at least three times larger. Then they brought in work crews to strip out the building, and I do mean strip to the bare boards. Now the whole place looks as if it is a new build. According to the specs, a new setup was put in place to open or close the roof."

"Hardwood floors sit on a hydraulic platform electronically moved from storage to the performance arena. This space can be a ballroom or a basketball/volleyball court. Under the main auditorium floor is a cement one that a roller rink can cover if someone needed it, and there is storage to put chairs and bleachers in if they planned a performance. The floor you see here will roll under the main entry floor once all bleachers and chairs are in their cabinets. There are dressing rooms for performers and good sound equipment, which brings versatility to the building. Shops where things can be sold, like food, promotion items, and the like, are available in the foyer. The curtains on the stage are all new since the folks said they didn't want last year's dirt in this year's productions. They replaced everything. Motors, seats, all of it, even the backgrounds are new. They planned that they would have a grand opening in two months with all bills paid. Now the advertising is done without a program to present," explained the agent.

"Show us the basement and give us the price," said Mara.

"Didn't want you to think I was putting you on. There are seven such properties for sale in this town. Each will go for one dollar to the first people showing interest," responded the agent.

"Give us your name and take an oath, please," directed Mara.

The woman complied. She was Kari Garentine, age twenty-four, with a two-year-old child that was sick a lot.

"We need to close on this property immediately and be taken to see the other such properties someone directed you to sell. What are they, where are they, are they like this one in condition?" asked Mara, who was getting excited. The stadium was only about ten miles from the house if they used a backroad.

"Certainly, would you like to have me ride with you, and you can drop me off when you finish? That way, I can answer questions and give you information as you move from one location to the other. It amazes me: no matter what you pay for the units, I still get a commission based on the local market. If all of them sell, then maybe the baby can see a doctor, I can take some time off to care for her, and we won't starve in the process," said Kari.

Randy was looking at Mara with a question in her look.

Mara gave a slight nod then said, "Wait," to no one in particular; it seemed though Randy got the message.

They saw the seven properties, and Mara purchased them all. She then asked if Kari would object to having dinner with them before returning her to her pickup point.

"Right now, a sitter is with Kelly. I have to be home in three hours; however, until then, there is someone to watch over her," responded the woman. Keri was thinking about how nice a hot meal with a pleasant company would be.

"Quad," said Mara into her speakerphone.

"Quad Leader," replied Shandra.

"When will you be done?"

"Just finishing the last question, hold on," whispered their lead guard.

"Yes, we are done. Would you object if we left now? Any other tests will have to happen when we return for duties take us out of the area for a time," Shandra told the man overseeing the testing.

"They said that too. Okay, go ahead. When you come back,

we will do the instruments and equestrian as they don't have the horses or instruments. The University band is on the road and thus so are the instruments," he told them.

"If you have no objections, we can bring our horses and instruments," replied Shandra.

He agreed to that arrangement

As they departed the building, Shandra signed for silence. The group loaded into the van they were using, and when off the University grounds, she stopped the vehicle and got out, then asked Mara where she was. Once directions came, they were on their way.

When the second van drove up, Mara excused herself and went out to speak with Shandra.

"Hello, fancy meeting you here," she chuckled.

"Yes, imagine that," laughed Shandra.

"We are going to eat first and after that want two drivers to take Randy and a woman to the woman's home. She has a sick child. If Randy says the child needs constant care, you can bring the Mother and Child home with you. We will see what needs doing from there. Thunder approved the action. However, you need to be aware of other things that should be at another time. How did you do on the exam?"

"The tester said we maxed them all just like you did. Poor Kennet isn't sure what he did yet is about to bust his buttons, and I know how he feels," replied Shandra.

"We still have to take instruments and equestrian as the band has all the instruments and they don't have horses. Said we would do it next time," commented Cherry.

"That works, now let's go eat," said Mara as she hugged her son.

They sat down with the others, and soon all were chatting away like old friends.

Chapter 3

Packing up

"Tell me a little bit about your daughter," Randy asked, for she felt an urgency to do what she could for the woman and her child.

Mara quickly picked up the urgency, and though they didn't rush dinner, they were soon on the road to the young woman's home. It was a rundown rental in a rundown part of town. Kari ran inside to let the sitter know she was there and check on her daughter.

The others followed and then waited at the door.

The young woman came from the back, carrying a red-headed child who did not look at all well.

"Please, may I hold her?" Randy asked, and the rest of the family moved out of the way while she did a quick exam.

"What do you sense?" asked Mara into her speaker.

"She has to be removed from here immediately. Take nothing. Allow Kari important papers though they will need replacing; however, nothing else. I am leaving with the child to get some fresh air, so tell her not to be concerned," responded the Doctor.

"Kari, you need to gather up any important papers you have plus any cash on hand. We are taking you and the child to care. Lock the door and notify the landlord. You will not be returning. No, not even clothing. Kelly will get new clothing as soon as we can reach an open shop," Mara directed.

The young woman did as directed, although it was like

she was sleepwalking. They found a store that had clothing for the young woman and her daughter. At Mari's direction, the team purchased luggage, and into it went what would be necessary for the Mother and her daughter. Randy noticed that Kari was crying.

"What is wrong, dear?" she asked.

"This is the first new anything we have ever had. Why are you folks so kind to us?" asked Kari.

"Because we can, and you need it. You are going to our home, and there you can both heal. Do not take any of your clothes or Kelly's with you. We have to burn them, and I will take care of it happening. Mara is holding Kelly and will be just outside the dressing room. Now let me help you," said Randy.

Randy handed a bag to the store manager and directed her about what to do with it after Randy identified herself as a doctor. It was immediately taken to the incinerator and burned.

"I will need to go get my car," said Kari halfheartedly.

"Give me your keys, and I will take care of it," said Michelle with concern.

"That vehicle has to be taken to police impounding for isolation where it will be emptied and inspected. We can get another later. Whatever affects those two has to be stopped here," Pat advised though Michelle still took the duty. They picked her up on the way home.

When they reached the ranch, Kari got a suite for her and Kelly. Randy followed them inside and directed that both needed to have a bath, which she aided Kari in accomplishing. She also helped them in putting on nightclothes, after which both went to bed. Another set of clothing would need burning. Randy put a clean set on the dresser for the following day.

"I will check on you two from time to time, and my room

is next to yours. I am a medical doctor, as is most of my family. Trust us and heal. We will talk more when you get up. We are going on a trip, and you both will be going along," Randy advised.

"Thank you for being so nice and the rest of the people as well. Tomorrow, the company I worked for needs to pay me and will advise them I won't be working there anymore," said Kari, who was asleep before the next breath.

"What do we have?" asked Mari asked as Randy sat down to chat.

Someone or something is poisoning them. The product used will affect anyone in contact with it, so I asked that a protective shell be placed over them until we could get them cleaned up and in a better environment without anyone else exposed. That home will have to have a controlled burn. I have the numbers and will call them in when our conversation is over. The so-called babysitter was not there when we arrived and no telling how long that person had been gone. I gave them both their shots and added in a counteractive for the poison detected. They are just going to disappear by leaving when we do. Neither of them will live long if left here," Randy told Mara.

"Their passports are on the table over there. I have their adoption papers for you. They have now become my grandchild and great-grandchild. Don't spoil them; encourage them, and help them become good solid citizens. If they remain with us, it has to be because they wanted to, not that they felt compelled. Joy will help as soon as she knows they have needs and what she can or can't do. For now, told her to stay away until you had a handle on things," Mara told her newest daughter, who would fill the slot that Star had held in the lineage.

Mara adopted Star's children along with the four they brought back. That gave her eight children, an adult daughter, two grandchildren, and one Great.

Pat only had four older kids.

"However, we haven't left home yet," chuckled Mara as she sorted her family.

Eva fit in with Grace so well that it seemed like she was her actual daughter; therefore, Mara left it that way. Her Mom wouldn't be alone, and they were both learning as they moved through life. Soon Joy and Kari would also be considered adults in the Clan though Joy had proven she was one as she raised Joey and Randy came as an adult. Included in that count were two sets of quads and one set of twins. Mara was very excited about taking her family overseas. They were moving as a band while handling the family business.

"We needed the makeup artist if she is well enough to handle it for our trip. We have a lead guard to look after the property. He will have to keep an eye on the properties we purchased too. That was quite the find though I think it was Thunder's connections that got them for us," Mara told Pat.

"I fully agree. Hey, you have a lot more offspring than I do," said Pat with a smile.

"You have the heavy hitters, and we needed them. What are we going to do with Gary and Jerry? I know Gary wants to run a leather shop. Price wants a place where he can do his goldsmithing though he too is family. Have plenty of places to offer them. I thought they might both like to see some of this world before settling down. I suppose we could take Chester too; only someone has to hold down the fort," laughed Mara.

"If that is all you are worried about, why not use those that are in place already? Give him the means to contact them while we are gone, and he can go as well. Due to the real estate we recently acquired, a fully armed force is necessary. The AI can take care of feeding and cleaning in all the stables. Pi advised them that we were going to be gone and for them to watch over the place. When we bring the three invalids home, you are going to have to help Granda with packing. The other two don't have anything to pack," said Pat.

"I asked for their sizes the last time we visited them and picked up a suitcase they can use until they have a chance to choose what suits them best. Both the guys needed new shoes. They need fitting to have a good pair of cowboy boots or two. I also packed all the kids in luggage for each of them. Since we will perform in western wear, that is what they have. Later they can use those clothes for work duty at home if they are not what they have a liking for," Mara told her twin.

"This is great; I have the easy ones," said Pat to tease.

"Not exactly; your duties also include any contact with law enforcement. That leaves you free to help me with my brood," laughed Mara.

"Why are we performing publicly?" Pat asked.

"Have you noticed how often someone contacts us at the restaurant? It is the only public place our family goes. Therefore, it was an excellent starting place. Now suppose, we need to hire guards for each of the properties, why not put Chester in charge of such a business and let him keep busy with those duties? The problem is finding reliable help. If we had a concert, it would be easier for them to find us. I may be wrong; however, I am thinking that these men will be marrying into the family. On a guess, the women will not want to change their last names; therefore, we need a separate branch for those men. Make them related. However, twelve times removed or something allows them to take the woman's family name when they marry.

The pair continued to tease one another as they made a list of what they had to take with them. At the top of the list was a Passport and shot record, followed by musical instruments. The first two would all be kept together and used only for identification when required. The lead adult would have the documents hidden in their clothing someplace where they would not get stolen.

The tutors agreed to watch over the small ones as they traveled, for they would still need teaching. Kennet would not be on that list, for he had now passed his Master's Degrees to match the lead twins. Dan and Gwen would get tested when they returned, and maybe Eva as well, plus the Quad under Pat needed to finish their tests.

Thursday had all kids in school except Kennet and the two babies. Kari was to remain home, for Randy was very concerned and would stay as well.

The Quad and the twins went into town. They needed to check to make sure the latest property had a clear title. They also told Keri they would pick up her check on the way. She signed a document to allow it. It was in a sealed envelope, which they expected.

When they reached the business that employed the young woman, Mara asked for the woman's paycheck.

To be sure, Mara touched the sword with the envelope in her hand.

"Is this the full amount? She needs to close out her employee account here and get her severance. She has a very sick child, and there is a medic with them full time now," Mara told them.

"Oh, I thought she would be back," said the woman with a bit of fluster.

"No, she needs to get all funds due to her. She sold eight properties yesterday, has a paycheck due, has a reserve on record, and all of it needs to be paid by one check, please," directed Mara while Pat stood to watch. The Quad was also in the area.

The woman departed to the back, where she spoke with the director of the business. They could hear the conversation.

"Of course, she gets her money. Yes, all of it. Why would we withhold what she has due? No, we are not waiting for any amount of time. You knew all along that her baby was sick, and yet she tried to do all we asked of her. Pay it and even put in a bonus for clearing those new units all in one day," said a woman who was rather upset that the bookkeeper even had to ask.

Soon the first woman was again headed their way, and with her came the other woman that spoke.

"I'm sorry about the misunderstanding. I am Jeroldine (Jero Firestar. I manage this enterprise; however, they don't seem to like the way I do business. It is time I quit. Make sure that check is for what it should be. Would you please wait for me outside?" asked the woman in charge after Mara complied.

Mara was shocked at both the amount and the woman speaking, yet didn't let any of it show.

"Certainly, we will do that. Thank you," responded T1.

In a short time, Jero departed the building. She looked around for the group, and they stepped up to the sidewalk, where she could easily see them.

"I submitted my resignation a week ago yet was asked to stay until today. I do not like the way this bunch does business. I'm beginning to think there aren't any honest businesses out there," Jero told them.

"What are you trained to do, and what kind of work would you be looking for?" asked Mara.

"My dream job is to run a stadium where I would be able to see the shows, to meet the performers, and to have honest bosses."

"You are hired. Now get your car and follow us if you will," said Mara.

"On my way," said the woman who suddenly seemed like a very young woman.

They led the way to one of their favorite stops, the pie house.

Since the staff knew them, a table was ready for them as soon as they were seen and counted. The waitress asked Kennet what flavors or if he would like to try something new. His eyes sparkled as he asked what kind they had. She took him to the pie display case so he could decide.

"Jero, we need an oath from you."

Pat led in the oath.

"Here is what we can offer you. We purchased some new businesses recently. In the purchase was a stadium. We would like you to run it and a few other businesses for us. However, before you do that, would you like to go out of the country for a while? Are you married, and do you have children? Now your turn," said Mara with a smile as she saw the open mouth and sparkling eyes looking at her.

"Are you serious? Yes, I would willingly work for you, ladies. Out of the country? Oh, what a joy; I have never been beyond our state border. Yes, I have a passport, for it was something I wanted to do; however, either short on time, money, or both. Am I married? Not anymore. He decided to clean out the bank account and planned on leaving with it. I still have the money, he is still in prison, and I am much better off since annulling the marriage. I have a business degree then added on a management course. Have one for working with real estate. Graduated from the University here with four degrees, does that answer all your questions?" asked the woman.

"Any children and you will have covered them all," responded Mara, who had all she could do to keep from laughing.

"He didn't want any, which right now is something causing

me to be thankful."

"Let's order," suggested Pat.

"We will discuss when we get home. Hold questions until then," said Mara, and it was because they had half of the restaurant to themselves that she said anything.

"Sis, keep an eye on the two vehicles. There are going to be repercussions on this one, yet Thunder feels it is the right decision."

"Thunder, you know her?" asked Jero in a whisper.

"You could say that," replied Mara as softly.

"Mom," said Kennet, and she immediately looked where he was.

They stood up and moved outside after telling the waitress to hold their order; they would be back.

"Jero, stay behind us no matter what happens," directed Shandra as they moved out into a line facing the vehicles and those who were crawling all over them.

"No sight to any except for us and those we are facing," directed Mara.

"Is there a reason you are damaging our vehicles?" asked Mara.

"You have something that belongs to us," said the man nearest her.

"And what might that be?"

"You got a check the account should not have issued, and we want it back!"

"How did you conclude that to be the truth?"

"You threatened the accountant unless she gave you a big check. Now we are here to get it back," he replied.

"Won't be happening," Mara replied, for she had hidden

said check in a secret pocket in her jeans.

The men pulled weapons, which caused the women to each draw a sword.

They fired, and the women returned the bullets with their swords as swiftly as they came. When the firing stopped, all those challenging were on the ground wounded. The women remained standing as they had been.

The Thunder Court was called into session, and they found out that this was the 'normal' way of doing business at that particular company. No one ever got their money from the owners. They would have taken the vehicles if they didn't find the checks. Once everything was recorded and documents signed, with confessions, it was Pat's turn.

Pat called in the request for pickup of a 'Thunder' load. Patrol cars were there immediately. All documentation went to the officers.

"Pat, this is getting to be a habit; however, you have sure made our lives easier. Now, what else can we do for you?" asked one of the officers.

"Give our insurance companies testimony that we did not damage our vehicles and that these men should be charged with that as well as attempted murder on Thunder Press. The vehicles need immediately replaced so we can continue home," responded Pat.

"Consider it done. Were you having dinner, or are you done?" asked the man.

"They started this right after we placed an order."

"Then we will have them here before you finish," he told her with a smile.

"Jero, remove anything you might need from your car. It is going to get towed away, and a replacement is coming," Mara advised as she replaced her sword, and the other women did the same.

"We will haul their vehicles in as well, for they will also need replacing, though you know that," he told her.

Mara just smiled, for to her, it meant that the new people would all get new cars of their choice. It also told her that they now owned a Realty Company of some note though it would need a bit of time to be considered honest.

They returned inside the restaurant where the waitress met them to get their orders a second time, for she canceled the first ones while they were outside.

"How about giving us an idea of who you would like as a performer at the Auditorium," Shandra said, for she knew that Mara was taking care of loose ends: like two new vehicles that would be waiting at their home for Jero and Kari.

"I know of some groups that live in this nation and might be willing to come here to play. I'll contact them while we are gone; otherwise, I will take care of it when we return. I want to find a good family group that plays and has a draw," Jero replied.

"One of the units you will oversee has a riding arena in it. Know some folks who ride well and might be willing to do a show or two," commented Cherry.

"Write them down, and we will try to get the schedule filled as soon as we can though no shows while we are gone," added Gretch, who also knew some performers.

Pat and Mara were listening yet doing what they needed to. Granda even joined in their conversation.

"We picked up another Grace project, consists of seven units at a dollar each. The woman who told us about them is now one of us. Her name is Keri, and she has a daughter Kelly that is two years old. Both of them are quite ill, and Randy is caring for them. She adopted them."

"Oh, I'm glad you rescued the Doc. She is a special lady and will be a real blessing to us," Granda replied.

"We stopped by to pick up the check owed Keri, and another woman became involved when the accountant refused to give Keri what they owed her. The office manager quit her job today because the owners expected her to do business with Keri's check being the final straw. We intend to pack up tonight and tomorrow so we can leave Saturday morning after you and the guys come home."

"We are still going then?" asked Granda.

"Oh yes, on schedule. There have been a few changes while resting, which will catch you up when we get you home. Rest well for now, and everyone sends you their love."

"I will never understand why she seems so shocked that we include her," said Mara to her twin.

"Because they treated her like she was a black sheep all her life, and she didn't even know there was another way. It will be good to have her home again," responded Pat, for all of them had been very concerned when she was injured.

Jero was still sifting the action she had seen in the parking lot. Those women were deadly! She was sure glad they were on the same side. They even said they knew Thunder!

"Before I forget, would you take my check as well? They need depositing as soon as possible, or that outfit will cancel them," she warned Mara.

When the meal was over, they went outside and found a new van in the slot where the old one had been. Pat checked it over for damage or bugs, for she had rescued her kit before the wreaker service towed off, and the officer brought the keys inside for them.

At the bank, both checks were cashed, not deposited. Mara then secured the funds to put in the vault until the women needed them. She suggested that Jero close her account for her checks from the firm were cashed there, and it could cost her all she had. Jero did as directed and took all her money out, which went to Mara. Kari mentioned she wanted her funds secured as well.

"There were maybe five dollars in my checking account. Everything else I keep with me. Thank you for cashing that check. You are correct; they would have taken it back. I appreciate you taking such good care of us. I will pay you back when my health is a little better," the girl told Mara via the home AI to Granda.

When they reached home, there were three new vehicles with drivers sitting in the driveway. Mara signed for them and allowed the drivers to leave in their van, waiting for Randy to send her car with the drivers. Pat checked out each new vehicle before putting it in the underground garage.

Randy had a question of Mara once inside.

"Why do I get a new car? The old one ran okay," said the Doctor.

"We are trading out all vehicles so that we are not as easily found by those who seek us. Your ex no doubt had friends, and sometimes those are the greatest threat," explained Mara, who had already seen that in action.

"Thank you for explaining. Next issue to discuss: When do you plan on leaving? I need to know to prepare Kari and Kelly for the flight."

"Prepare them in what way?" asked Mara with great concern.

"Both have lung infections and will need some powerful drugs."

"Okay, the rest of us have no choice in going. Do you want to remain here with your daughter and her daughter? Are we endangering their fragile health by taking them along?" asked Mara.

"Here, they can remain home and rest to get well. The

air is filtered here, and no contaminants can get to them. On the plane is recycled air. That could be a problem for their lungs. If you take them to the hospital, they will be in isolation while we are gone. I don't particularly appreciate leaving them as they are now my responsibility. However, that seems to be the best option at the moment, for you are not leaving without me," responded Randy.

"Let's let that decision wait until after we get the other three home tomorrow. We still have to pack a plane and get ready to depart," Mara told her.

"Where is your pilot?"

"Shandra is our lead pilot though the Quad and Twins are pilots as well. Due to the distances we will be traveling; it may require everyone. I want you to think about something, don't give me an answer at the moment, give it some thought and get back to me. Someone targeted Keri and her baby. Regardless of where they are left, they will still be without protection. If with us, they at least have that. Oxygen is available on the flight; therefore, they won't have to deal with recycled air if that is a problem. Let's think about it and see if there is a better solution than leaving them here. We will talk again, though, after I get the three home from the hospital. Will that work for you?" Mara asked, and Randy knew it was Thunder this time. She felt the change as she spoke.

"Yes, I agree about that. Mara, I know that you won't jeopardize any of this family needlessly. I'm worried, and you need to know that as head of this group," replied Randy.

"Randy, let me tell you a couple of stories. Just listen, please?"

Mara told her about the shape Joy was in and Joey when they found them. Randy nodded that she understood but said nothing. She explained how Joy's body had been broken a bone at a time and how Joey could not even hear due to a lousy thump on his head by her stepdad.

When it looked like Randy was going to ask questions, Mara raised her hand and quiet continued.

Then she told how both children had surgery that took three days to get them to put them back as they should have been.

"The doctor who did the surgeries said it would be at least six weeks or as long as six months for them to heal with a possibility of up to a year in recovery. We arrived home two days later, and after getting x-rays on both of them, we removed their braces. It was apparent that they were both fully healed. Does Joy look injured to you? Have you heard Joey as he giggles every chance he gets, and it won't be long before he is talking?" said Mara.

"Are you telling me that Keri and Kelly will see a full healing by tomorrow?"

"That depends on you. Do you have faith, are you willing to trust, and do you believe me?"

"See you at breakfast and again after the three are home. At that time, we shall see if I do," replied the Doctor, who then returned to her patients/kids with a lot to give some thought. This group operated on a different level she knew. Now she was being asked to do the same. Was she up to it?

"Pat, what do you want to do about supper? We have about thirty people who need feeding. Also, there is an upcoming flight. How will we feed everyone during that time?" Mara asked for the Quads to remain assigned to Pat.

"Hold on, and I will ask. My solution might not be the right one. Shandra, meet me in Mara's quarters," sent Pat.

The two women entered together when Mara called for them to come in.

"Planning session," explained Pat.

"I have not had time to think about the plane and its requirements. We have to have food for thirty people, at least, for three meals a day coming and going. Then there needs to be some on hand for those who will develop allergies or cannot eat the food where we are going. Also, we need to keep the meds with us in case of various problems like poison, animal bites, plus the special meds that Keri and Kelly need. Those items have to be out of sight and for our use only. Otherwise, we could find ourselves in prison due to the laws in some places we will have to go. If each person going takes a suitcase, where do we put them? In the lower level with the horses, I would imagine. If Kari and Kelly have breathing difficulty on the airplane, are we equipped to handle the requirement? What is our order of flight? Do we go the farthest away and work our way back or start at the closer ones and work our way out?" Mara stopped.

"Have each person pack their luggage. If we need more, we can pick it up along the way. Yes, it needs to stay in the baggage section. Yes, we have oxygen on the flight, and if it is needed, we can order some to be ready for us at each place we stop. Food is already on board, for we stopped there while you ladies were registering the new acquisitions. We ordered what is required to be delivered tomorrow at six AM. Yes, meds can be a problem, so instead of hiding them, why not put a medical case on the bulkhead to carry those items? Then as Thunder, you can 'hide' it, and no one except us will find it. As to the order of flight, please tell me where we are going, and I will work out the way to go. We will need to know the nation, the town the airport is in and how far away we have to go to the place. What are we going to use for transportation when we land? How many are going? What is our chain of responsibility? I'm guessing that the Twins control while our Medic looks after everyone's health until on land where she is a guard with us. Do we take Pi and Shira with us?" Shandra advised.

"Yes, Shira and Pi have to go. If we get a call as Thunder,

we have to respond, which means they have to be with us. We can always pick up additional animals if we need to. The eight-year-olds might not have the strength to pack their luggage though I did get ones with wheels on them. Glad you took care of the food issue. Yes, to do as you suggest with the meds. Oxygen is a decision we will look at after we get everyone home. We will then have a grand council with all members participating in the decision-making process. If the food is to be at the hangar at six AM, we can stop there, go to breakfast, then pick up our people and return home. Here are the names of the places we have to go to and where they are on the map. The notes are the languages used, and we have to be aware of the laws. I leave it to your decision about what order to do this."

"We are not going to notify anyone we are coming. Remember the woman at our first ranch? We had just started a corporation to sort our first inheritance. Pat was with us as navigator; Joy and Joey were returning from having surgery. A Thunder Court session showed that we now owned the property. The woman who met us claimed that she owned it and had it for four generations. The property was in excellent shape; however, one of the studs gave the woman away. He hated the woman. I would guess that he was around when the previous owners lost the property and their lives. That is when Shira showed us where the bombs were after Law Enforcement came to pick her up. She went to prison, and we were able to secure the location after sending her to prison with a death sentence over her head when she tried to kill me. We no longer notify anyone we are coming."

"The chain of responsibility? From the top, Granda, me and Pat, Randy, and you four. From me on down, you step up as we step down."

Chapter 4

Their first flight out

"Okay, we can live with that. Now, where do the new folks fit in?"

"All the young children plus Joy and Joey fall under me except for Keri and Kelly, who fall under Randy, who falls under me. The adults Quad and Pat will also have Jero with them. We have six tutors and four men who will most likely go with us. If Granda is up to it, she will put those nine under her. If not, they will fall under me, or I can give her the tutors and keep the men under me. It will all work out as we go. No, Pat, you aren't being ignored, for you may have your hands full before too long. Be patient. The same goes for your group Shandra," Mara advised.

"Next item to think about: does everyone have a vehicle now? Shandra and her sisters did not have any when they came, yet we keep getting vehicles, so is there enough to go around now?" Pat asked.

"No, there isn't. All women have vehicles; however, none of the men have them. The tutors came by cabs and will need vehicles as well, I would imagine, or we can make sure one of the vans is available for their use to take kids on field trips and such. They could even use it if they need to go into town for a meal or an errand. Their off duty hours are their own, when we are home," Mara replied though she knew that vehicles were on their way.

They then looked at where they were going to have to go, made sure they had not missed anything from the reports the AI had on file.

"One thing I would like to see us do is to wear bulletproof vests. We have become the number one target for some people, and while we can protect with Lightening, how about those who use scopes and try to get us out of the way?"

"We definitely shouldn't make it easy for them. I don't know about you two; however, the four of us are fully armed, with the sword being a welcome addition, however not our only weapon," replied Shandra.

"Oh, none of us are ever unarmed. We also have several black belts to our credit. All of us received training to use whatever comes to hand and to do it well. Check your memories on that one, and you will find it to be true," responded Mara.

"Never would we doubt you. Believe me, if anyone had told me how well educated we would be in less than a month, I would have asked what they were on!" Shandra told them.

Mara laughed and laughed. It felt good as so much happened that she was not laughing as much as usual and that had to change, she knew.

When their little meeting was over, they loaded the Quad and the Twins plus Kennet to make a run and put things in the plane that they would need. Dan and Gwen said they would help, so they soon had two full vans of stuff that would need to go. Joy offered to watch the quad of eight-year-olds.

"Shandra, I have been searching my memory as I have a curious nature. Why do we have two planes when we can't fill one?" asked Mara as they were working.

"The second one is backup; if something goes wrong with the one we are using, we can always pull the second one to get the job done. We will alternate which one we use to keep both in use. A couple of mechanics need hiring to take care of them; however, they also have to be able to do other things like serving as guards, so they have full-time employment."

"Okay, in plain English, what are you trying to tell me?" asked Mara with a chuckle.

"I can get you four new people at a call. They are former Military and can easily serve as guards on the ranch though I think they may have many talents we could use. The thing is, they are all females," she said and waited.

"Why didn't you say so? Get them here, so they are on the flight."

"I think they can be here quickly; however, they have to see how they relate to Mom. That is where they will fall, I am betting," replied Shandra with a smile.

"They will also fall under you, so what are your thoughts about them?"

"This particular bunch each held positions of responsibility. Each is looking for a place they fit. They are honest, hard workers, love to ride, and all four are receiving their discharges today, here," responded Shandra with some caution. These were people trained in ways that most folks might not want to hire. To be honest, so was she.

"Give me the information on them. Does this group have passports? How soon can we meet with them? Are they willing to make an out of country visit immediately? What do they expect in pay? Where do they live?" began Mara.

"Whoa, you said, call them, which I will do. These don't live anyplace due to being discharged in about thirty minutes," said Shandra as she asked the AI to make the call and connect her.

"This is Commander Shandra. May I speak with Petibone, S?"

"Major Petibone here," said a voice they could all hear.

"Sharna, this is Commander MB Tridine. I need a favor. Round up those on your list, and I will send you transportation. You will be going to a hangar on the civilian side of the airport tarmac. I have an offer of employment and some other nifty benefits. Please come and listen for it will be worth your time, I'm sure. It has to be as soon as you get discharged. Please don't talk to anyone else until I see you. Yes, it is honest work, and no one can record or even hear this information except you," said Shandra, and she disconnected.

"They will be here as soon as they can catch a cab. Presently those four are at Fifteenth and Corso. Hey, that is just around the corner. Let me go get them," said Shandra, who called for Cherry, and they were on their way.

Shandra jumped out of the van and ran up the courthouse steps. Standing at the door was a woman in Major's uniform. She had a duffle bag next to her, and three other women, each holding a high rank, were standing behind her.

The Major saluted the Commander as soon as she recognized her. Shandra returned it in kind.

"Put your gear in the back. We have an appointment to get to," said Shandra, and they quickly did as directed.

Once Cherry maneuvered the van out of the parking lot, Shandra checked in all directions to see they were not followed and asked they be lost. She did not want anyone following them on this one.

"Ladies, you may or may not know one another, although that is not a problem. I want to introduce you to some folks that need your services. It won't be as officers, do you mind getting down and dirty?" asked Shandra.

"Shandra, tell us straight, what is the deal?" asked the Major.

"I cannot, for it isn't my story to tell. You will be oath-bound, and those we are meeting will fi ll you in fully. You will become part of our family. Housing comes furnished, you get paid according to what you do, and we depart Saturday," responded Shandra.

"I highly recommend you listen closely. We are here," said Cherry as she identified at the gate then drove to the hangar where the door opened as she got close, and she went inside.

"Leave your gear in the van for now. We will take you shopping a bit later if you decide to stay," she advised.

The four women were in the six-foot range. Upon departing the van, they lined up and faced those waiting. Four women who looked like copies of Shandra were facing them.

"May I introduce your applicants: Sharna Petibone, Betty Pretine, Darna Porca, and Carol Scorby? Their gear is in the van. You know what I told them," said Shandra with a smile.

"I am Mara and the leader, if you will, of a family group. Our youngest is one year old, and the oldest is fifty-seven. We need a chef, female guards, and mechanics for airplanes, which you see here. It will help if you ride horses though we will teach you if required. Do you like to play musical instruments? How strong is your faith? We are armed at all times with permits to carry concealed. Does any of that sound of interest to you?"

"Would you allow me to try out your program? I have been Military for a long time and don't know how well I will do as a civilian. I believe we all feel the same way. It is necessary to make the transition though would like a friendly environment to do so in," replied the Major for often families did not want their female soldiers to return home.

"Pat, please take oaths," directed Mara as she moved to one side where she submitted the names for passports that they would need the following day. They would also need identities.

"Sis, they fall under you if you don't mind. Their paperwork is on the way. Vehicles we will deal with upon our return. Suggest they allow us to secure their funds. I will have enough on hand for any expenses, as those we are meeting will expect me to do that. Our AI will keep track of everyone's expenses and will figure it out when we get home. Thank you for the satellite that will keep us connected with home," said Mara.

"The four of you just changed identities. Your last name is N-Sign. You keep your first names if that is your desire. Passports are being issued and should arrive at the house this afternoon. Pat is now your Mom, and I am one of your sisters. The others are the driver Cherry plus Michelle and Gretchen, known as Quad-A. You are Quad C, for we have a set of eight-year-old Quads under Mara. If you want to remain, that is," explained Shandra.

The Military folks began to laugh. Freedom, now they would have it.

"May we change clothes?" asked Sharna.

"Certainly, the door is locked, and we are all females. No one can enter here without our presence and consent," replied Mara with a smile. She had checked them with Thunder, and they were ready to go.

"Oh, before we forget, weapons are to be worn. If you don't have any, we will pick them up along with your clothing. Also, you will be taking some University pretest courses as soon as we find the time."

The new group changed into jeans, boots, and western blouses. They became part of the N-Sign Clan and no longer looked anything like they had while in the Military with the change. Since the Military kept all the arms they had permits to carry; they would have to purchase new unless they happened to purchase their own along the way.

"In case you are wondering, we volunteered as soon as you requested oaths. The only thing that would have made it better if we could change our first name as well." Betty laughed.

"If that is your desire, it can be done. What do you want me to call you?" asked Mara. She already liked the new group, and she didn't see the stiff-necked officers she had met previously.

"If you are serious, my middle name is Rachael, and was called Rae," replied Betty.

"I'm Sharna Josephine called Jo," commented the former Major.

"Wouldn't want to be left out. Folks call me Spicer though my birth name was Carolyn Lenore," added Carol.

"Let's make it unanimous, my birth name was Christine, so I answer well to Chris," laughed the fourth of the group.

"Okay, ladies, we have work to do. Split into the two vans and mix yourselves up so you can get to know one another. Shandra and Cherry are the drivers since they already know everyone. The first stop is the bank. Cash the checks with your pay. Set up accounts for your Military retirement to go to, and here are the numbers. Though only put five dollars in each account. The rest goes under your names in a different secure location. We have seen an account drained in three seconds if someone wants to find you. Our funds are not left where anyone outside my family can find them."

After completing the banking, they took the four new ones shopping for weapons and clothing. They needed to pick up permits at the same time, for the Military ones were gone. Then it was time to make a run home to feed the kids. The new women sat at a table in the dining room and wondered why such a large dining area.

They heard the noise before they saw the incoming. Kids seemed to be coming from all over. Joy and Joey arrived first. Joey went into a highchair; then Joy moved to the kitchen to help with the meal. Randy showed with Kris and Kelly. Kelly, too, was placed in a highchair. Kennet took his place by where his Mom sat. Quad A sat with a space between each of them. That is where Quad B would sit. Dan and Gwen flopped in chairs at one end of the table that Mara headed currently, for when Granda came home, she would again have the head of the table.

"Grab a seat. There will be more here tomorrow. Oh, here come the tutors. I am not going to try to introduce anyone. Just know they all belong and if you wish to know someone's name, ask," directed Pat as she began to put food on the table. They had set up crock pots the night before. Now the food was ready to eat. Even with the new ones, there would be plenty to eat.

"Okay, I am going to call your names, then we will have the blessing. When I call your name, raise your hand. I introduce my daughters: Gwen, Nancee, Tracee, Joy, and son Joey, Randy, and her daughter Keri with her daughter Kelly; my sons Kennett, Dan, James, and Pete. Randy is also our resident Doctor in case of need. Pat your turn," said Mara.

"I have two sets of quads to your one," laughed Pat before continuing.

"The first set is Shandra, Cherry, Michelle, and Gretch, followed by Jero, then the third set of quads called Jo, Rae, Chris, and Spicer. The last group to arrive is the tutors for the kids. The men coming in the door are Price and Chester. We have three people in the hospital due to surgeries, and they will be home tomorrow. Okay, Sis, back to you," said Pat.

Randy said the blessing over the meal, and everyone began to enjoy the meal. When the meal was over, the eight-year-olds took the plates to the kitchen, where Gwen, Dan, and Kennet put them in the dishwasher for cleaning. The adult folks cleaned the table, set the silverware in place for the next meal, added cups and glasses, filled salt/pepper and sugar containers then swept the floor. By then, the Tutors had put the dishes away that came from the dishwasher, and they were ready for the next duties.

Everyone returned to their place at the table, and the new ones followed along.

"Here is the plan for the next three days. We are going to be going on a plane ride. Adults, bring your gear to the vans in the garage with your name on the container. Randy, would you pick up the luggage for Joy and Joey when you take the gear for Keri and Kelly? Thank you. We will move it on one of our trips to the airport. Kids, you are packed, and it is on the plane."

"I have everyone's passport and shot record. Do not take money with you. Leave that duty to me. On the plane, we are family and can relax. Once we land, you will have to be cautious in what is said and done or even how we look. Answer no questions of anyone. Refer them to me. If in doubt, ask your Mom to fill you in. If she doesn't have the information, she is to contact me."

"At six tomorrow morning Quad A, Mara and Pat, the twins, and Kennet will be getting the rest of our group. They are coming home to rest a bit before the flight out. While we are doing that, the next group needs to take the exams at the University. That would be Quad C and some extras. Kids return to studies; yes, the tutors will be going with us under the current plan though everything is subject to change if the information changes. Ranger, you can join the men at that point if you wish since you have so many women in your group," Mara directed, for there was only one man in the group of Tutors.

She looked at Pat and received a nod and a smile.

"Okay, everyone returns to your duties, and we will see you later today or tomorrow when we bring the patients home," said Mara.

By Thursday morning, the airplane was ready and seating assigned. Play areas were available for the kids to include games. Quad C had taken their testing at the University with the extras.

Quads A and C had a meeting in the hangar before returning after the last load.

"Now you have seen those who will be working with you. Have you any questions?" asked Mara.

"How do you manage so many?" asked Jo.

"With love," replied Mara.

"You don't look old enough to be the Mother of this flock," said Rae.

"I am… no amend that I will be… eighteen in November as I recall. I graduated from HS at fifteen, college at sixteen, took masters at seventeen, think that about covers it. The twins and Quad-A have around twenty master's degrees. That has to include my son Kennet. Any of you who wish to take the exams may do so, or if your name comes up, you can ask me to remove you from the list. Since you have all taken the same exams, you have the same degrees. Only those with that knowledge can remain as part of the lead group."

"Jo's Quad, Jero, and Randy will be taking the Exams. Some group members have to finish their testing while others still have to start theirs, although those four, also called Quad A, finished their testing today. Anyone who has not taken the exams is to do that tomorrow morning while the rest of us are busy picking up those at the hospital."

"There are babies that will need care while many are busy. Take horses and instruments with you if you are testing. Also, tomorrow morning would a couple of you be willing to take over breakfast for me? We have to be at the hospital at six AM and should be home by ten. Have to take the men from the hospital to pick up their gear for the trip. Everyone has current x-rays, been fingerprinted, and blood work is current."

"Those records will remain in a secure area for that purpose. The reason for blood tests is in case anyone decides to marry or if we have to compare what someone had as normal with something that comes up. I do not want any to have problems with an unknown relative entering the picture. Dr. Meranda takes care of those areas."

"Wear whatever you want to on the flight. We use western wear if we perform or to go to a ranch we own and have to claim," Mara paused for she was thinking about something.

"Quad C, would you fill me in on your talents? I feel you play instruments, have managerial training and knowledge in some new businesses we may be picking up. We also may have to use a few foreign languages before we finish. Any suggestions?" asked Mara.

"I was director of events for the USO. We booked those who did the show tour. Then I became one of the officers for the first overseas deployment to Cataranga. As a result, it fell to me to make the decisions relative to troops movement in the Company I was over. Upon our return, some things came to my attention that caused disquiet in my spirit. I took as many language courses as I could, even listened to them at night while sleeping."

"I took some of my money and purchased a car dealership. It was necessary to hire a manager to oversee the business while I worked. In my off-duty hours, I ran it. I still own the enterprise, and the manager remains in charge until I contact them about what I want to happen."

"Somehow, we also managed to take the Master's Pretest exams and passed all of them, to our amazement," said Jo.

"I'm sure we each have a similar story. If you have a need, call us together and tell us what it is. Most likely, we have some knowledge in that particular area," said Rae.

"That also applies to Quad A," commented Shandra.

"Jero is the director for the stadium and six other businesses we purchased a few days ago. If you have ideas in that area, let her know. Seven of us are Doctors. If there is a need, make us aware of it. All of us are Pilots in this group. We ride horses and serve as Law Enforcement Officers from time to time. Three of us are Judges and Lawyers. We never know when action will be necessary. The lead group is Pat, me, Randy, and Quad-A with a woman you have yet to meet, Granda, who is over all of us. She is our mentor and my Grandmother. The N-Sign Clan leaders are Pat and me, although I am the senior in the position. Jo, your group, will serve as a backup if anyone is injured or ill when that need comes up. Kari is a makeup artist and will give us a makeover if it is needed. In some areas, women are not allowed to own property. The names we use will not make it obvious that we are females. The lead group, excluding Granda, makes it necessary that each become two people. Trust it is so. We are trying to catch you up a little at a time not to overwhelm you. When we are in public, we do not discuss any business. We have had our vehicles bugged more than once. Pat has to check them each time we depart and return. Okay, that is enough for now. Did you pick up the gear you wanted to take with you?"

They made a few stops to be sure all was in place for the flight out. Then it was time to show them their new living quarters.

"Come on, we need to show you where you will be living," Pat said, for they were now under her.

As there were four doors open in the hall, the women entered each one and looked around.

"Pick the one you want, for there is one for each of you. Your gear will arrive, and you can sort it, put it away, except for what you will be taking. Carry minimum luggage on the trip. Leave your Military clothing here, for being Military might not be a plus where we have to go. If you want to keep your Military ID with you, it needs to become part of your clothing or be given to me to keep it secure. Any of the new properties that give us problems will sell after removing whatever we need to. Quad A, which are your new sisters, have suites across the hall from you. Names are on doors to help us all remember who is where. Welcome, and so very glad to have you and your expertise. I am in hopes we will get to know one another better on the flight over," Pat told them.

Mara was checking to be sure she hadn't forgotten anything. Kid's stuff was aboard, check. Then she started laughing. The things she had not gotten done was Granda's stuff and her own. Best get it done now before she forgot again. She moved to Granda's suite and began checking her clothes.

"Granda, what do you want to take with you? I am packing for you," asked Mara.

"I keep waiting for the trip to cancel; why is that?"

"You and I will have gear on board in an hour. One set of Quads has to get their stuff sorted and packed; then everyone should be ready. I have Joy and Joey's gear by the van for loading. Kennet took a suitcase last trip. The Quad B has their gear aboard, as do the men, except for those where you are. They will have to go shopping on the way home as it is difficult to buy for someone else when you have no idea of sizes," explained Mara. She had tried.

Granda told her what she wanted packed. Next, Mara moved to her suite and packed her gear. She knew that Keri would need all new everything. They even had to burn the clothing mother and daughter had on from the store. She made a list of items that she knew the baby would need and headed for their suite with that in mind.

She knocked and was not surprised to have it answered by Randy.

"Is it time?" asked the woman.

"I've been checking all my lists at least twice. I'm here to see if it might help you to have me purchase for Keri and Kelly while you stand watch. That way, we can get everything aboard for an early departure. Is your stuff ready to go?"

"Actually, yes, it is. Put it just inside the door. Will you be going by an arms broker? I need a thirty-two and maybe a three-fifty-seven. Know how to use them both and have a permit for a dream said to do so. I intended to pick up the weapons only we picked up Keri and Kelly," replied Randy.

"Will pick them up when we get the ones for Quad C, who will be in a van themselves. Jo can do that since she is knowledgeable. I will sign for you if you want. It seems you have enough to do here. Sign your name on a piece of paper, and your Mom can handle that. Also, have to pick up clothing for Jerry and Gary, so best they are along to do that. We need to be at Gorman's at eight. The owner said we could get in early to get what we need for all the men. There is a kids' store nearby, so that should meet Kelly's needs. We will need sizes for both Kelly and Kari. Now that I own a few businesses here, the perks that come when in that position are amazing. Pat and I got appointed to the business board for the area, won't take the duty until we get back."

"Dear one, don't you have enough on your plate without adding more?" asked Randy with concern.

"I asked for this duty and agreed to do what they tell me. The other members do not tell me how only to do it. I'm thankful we took the Masters series of exams, for we needed the information," Mara explained.

"You have done a great deal. I'm so thankful for you and the timely rescue. How can I aid you?" asked Randy.

"By being my daughter, by caring for Keri and Kelly, and loving all of us. You watch our backs, even took on the sword when asked to though I know that Physicians usually do not use weapons, yet all of us have that requirement. You fit as you have always been with me. We are truly family, you know. Being responsible for all of you is an honor, and I would not give it up for all the gold there is. When we return, we will set up a panel to govern what is now controlled by this family. I want to wait until Granda is with us again, though. I'm concerned about her. She is afraid, yes afraid, and she wasn't before. The beating took a lot out of her, and we have to give it back. We need her. Unless we can do that, she won't be with us for long. True, I can now do the duty; however, I would prefer that she take part and feels loved and cared for with a job to do that is important."

"Eva will not join us, for she has now become me. My Mother will train her and care for her to the best of her ability. They fit better than Mom and I did. I am glad it has worked out this way, for I'm at peace with who I have become. It is an immense blessing to have as many children, grandchildren, and even great-grandchildren as I have. We have been much blessed. Not the family only, we also have the funds to support what is under our control. We need you far more than you realize. You rescued Keri and Kelly, who would be dead without your intervention. A doctor is needed to travel with us in case of other such events. Granda needs to get her feet under her once again."

"On this trip, I will be leader, pilot, Mother, and all the other titles given to me. Hopefully, my education will help me to do the best I can. Help keep me on track for that maturity is needed to help me keep balance. In time I will develop my own; in the meantime, how can one learn unless someone teaches?"

"You mean that, don't you? When I asked Granda what to do, she said trust and where to find you. I've never been sorry she gave me the direction. You are stuck with me for both our lifetimes. My life would have been over if you had not allowed me to join you. Now I still have my career, a family, and those who love me. All of which I lost as a result of a bad decision. Why would anyone want to follow me? Suddenly my decisions are second-guessed, for I no longer trust my judgment," Randy said.

"Have you asked Thunder?" asked Mara.

"Have I asked who?"

"Let me show you. Put your hand on Lightening. No, don't draw it. Just rest your hand there. Now mentally ask your questions directed at Thunder and see what you learn. My questions are different though I will do the same."

The two of them stood as in a trance for some time. Mother and daughter smiled at each other, exchanged hugs, and returned to their duties; for now, they knew what needed to happen.

A short time later, Randy again went looking for Mara. She was found in the kitchen, setting things up for breakfast.

"You were right, and the trip will happen. Keri and Kelly are fine. Keep teaching Mother mine, and I will continue to learn. Love you," said Randy, who then departed with the message delivered.

Mara sat down on the first available space and stared after Randy.

"Thank you," she whispered.

Those around her so humbled her.

None of her family saw her as a teenager. They saw her as their Mom. She did her very best for them, yet she had times when her faith felt weakened. She felt very inadequate to the task before her. Randy had given her the necessary answer; therefore, she would continue to do her best and trust it was enough.

By seven that evening, everyone was in their rooms, making one think the building was unoccupied. They gathered up the luggage waiting by the vans and took it to the hangar where they joined those already aboard.

"Would anyone object if we took a break?" Mara asked for

Quad A, Kennet and Pat were with her.

"Name the place," replied Shandra.

"Pie, please?" asked Kennet.

Mara laughed and agreed, so that was where they went.

They were chatting as they moved into the restaurant, though their car was in plain view of where they would sit.

"Everyone is healthy at the house, and we go on schedule," she told them. All understood.

"What can I do for you, ladies?" asked a waitress who tried to be their server whenever she could.

"Two pieces of pie and whatever is new," requested Kennet.

The rest placed their orders and sat back.

Mara closed her eyes and thanked the power for watching over her and her family. She loved every one of them and was so thankful for them all. Others would join over time, yet each one would be a separate person and loved and cared for by Mara.

When she opened her eyes, she saw the waitress was waiting at a nearby table to serve them. With a smile, Mara nodded at the woman and put the orders on the table.

"Thank you," she told the waitress.

"You always honor others and never get upset when your meal is interrupted. However, I intend to remain courteous. I am a waitress to finish my education and raise a set of twins. Cameron didn't want to be a Father, so he left, and I have them independently. Not everyone is polite to us, yet I understand how much pressure is on some folks. You have come with your family, and when you leave, you have more with you, for you never turn down a request. That is the kind of person I would like to be," said the woman with tears in her eyes.

"We are here often; why did it seem that today was the time to speak with us?" asked Mari with compassion and understanding.

"Maybe it's because I cannot keep up this pace much longer? Or maybe it was that I'm overwhelmed with the kids, school, and work. Something told me that it had to be today, or I might not get the chance at all. Please will you allow me a chance to learn to be like you?"

"Plan on a week's worth of clothes, and that is all. Please give me names for you and your kids so that passports get ordered. My Doctor will make sure you have the necessary ID's as well as shots. Bring any funds and important papers you have with you to the house. We will sort everything there. Give me the names of your family," said Mara with a smile. She knew this was another they would need before the day was over. Her weariness departed, and she was ready for whatever came next.

"My name is Susan Cloe Finright. My twins are a pair of girls. They are Georgine and Richley. Both of them hate their names and call themselves George and Rich. They are ten years old. I will have to take a leave from my studies at the University," Sue explained.

"I'll take care of that. I know that normally you can't leave in the middle of a shift; however, you have backup this time. You will need the time to change addresses, pack, and learn what you need to know for what is ahead. Tomorrow will be a busy day, and we have to be on the road at five AM. We won't be home until at least ten tomorrow morning. Suggest that your kids get equipped with jeans, boots, a hat, and western shirts in addition to whatever they use for play clothes. A meeting has been scheduled for when we return", Mara explained.

"I'll get Myrta to give us a ride. My car died, so I usually walk or have a friend get me to and from work for can't afford a different one at the moment. You know nothing of me, yet you offer to give me a vacation?"

"It will be a working one; however, we also hope to give everyone a good time. There may be some bumps for the leaders though the rest should be well protected. When we depart, you will receive your severance, and the replacement will be here. We will wait for you outside and take you home. That way, we can meet the kids, and by then, we may have another solution," Mara said, for she thought if the kids were still up, maybe they could take them all home tonight.

"Joy is asleep. I just checked; however, my sleep time is up; therefore, the Doc will be waiting when you get here. What suite do you want them in?" Randy said, and Mara heard her.

"We fill as they come."

Though they departed home with the last load at seven, they found the clock still read that time. Mara chuckled, and they ate their treat, then paid the bill and moved to the van outside.

Pat checked it out then stood to watch until Sue joined them.

"We will put them in the next open suite in our hall. It is a good thing the men are in a different wing. Don't let the kids talk you into taking a trunkload of their favorite toys. They take only one suitcase each; the rest will be home when we get there. Something else you might want to know, we have tutors that are teaching our children. Your two will join those in classes," Mara told them.

Pat had administered the oath to Sue as she would fall under her. Now the twins had an equal number under them.

When Sue had her seat belt on, they followed directions to her home. It must have been five miles she walked to and from work if a ride wasn't available. When they stopped in front of a building that looked like a residence, Susan told them she rented a basement apartment as that was all she could afford.

Chapter 5

Granda and home

"Mom, should we wait here and not overwhelm the youngsters?" asked Shandra.

"That is a good thought. You do that, and we will see if the children are up."

Mara and Pat were the only ones to go in with Sue.

Sue unlocked the door and was attacked by two girls in their pajamas.

"Mommie, you are home early. Are you sick?" asked one of the girls.

"No, I'm not sick; there have been some changes for us," replied Sue.

"What, Mommie?" asked the second twin.

"We are moving to a place where you can go to school with a private teacher. I will be gone for a week, then will come back and will see what to do next," Sue told them.

"Don't you work at the restaurant anymore?" asked one of the girls with a frown, for she knew that their Mother had to work for them to eat and have a place to live.

"I've been offered a new job and need to take some training. We are leaving now. Get dressed and let's go," said the Mother with a satisfied smile.

The twins ran to get dressed while the Mother paid the sitter and located a pair of wheeled suitcases that she had forgotten she had. Sue did as directed, and by the time the kids dressed, three bags were sitting by the door. Pat took them out to the van.

"Sue, take what you feel you want to keep. You won't need the groceries, laundry, bedding, or any of that stuff. Your suite is fully furnished. What you need, we will get. Just lock the door, give the key to the landlord, and by the time you get to the car, they will have inspected the apartment and given you your refund."

The woman was astonished that she got her money back.

When they reached the Ranch, the lights were on outside the building, and the garage door opened as soon as they were close enough to be identified. Shandra put away the unit she was driving, and Cherry parked the other one next to it.

Randy entered the basement door and waited for Mara to approach.

"What have we got?" Randy asked.

"A very weary Mother and two excited kids, the kids may need some items, so perhaps one of the tutors would be willing to go shopping with them. Would you be willing to do the brief? She gave an oath, and the kids need to do the same. She needs to plan on being tested at the U after breakfast. We left at seven now the mother's gear is on the plane. The twins will be going with the rest of our students. It is now seven by our home clock, and I am exhausted. Would you mind if I went to bed?" asked Mara, something she had never done with anyone except Granda.

"It is nice to know you are human after all, goodnight Mom," said Randy with a loving smile.

"Oh, these are under Pat," Mara advised, then departed for her suite with Kennet.

"She is your Mom? To me, she seems only a child," said Sue, who was in her thirties.

"She is that too. I am Dr. Meranda, also called Randy. First thing tomorrow, we will get the medical information on your two and bring shot records up to date before you need to make a trip with our last group of students. The day after is our scheduled departure. For now, come with

me, and we will get you settled in," Randy advised.

"We will need our luggage," replied Sue.

"It is in your room," was the response.

The twins and A Quads were up at four. They knew that there was food in their suite for a meal if they so desired. When the twins reached the basement, they found Quad A in place, for they would be the drivers and aid in getting the patients in and out of vehicles. Quad C was getting up to start breakfast when they drove out of the garage for the next group had an eight o'clock appointment for testing. Mara was thankful that Randy would be there to answer any questions.

"Please tell Granda we are on our way when she awakens," directed Mara, who sat with her head bowed for the trip to the hospital.

If she had looked up, she would have seen that the only one not in an attitude of prayer was the driver. They were all praying that Granda would bind the fear and cast it into the sea of forgetfulness. They needed her with nothing to inhibit her actions and decisions.

When they reached the hospital, they entered by the emergency room door, and there sat the three scheduled for pick up. Each was in a wheelchair with their x-rays and discharge papers on their laps. Looking on with a smile was the Hospital Admin, Katrina.

"You are right on time, I see. Your group is ready and have x-rays as of today. Have a wonderful trip and see you when you return," said the woman.

Mara scowled.

"She is already oath-bound, and I told her," said Granda with a smile, for she understood her Granddaughter's concern.

"In that case, let's get everyone in the vans. We brought two due to your casts," commented Mara. She was tired, however, not as tired as she would have been if Randy had not taken over the new woman and children.

"I'll make a bet with you," began Granda once in the vehicle.

"And what might that be?" asked Mara.

"You didn't eat breakfast; none of you did, though that was your order. Neither did we, for we are tired of hospital food, let's go eat," finished Granda.

Everyone laughed, and the drivers took them to the nearest Restaurant.

Those with casts used their walkers to move. Granda did not have one and walked under her power. They left the wheelchairs at the hospital, for Mara knew the patients would not need them.

The restaurant was nearly empty. Service was slow as a result, for those on duty were most likely doing side work that needed catching up before shift change was their guess. A young woman came from the back and directly to their table.

"I'm sorry, the cook just dropped a pan in grease and was burned. I've been trying to take care of her."

"Put her in our van, and we will get her to the hospital immediately. Meantime we have a medkit that carries some stuff called no more burn. I will use that now and give her some relief. Do you need a cook?" asked Mara, who was instantly alert.

"We have one coming though it will take them an hour to get here."

"In that case, let me take care of that. We will feed our own and any others that come in until the cook arrives," said Mara.

"Thank you; I'm at a loss. I always wanted to be a Chef but never made it. My life is just starting, so the possibility is there to do it. My name is Merry, and I started yesterday."

"I am Mara, and this is my family. With the attitude you have, you will go far. What is the cost of such a school these days?"

"There is a school in France that comes highly recommended; however, so is the fee to enter. Also, there is one in this state that graduates people in the Restaurant business. My dream is to work for a family that is large and will allow me some freedom in what gets cooked," she told Mara.

"You are hired. Give me the names and locations of those two schools. When you return, you are to go to this address and begin work," said Mara.

"My goodness, just like that, a dream comes true?" asked Merry.

"We have been looking all over for a Chef to feed a family of... currently thirty or forty. Would that work for you? Won't be here for a month or two due to business out of the area, and by then, you should finish with school and be ready to be put to work," Mara told her.

"For now, I better get to work, or I'll get fired. Yes, I would appreciate it if you could get the cook to the hospital. Also, accept one of you to aid by taking her place until the cook replacement gets here. I'll return for your order," said the woman who hurried off to take care of a customer who wanted to pay their bill.

Mara got the orders from her group and went to the kitchen to take care of them. The cook was on her way to the hospital, and some breakfast customers were beginning to arrive. The waitress was hurrying to get everyone's order. The orders from the kitchen were pleasing to the eye, and customers commented on the excellent food.

"Merry, you have a special delivery in my office," called the Restaurant manager.

When the woman returned to the N-Sign group, she had a puzzled look on her face.

"I just received a grant that will pay for both schools I mentioned. Now I need to get a passport and figure out how to purchase a ticket to France. Did you have anything to do with this?" she asked those at the table.

"No, however, if you would be willing to leave tomorrow, I know how you could get there without going in debt," said Pat, after checking with Mara.

"I was going to stay with a friend until my first paycheck from here. Looks like good timing to me," laughed the young woman.

"What time do you get off work?" asked Pat.

"My shift is six to two."

"We will pick you up at two and take you to our place where you can meet some of the family," advised Pat.

"Thank you, gotta run an order is up," said the young woman who didn't run. She hurried to take care of business.

An hour later, the person who told Merry of the mail came out and looked around.

"Merry, where is Gena? She was supposed to be helping you; however, she just called in, said she overslept. I also got a call from the hospital, and they said our cook is there with burns on both arms. What is going on?"

"The cook dropped a pan in hot oil. A customer offered to take her to the hospital. I accepted. Then another customer said they could cook until the relief got here, which would take an hour. I took her up on the offer and have seen some nice looking meals come out, plus the customers are praising the food today. Here comes the cook now.

Everyone has ordered, and the side work is ready. Today will be my last shift, at this time, as that letter you gave me was acceptance to a Chef's college in Paris. I leave tomorrow," said the young woman with a smile.

The woman asking questions was in shock. Merry was just seventeen and had accomplished all that in one hour? Why had she not kept an eye on things, as she should, being the Office Manager? The youngster had completed a lot more in an hour than the manager had in the last four.

"I will see that you get a good recommendation, and your paycheck will be ready when you go off shift, as well as a bonus for all you have done to keep things going smoothly today," replied the manager, who then went to make a call to the owner.

Mara returned to the table when the cook took over. She had her meal in hand and sat down to enjoy. Shandra joined her, for she had taken the cook to the hospital and returned to eat.

"What is going on?" Mara asked her twin.

Pat filled her in.

"Merry has earned that money. She also caught up on the salad making, put a dozen pies in the oven for later, and caught up the dishes. It seems to me that there is only one on the shift."

"And what were you doing, sister mine?" asked Pat.

"This place has a fast pickup for food. Delivery boys were here as soon as I entered the kitchen, and I have put out about two hundred meals in one hour, and that is in addition to those ordered within the place," laughed Mara.

"You didn't make the pies, though," said a disappointed Kennet.

"If we have time this afternoon, I will make you a whole pie just for you," Mara said, then she got up and hugged her son.

"Thank you, folks, for all your aid. I could not have done it without you. They just told me I have the rest of the day off and get a paycheck for a week of work. The reason they gave was: to give me time to pack if I leave tomorrow. You get two hundred dollars for your part in keeping things going," she told Mara and handed her the money.

"Why don't you keep that too and use it to buy something you want in Paris? Get whatever you have here, and if you have a vehicle, we will follow you, then take you to our house after you pick up your belongings."

"I have an old car, but it runs. I only took an overnight bag, as I did not know for sure if this job would work out or not. The last few minutes have shown me that I can do this and no reason to be concerned next time."

"Ours is the red van. Cherry, would you be willing to take her car to the house? We still have to get some shopping done, and she might want to pick up some items for the school. You know where we will be; if you feel you want to rejoin us, one of Quad C can bring you to us. Merry can travel with us for now," Pat advised and saw the nod from Shandra for Cherry to return.

When they reached the men's store, they found the owner pacing the pavement. He ran to the van as soon as it stopped.

"Oh, thank goodness, I was afraid I missed you. Bakker can't get in due to a wreck on four-forty. Therefore, the register will be my duty," he laughed with relief for the income was needed.

They unloaded everyone and moved into the building. Each of the adults aided an adult, and it was soon a done deal. Granda was looking in shop windows as they passed other stores.

"Now, there is something I've not seen in years," Granda

commented to her companion as they slowly walked to the men's store.

"What is that?" asked Mara.

"A traveling dress like Mom used to have. It is cool in summer, warm in winter, and easy to wash. Can even roll it up and put it in a backpack yet shake it out and put it on," said Granda.

Mara saw Pat looking her way and nodded. Soon Pat was chatting with the man in the men's shop, and later she departed with someone else. She took Michelle with her, for none of them were to travel alone. When they reached home, there were two of those garments on Granda's bed as well as each of the adult group found two in their favorite colors and patterns waiting for them.

Once the men had what they needed, the women moved to the kid's store and picked up a full wardrobe for Kelly.

Mara had noticed that Joey needed diapers, which were getting low, and he was growing out of his clothes. Kelly needed a car seat as Joey had one. Pat began to chuckle, for in the door walked Randy with Cherry, Kari, and Kelly. Now they could fit the clothes to the need. Merry was to purchase what she needed, and since she was now on the N-Sign payroll, she would have the money required. When everyone had what was needed, they made a final stop for Jo was the one who volunteered to return with Cherry, and due to those going with her, she remained with the group. They stopped at the weapons store and picked up the extra that group members needed. When all errands were complete, they returned home.

It appeared that someone had lined the drive with horses.

"Hey, Granda, your welcome committee is out," laughed Mara.

"I should say," she rolled down her window to speak with them.

"Hello there, Pi, Thunder herd, thank you for the welcome. I have missed you all," said Granda with a smile. The horses whinnied and danced to welcome her.

The vehicles went into the garage, and the group took the elevator to the level where various ones lived. The men had help in reaching their quarters. Granda was assisted by Jo and Mara's suite, for Pat received a call from one of the younger kids.

Once everyone was settled, the packages' inspected, and the receivers' surprised, they could stand still a moment.

"Granda, I have to take care of a piece of business then will come to visit for a while," said Mara.

She ran to Randy's room and, getting no response went to the medical suite. A tap on the door brought Randy on the run.

"Can we check the x-rays?" asked Mara with excitement.

"It is as you said. We can remove all casts and let them move on with life. All are one hundred percent healed," said Randy with a look of amazement on her face.

"I'm bringing the men first; then we can make a to-do over Granda. She seems to be doing well. However, I'm not taking any chances," commented Mara.

"Pat, could one of the Quad C bring in Gary and Jerry? Will meet them in the medical unit," said Mara. She was so excited she was hopping from one foot to the other.

Randy had gotten a full medical facility when the door opened; therefore, she had all the tools she would need to do that job. There was even an x-ray machine and a means to read said x-rays.

When Gary hobbled in the door, he headed for the first chair he saw to set down. He had a body cast from his toes to his hips. Although his casts were only to his knees, Jerry had the same, and both men wore shorts to accommodate the devices. They had guesstimated their shoe and boot sizes as they could not try them on in the store due to the casts.

"Jerry, let's take a look at you," Randy said, and he went to a private room where they removed his casts.

"You need to remain here while we take care of Gary. You are now fully healed and can walk normally. It will make the trip tomorrow much more enjoyable. When I finished with the three of you, you need to take a nice warm shower and get into some clean jeans. That will tell you if you as healed as we believe you are," Mara told him, for both men had worn shorts after their surgeries.

"Gary, your turn to be checked," said Mara professionally as she led him to the room where Randy waited.

He cried when he saw his new legs. They were firm and not an injury or scar to be seen. They left him to enjoy while they moved to Granda's room to get her. She was brought to the clinic and given the same information.

"The x-rays show your hip completely healed, and you should have no more problems," Randy advised.

"That hip has bothered me for years. Thank goodness it won't anymore," the woman said with a smile of joy.

Mara went to get the men and took them to the waiting room, then returned for Granda.

"Welcome home fully healed family members," said Mara while Randy looked on with a huge smile.

"Anyone want to dance?" asked Randy in jest.

"Oh yes," was the response from all of them.

"Need Quads A and C to join us in the Med Clinic," said Mara.

Pat gathered up Joy, Keri, the adult Quads and went to see what was going on. It was nap time for the littles.

A bit of music was playing in the background, and soon everyone was dancing. It was a wonderful memory for all who participated. The AI piped the tunes throughout the area.

"I'm going to go play the piano," said Granda with determination, so the entire group followed her to where it sat.

Before long, there was a full jam session going; some didn't play but danced, and some did both.

Two hours later, Mara called a halt, and the group sat in comfortable chairs to have the meeting just as the last group returned from their testing.

"It is time to catch everyone up. Meet Granda, my Grandmother, and yours as well. Granda, you need to know: Quad C introduce yourselves please," Mara told them, and they did.

"Jo."

"Rae."

"Chris."

"And I'm Spicer." Each replied.

"Now Keri," directed Mari.

"I am Keri, and this is my daughter Kelly," said the young woman as she stood.

"Susan," directed Mari.

"I am Susan and have twins, George and Rich, though they are girls," laughed the woman.

"Merry, your turn."

"I am Merry and am hitching a ride to Paris with you to attend Chef School so I can come back and be your Chef," said the young woman from that morning.

"Guys, I think you remember Granda; however, this is Gary, Jerry, your fellow Hospital patients. Then, Chester will be our outside lead guard, though he will be going with us, and the current staff will continue until our return. Price has also asked to travel with us and think that covers everyone."

Pat and Mara looked around at the group and saw only nodding of heads.

"Granda, I think you know everyone now. Today I have some promises to keep. There are pies to make for lunch, with one for Kennet alone. Everyone is packed, and those items are on the plane, which is fueled and ready to depart. All vans we use to get there will remain in the hangar for when we return. We will take all the vans we have as we never know how many will be returning. There will also be a truck and horse trailer so that Pi and Shira have a nice ride. The horses know the plan. You need to plan on an early night for we depart at four AM. We will be eating out in the morning to save on prep time. After that, we board the flight. Shandra…"

"Our first stop will be in Nashville, Tennessee. How much time we spend at each location is up to the leaders. The second stop is Texas; then we go due south. What that tells you is that we will be going into diférent climates, with a lot of them cool this time of year. Dress comfortably. It is a four-hour flight to Tennessee. We rented a hangar for the time we are there so that no one except us has access to the plane. The same will happen at each place we stop at for a time," said Shandra.

"May I make some suggestions?" asked Jo.

"By all means," replied Mara.

"The Quads should stay together, especially kids. My group can take care of them if you give permission. Randy is guarding, I understand; therefore, put Joy and Keri with her along with their kids. My understanding is that

Kennet moves with the twins. Dan and Gwen can watch over Granda while the men watch over all of us. That way, no one can take off with any of our group."

"I ordered a truck and trailer for our four-footed friends. It will be waiting at the airport in the hangar we rented. No one needs to know that they are on the plane," said Mara.

"With forty of us, I rented four vans for Tennessee and Texas. Out of the country, we will do whatever we have to with what is available. The weather in the south will be the opposite of what you have here. Dress accordingly. Tennessee and Texas will be hot; therefore, all vehicles come equipped with air-conditioning, as does the truck both in the cab and the trailer. No one moves alone, kids, that means you especially. Stay with the adults. Quad A, your main duty is guarding the airplane. Once South America business is covered, we will stop in Australia then fly to Paris, which also requires us to check out two ranches, which we will require a bit of a drive. Then make a stop in England as well before we return home."

"During the day, kids will be with Tutors. When we land at an airport, only a few of us will leave the plane at that time. We need to see where the places are that we have to see. Also, we need to decide as to what has needs done and our welcome. Once those duties are over, we will all do a tour of the city. If you see something of interest, notify the driver, and she will relay it to me. We will decide if we stop or not, although the business has to come first."

"I also have a suggestion," said Granda.

"Go ahead," said Mara with a smile.

"The T Twins need to also travel with guards. If the kids remain at a motel with their teachers, two guards would be enough to leave them if they do not go wandering around until we are all together. Meals can be ordered in and billed to the room. That would free up Quad C to move with the Twins if Quad A is to guard the plane. Now you see why we are doing some stateside ones before we try the out of country ones. We can work out some of the bugs and make sure all bases are covered," offered Granda.

"Granda, why do I get the feeling we should leave the kids and their Tutors home, except for Joy and Keri or maybe including them, plus Kennet has to be with us? We will have Jero, Sue, and Merry with us. Sue's two can remain with the Tutors. Why not leave them while we do the two nearest? That will give us a chance to look at what we are doing and what might need changing," Mara suggested in turn.

"That would be my preference even if it means that Quad C remains as guards," said Jo.

"Let me check out some things; then we can make a decision. Right now, I have pies to make. Could we discuss this after the meal?" asked Mara with a smile.

"You are in charge, so do it any way you want to," said Granda with her great smile.

"Thank you all for the input. I will talk to you again after we eat. Enjoy your free time until then. I appreciate and love each of you. Without you, this is a task beyond me; with you, it is doable, and we will give it our best shot," commented Mara.

Pat and Granda just smiled and nodded their heads.

Mara headed for the kitchen, and everyone else vanished. Granda returned to the kitchen once the others had scattered.

"Welcome home, Granda. Oh, how I have missed you," said Mara as she ran to hug Granda.

"It is good to be here. It did give me a chance to look at the care one gets in that hospital. Understand it has changed a great deal since you took over. Some of the patients have been there a while, and they said it was a huge improvement to no care and big bills," Granda informed her as she returned the hug.

The older woman sat at a small table by the work area of the kitchen. Mara got out the ingredients she would need as she continued talking with Granda.

"We have a wonderful family, and with their input, I should stay out of trouble. I'm learning, though not fast enough, it seems."

"What are you going to do with the stadium?" asked Granda.

"Thought we would have concerts with the family. However, I am not sure now. We also inherited a couple of stadium managers. They are already setting up events to start when we return. There is also a riding arena for riding shows. That might be what we would be doing; however, we now have the possibility of having many horse breeds to put on a show if we so desire. Right now, my only push is to take care of this property."

"Then why not take Quad A, Doc, Kennet, Pat, you and me? That gives you guards and the necessary team?"

"It excludes Pi and Shira, though. It would be nice if we could write in those locations and ride our horses there. The problem with that would be someone would recognize a horse, and we would be in trouble again. Someone suggested that we hire some folks whose sole job is to go to these places and check them out. We can claim them through the mail or courier mail, then have our team check everything out for us. That seems like the best idea to me. The problem is no one knows who to hire," Mara told her.

"What do you mean? I thought that was why we acquired Quad C. Why not have them do contact and check. You will have only four people moving, the property will get a full inspection, and those ladies have the training to wear weapons. I saw what Jo purchased while we were at the armory."

"Since Jo is used to being in charge, why not send her as leader of the team, and they can change ID as needed by contacting me if they need to? Once the properties are taken care of, you can decide if you want to pack up the family and go sightseeing in a foreign country after solving the property issue. It would put fewer people in danger, for they would be representatives, not owners. Have you asked them if they would be agreeable?" Granda asked.

"It is not my intention to listen in; however, maybe we need to offer a different suggestion," said Jo as she entered the doorway.

"We are discussing that. Sit down and talk to me while Mara gets those pies in the oven, or we will have too much of something and nothing of something else," said Granda with a chuckle.

"What you now call Quad C consists of four ladies that knew one another before, although I did a background on all of them. They were undercover agents in a few places and knew their craft. I am trusting that our oaths to you will cover us as well. Remember, this is not public information. Each of us swore to follow the directions of those who would rescue us and think that will have some bearing if you do send us in. You could not pay me enough to take my kids to the places you will have to go. Yes, we will follow whatever orders you give, though we will also warn of danger if we are aware of it, as in this case," Jo told them.

"One of our concerns was traveling with weapons and animals. You see, Thunder Twins and Kennet cannot travel without their mounts and Shira. Quad A members have the training to replace the twins if something goes wrong. They are also our pilots, as are Pat, Mara, me, and Kennet. Oh yes, and Randy has the same training," Granda explained.

"What training do you all have? Perhaps we have some of it as well," responded Jo.

"Mara, give her the list, or should I call for Pat?" asked Granda.

"Just a second, and I will have these pies in the oven then will give it."

After setting the timer, she sat down to answer.

"Accountant, Bookkeeper CPA; Administrator of Hospital or clinic; Architectural Drafting and Design for homes, business and aircraft; Business; Chef; Computer Tech; Equestrian; Lapidary, which is precious metals and stones; Law enforcement; Leathercraft Master; Legal - Attorneys, Judges; Managers of Business such as stadium, corporations, and ranches; Martial arts in at least four disciplines; Mechanics of our planes, vehicles and most equipment; Medical Doctors including Surgeons and Ortho; Musicians; Pilots; Real Estate buying, selling and renting; Veterinarians; Weapon assembly, disassembly, and marksmanship; writing and think that about covers them. Have you some you want me to add?" asked Mara.

"What type of degree do you have?" Jo asked in surprise.

"Oh, those are just the Master's Degrees, and all of us have those, which is around forty as I recall. Today, everyone of age is trained with that knowledge and have taken the Master exams," she replied matter of factly.

"Is she serious?" Jo asked in surprise, for she took the tests yet didn't realize the impact of what she was taking.

"Yes, you see, they need the certification to show when they have to deal with problems. Only family members will know how fully qualified they are. They only share what they must in a given instance, like when they acquired the hospital and Clinic. We keep getting new members like you four, and she wants everyone as well trained as she is. However, she remains in charge, and that will give her more different points of view from which to make an educated decision for each person learns differently and uses those skills differently as well," explained Granda.

Chapter 6

AC Quads on duty

Randy tapped on the door frame.

"Room for one more, what is for supper, Mom?" asked Randy, who never mentioned that she was in the conversation the whole time.

"Let us have soup and pie since we are undecided as to what tomorrow's schedule will now be," replied the girl. She had put some crockpot soups to cooking before leaving to get the patients. Since nothing was frozen, it should be ready for the meal.

"Sounds good to me. Do you want me to throw on some dunking bread?"

"I'm for anything that is homemade bread," laughed Mara.

Randy took out the ingredients and soon had the required items in the oven.

"It has been suggested that Quad C become property managers until teams get hired or the property sold in various areas. I know we want to bring home some of the horses to keep the breed pure though not sure how to do that. It will mean setting up some ranches locally," began Mara.

"Oh, I forgot to tell you, picked up that ghost town and found out it is an entire valley, so got it all. It seems the state is getting rid of Real Estate that is not productive, and this fell in that category. Understand there are other such places in our area as well; therefore, picked them up before someone else did. We could probably put a couple of dozen ranches there as well as the shops you mentioned. Didn't Jero say that you would have a lot of shop space in the new buildings you just got?"

"Yes, however, not sure if we need to keep them open all the time or only at events, which would mean factoring in employees, and that is a whole different ballgame. We need a board to make those kinds of decisions. With all of us having the knowledge we need to share the work," replied Mara.

The pies came out of the oven and went on racks to cool. They could smell the quick-rise rolls baking.

"How long would you ladies need to cover South America?" asked Mara of Jo.

"No idea since we don't know what we have waiting for us. Fortunately, I speak the lingo," Jo replied.

"Oh, that is what I forgot! We are linguists and have around thirty, or is it forty languages in our repertoire? We are also chauffeurs and drive anything with wheels, wings, or tracks. It seems reasonable that we might need them in dealing with these properties," said Mara as she continued with supper.

"I don't have that many, but do have a few," laughed Jo.

"You have as many as we do. You see, you are now part of Thunder Press and family. We all do because what one of us has, we all do. Except for a few tricks, I keep to myself to rescue us if it becomes necessary. You will have to learn the sword drill before you depart, I think. I will get the mail going to claim the properties and make sure you have copies to show your authority. You will each have dual passports to be sure they don't refuse to deal with you because you are females. You depart at six AM on the current schedule. Do you want to try the Tennessee one and Texas, or do you prefer we do them?" asked Mara.

"I think your idea to try the ones in this nation before going to another is sound. We will do that if you don't mind. Would you allow a rental car or two in each of those states?"

"Yes, you will have the vehicles, and a private jet is going to take you where you need to go. Shandra and Cherry will be your pilots. Due to the distance, you will have to take Mitch and Gretch with you as well. In time you will also be pilots; however, for now, these are certified. You have passed the pilots exams; however, now you have to take an actual flight with an instructor to be tested for your license. They can take turns securing the aircraft. Before supper, we will check out the jets and look at the new permits for both personas. Do you have makeup kits, or should I order some from Kenders?" asked Mara.

Jo's eyes got bigger at each bit of information.

"Oh, by all means, order the kits," she smiled.

"Randy, do you want to go for a ride with us? Need Quad A, Quad C, you, me, Granda and Pat, oh and Kennet."

"I notified them, and they are at the vans," said Granda.

"Your sisters will love you even more now that you are going to allow them to fly, which is their first passion," laughed Mara as she ran for the door.

Everyone loaded up, and Shandra drove them to the hangar. Inside were two new jets with seating for twenty in each.

"T1, you keep this up, and you will need an airport of your own," laughed Shandra.

"Suppose we can work out something," laughed Mara though she had already factored in one within the valley where they would build the craft town.

They checked out the aircraft and found them to be new. The titles were in the same name as the other two. Shandra pulled out her pilot's license and noted that it showed her as proficient in this one and the others. She smiled and continued looking things over.

"Jo, if you want to, we could probably leave right after supper. It means we would get into Tennessee late; however, you could sleep in and go from there," suggested Shandra.

"We have a lesson we have to do after supper. After that, we can go," replied Jo.

"What lesson is that?" asked the pilot.

"Something to do with a sword," Jo told her.

"Not a problem; we are the teachers."

"Let's go eat, or do we do the drill first?" Jo asked, not because she was hungry, she wanted to be on the way.

"Might want to do it here where no one is watching, lift your right hands, if you are right-handed and the left otherwise," laughed Shandra.

Jo did as directed immediately, for she could begin to believe with all she had seen. The other three followed her action. When the shielded swords were in their hands, they waited to see what was next.

"All of you do as one of us does; however, you have to be slightly behind us. Never let a friend in front of an unshielded sword called Lightening. Your swords are not activated," directed the lead Pilot.

Shandra began the drill, and each sister replaced her at the end of five minutes. When her turn was up, she aided the rest in doing what was required then returned to the lead spot to take another turn when some were having difficulty.

"Did anyone notice what time we left home?" Mara asked for they all needed to trust, and at the moment, she did not feel they were.

"Yes, it was at three. Isn't that about the time now?" asked Randy, who caught on quickly.

"It was a bit before that. If you have the drill down, we can stop by the flight tester for certification, then go home and eat. You might even be in the air by three," commented Mara.

Jo looked at her with a raised eyebrow yet said not a word.

"Have Faith," said Randy, who had so recently learned about faith and trust.

"Okay, let's eat then."

"We need to make sure the jets are full of fuel, then we can go," said Shandra.

The tanks were full, so they left the jets in the hangar. They did the testing for a pilot's license and went home for dinner. Everyone had their permission to pilot now. However, some hands-on would be appreciated.

Dinner was as good as expected, and everyone ate their fill. The lead group learned that there had been a change in plans and only Quad A and C would be going. The third Quad was enjoying the learning and didn't mind at all. Dan was getting the hang of knowledge, and Gwen was doing her best to beat him. Now that they, too, had been tested, they could quit the learning. However, they wanted to continue and didn't realize they knew what Mara did.

Mara was amazed that no one objected no matter what she told them the plan was, so she didn't do that anymore. She told them when to be where and let it go at that. True to her prediction, the first jet was in the air at three local times. In minutes they contacted her to say they were in Tennessee and staying at a local motel. They had picked up the rental units, and there was a restaurant nearby for breakfast. The women were a little tired. Therefore she directed them to rest and be ready to go tomorrow, even though it was early.

"They don't realize how much they did in fifteen minutes.

In my research found that most of the ranches carry the same name. As a result, we have checked for all ranches on this planet under that name. There are twenty-four. We hold title to all of them. Jo will have to hire managers for each location unless she feels we should keep it and maybe the managers, while Quad A will test those who apply. I will locate a plane equipped for moving horses and dogs when they let us know what they are bringing home. All ranches may have the same kind of animals."

"I'm not at all sorry about any that have joined us. The expertise of our new members has added to ours as what we have has added to theirs. Jo has a good head on her shoulders and is not at all averse to taking on whatever project you assign. It is not her plan to take your job for having been the one in charge, she knows the challenges you take on always, and the fact that you are younger is also in your favor with them. Each member of that group has a specialty. They are doing what they were trained to do, yet with someone over them who has the training for overseeing one with those talents.

I'm looking forward to the reports they send. Shandra will make them aware of how to use the devices she took to issue them. They will come in on a separate line to us so that only we four will know what is going on, other than them," Pat responded, for she had worked with the AI to get the calls where they needed to go.

"I have a directive," said Granda. "Everyone in this household is going to bed, and no one is to get up until fully, and I do mean fully, rested. Good night!"

Granda told the AI they were offline until the following day, and everyone did as directed. Mara was thankful for she was exhausted and needed to give her body some rest and a chance to adjust. She woke up once in the night and listened to a conversation with the group that was in Tennessee.

"Mom, someone is messing with the vehicles," Shandra

was heard to say.

"This is T1; you have two options: confront them and hold court to keep down the numbers that could give you problems or let them do what they will and file an insurance with the rental company when you get up," responded Mara.

"We are on it," replied Jo.

Mara went back to sleep without even realizing she answered them though they asked for Mom.

At eight in the morning, Mara rolled over and looked at the clock. She had to admit that she felt better. A quick shower made the kitchen next, to begin breakfast. Everyone was to sleep in, and she hoped they were doing so.

"Mom, I'm hungry. Can I have some of my pie?" asked Kennet as he wandered in with a wet head, which told her he had showered.

"You are going to turn into a pie if you keep this up," said Mara though she nodded at the pie for him to go ahead.

"Will we be busy today?" asked Kennet after he swallowed the pie in his mouth.

"As you well know, we have no idea until things happen. Why, are you bored?"

"No, though I might catch up on riding, music, and running," he told her.

"Why running?" she asked.

"Pi ran with me, and it was fun," he responded.

"Okay, though I do not recall that being part of the training. Nonetheless, we will join you after our breakfasts settle."

"Why not wait for breakfast? The rest are at the stable now," he replied.

She chuckled then told him, "That kind of activity should have been before our showers."

"I know, but then I wouldn't have gotten my piece of the pie," he laughed.

Randy entered the door.

"I put Jero to watching the small ones and sent the rest to the stable. I thought you might be here. Are you going with us?" asked Randy.

"My son seems to think I should, so breakfast is on hold."

As the three moved toward the front door, they met Granda headed in the same direction.

"Time for exercise?" she asked them.

"That is the rumor I received as well," Mara commented then they waited for Keri, Joy, Susan, and Merry to catch up.

"Race you all to the stable," called Kennet, and they were off and running.

Everyone was laughing when they stopped. It felt good to be doing the running. Mara breathed deeply of the warm summer air and was thankful for her home and family. Feeling a bump, she turned to find Pi wanting her attention.

"Yes, dear, I'm sorry we have been so busy. Now that we have A and C Quads, we have some time to spend with you and the rest of the herd. I'm thinking about getting some miniature horses for the younger ones to ride until they need a full-sized mount," Mara explained.

Pi spun on her hind legs and took off running.

"What did I say?" questioned Mara herself.

Soon they saw Pi returning, and she had a herd they had not seen before.

"Pi, where did you find these? Who owns them? Yes, they

are what I had in mind though the eight-year-olds could use some a bit larger. Joey and Kelly could ride these, I'm sure," Mara told her mare.

Pi whinnied to her herd, and they moved to the fourth stable and went inside, for it was empty. She then led Mara to her saddle.

"It looks like Pi wants us to go for a ride. Saddle up everyone," directed Mara.

They did as directed and soon were riding alongside Pi for the pasture gave them room to do so.

The house was gone from sight by the time they reached the destination that Pi was going to. She had stopped at a gate to allow it to be opened and closed. The next time she stopped, there wasn't a gate. It appeared to be flat land. The mare stopped, so Mara dismounted, and the rest followed her lead. Pi walked to a dip in the area's rolling hills then took a trail downward with riders following their mounts.

"Why do you think they belong to me? I wish that I could understand what you are telling me," Mara commented.

::Then why didn't you ask?:: said another horse.

"Okay, I hear you, now please explain."

"An older woman lived here and cared for the animals. A month ago, she was taken away in a vehicle with lights flashing. Her spirit had departed. We were visiting over the fence with Pi, and she said that we needed homes before winter. All of us agree that being out in winter without a caregiver is not good. That is why she brought us to meet you. We need help." A palomino mare stood next to Mara, and she knew that was the one speaking.

"How many of you are there? Who owns the property? I will need to acquire you legally to do what this requires."

The mare left and returned with a can in her mouth. She

gave it to Mari, who opened the container to see what was in it.

It contained a note and property title. The letter read: [If Star Gold gives you this message, she has chosen you as the next caregiver for my friends. With the note is the title for the property, which is now yours. That includes the land and the animals on it. It is a full section and was signed over to you when I signed the deed. Also, she can lead you to any funds on hand at this location. Love them, and they will bless you.] The signature was Mary Jo Preston Riley.

"Okay, that tells me who owns the property. It will be registered as soon as we can get to the office that does that. It will have to be backdated to when Mary Jo signed to make it legal. Since this property is adjacent to mine, there are some decisions to make."

"They will have to decide if we use the stables we have or put up new ones at the home place to accommodate all of you. Two of our kids look after the horses and dogs. We require horses for children. Would you allow them to ride you and learn the proper way to ride?" asked Mara.

"Yes, we are looking forward to it. Remember if you don't believe it limits those with special abilities, like your mare," said the voice.

"My name is Mara, and I'm the one in charge. I am learning, and thank you for being willing to teach."

"Would you ask your Stallions not to bother ours?" asked Star Gold.

"You have more than one as we do?" asked Mara.

"Each type of horse has its a stud. Just as I am Palomino, there are other breeds here as well," the mare explained.

Before long, the women were playing chase with the small horses. After all, Kennet said they had to run. The women were tired but happy and ready to have breakfast when they returned to the main house.

Sharron L Ensign P.O. Box 583 Helena, MT 59624
Mara Trains Randy
406-458-7091

Mara spoke with each of her studs and explained what was going on. They agreed to breed only with the larger horses and none of the small ones. Mara would need to be present at any mating, for there were records on every animal that continuously required updating. Suddenly she realized that this was indeed a ranch. Now to find someone to take care of the animals, mostly if she did what she planned on doing the next day.

They ate breakfast, and after Mara gave music lessons to those who wanted them and were not in school. Granda joined them because she liked hearing the instruments. They even asked Mara to play for the group, which she did, but only if Granda would play on the other piano. The house rang with the music, and everyone was happy.

Kennet was left to practice his guitar while Granda, Randy, Pat, and Mara had a meeting.

"All except the kids in classes will be flying out tomorrow. We are going to Paris to get Merry enrolled in Chef School. We should be back in a couple of weeks. There will be a train trip to London, a quick stop in Spain to look at some horses, then we return home. Someplace along the way, we need to hire a housekeeper. We have a Chef, once she finishes school. The little horses' visit reminded me that feeds for all the animals' needs purchased and the buildings made ready for winter. The stables will need a makeover to accommodate the smaller breeds. As I understand it, each breed will need a separate building. How many that means, I'm not sure. The stud will have a station near the building where his mares live. We also have to have personal gear for the weather ahead. All I brought was my summer stuff and my books. The complex needs thoroughly cleaned, which might mean hiring it done by a company that does that. Now we need to purchase some professional clothing as well as personal stuff . The freezer needs stocking to keep this bunch fed. So does the pantry. The planes will need winterized and stored for the winter. Adverse weather is part of winter, so we must do the same for all vehicles.

If any of you have things you need to do, do them. If it is something that needs ordering, add it to my list, and I will get it done," Mara advised.

"Since my work list is the shortest, at the moment, give me the list of what you want me to put on order, and it will happen. While we are in France, there are three things I would like to do, and it shouldn't take long. I want to have my picture taken at the Arch de Triumph. Would like to see the Eiff el Tower and see the river that runs through there," was Randy's contribution.

"If you see the First place, it leads directly to the second, and the river runs between the two as I recall," said Granda.

"As I said, it shouldn't take long," replied Randy with a smile.

"The Mothers of our group have not been out of the house at all. I want them to go with us, and if you say it is okay for the small ones, then that will work. The kids in school can have a week of stay over with the tutors if they agree, which means that Gwen and Dan remain with them also to look after the horses. They can take them to the park, go for walks, ride horses, and study. I'll. Amend that, Randy will order in some easy fix meals or catered for while we are gone, and Granda will approve the expenditure. Our AI will secure this wing, for no one has reason to be in here if we are gone. We should be back before the Quads. If we aren't, then Shandra can ID with the AI."

As if the speaking of her name summoned her, Shandra called in.

"Mom, we held court, and it resulted in another batch of businesses, however no ranches. We will be here a while to get it set up the way it should be."

"Not to worry. We will be taking Merry to France, and since we will be there, we will cover the two ranches on that continent. That will allow you the extra time you need," Mara replied.

"Thank you; I will tell Jo. If you get a chance, stop by and give us some input," said Shandra.

"We will, and thank you for checking in," said Mara, who cut the call.

"Not sure what that was about; however, we will be making a stop in Tennessee as they have something they do not know how to resolve. Granda, will you check with the Mothers and see if they want to go? Randy, let me know if the babies are old enough to fly. Pat, now that I am taking all incoming calls, would you please check with the tutors and see if they are agreeable to taking on the kids until our return? That means they will take on all of the school-age plus oversee Dan and Gwen who plan on remaining," directed Mara.

Everyone departed to handle the business assigned.

Mara sat and thought for quite a while. Now she had a better idea of what the requirement would be in Tennessee. It was a decision that Mara would have to make. She ordered vans to meet them at the airport in Nashville the following morning and then booked rooms where the rest of the group stayed.

The Mothers wanted to go along. The babies were approved to make the flight as well. Pat said the tutors would keep the kids until the leaders return. Gwen and Dan would watch over the horses while the Tutors watched over them. The kids would not move without an adult in attendance. Mara told them that meals would be available; however, the teachers said not to bother, for there was plenty in their freezers to take care of a few children, as they knew there would be times when the leaders would be gone.

As a result, those designated to go east left immediately. They had their belongings in the large plane; therefore, all they had to do was claim their luggage, put it in the smaller airplane, and they could be on their way. While

Mara was doing preflight of the jet, she asked Pat to see if there was stabling for Pi and Shira. A quick check said yes, there was, and they were in it. Mara called the tower for clearance, and the jet fell in line for departure.

When they touched down in Nashville, they saw the eight women waving from the meeting area, for they had secured their jet in a hangar, and the women told where to put the second one. The vans had been picked up and were also in the plane security building. The eight ran to the hangar once the second jet was in place. Everyone received hugs, and all then went to a meeting before they departed to do what was required.

"Each group will take a van, therefore load up, and we will join you as soon as we can," directed Mara.

Cherry was assigned one of the vans, and she took Joy, Keri, Merry, and Susan in her group. Soon Granda, Randy, and Pat joined that load.

Soon each van had a load, and they were ready to move.

Mara was with the Quads to answer questions about the previous night's activities.

"Okay, fill me in; what do you need me for?" asked Mara with a smile.

"When we took care of those guys messing with the vehicles, we picked up a group of felons that had a lot of funds and wants. The money is in our jet. The vehicles they were using are in storage until you decide what has to happen. However, some property was involved. Upon checking it out, it was not something you would want to keep. We did, however, check it thoroughly before selling. Even asked Thunder for input," said Shandra.

"Jo, what do you have to report?" Mara asked for she felt an urgency from the woman.

"In the buildings we inspected, we found car carriers. Each had a full load of vintage vehicles. If you have a use for them, they can probably be sent home. It looked like they were using a warehouse to stockpile items for sale. That building we still hold. The items came from all over the US and look like quality products. The puzzling thing is there weren't any stores in the inventory. That is the first thing we would like you to look at," said Jo.

"Lead the way," said Mara, and Jo took a different street to get them to the place.

Jo took them to the warehouse district and one specific building though they looked like a large metal snake with one structure after another all connected. Jo held the key. The vehicles were parked inside to be sure nothing came up missing. One section had pods in it, which were open and full. Jo reported around a hundred of them were stacked in rows though she had only opened the bottom of each tier.

Mara stood thinking for a moment, then looked at Jo with a smile.

"They have to be loaded on trucks and sent to the new businesses we have at home. There they will be unloaded and inventoried. There is more here than you know," she advised Jo.

"My thought is that they need moved as soon as possible and sent by various routes to their final destination. The backup of the group we stopped will be here in hours to remove this stuff before we can take possession," Jo told them.

They stood and watched as the pods closed and disappeared. When Jo seemed concerned, Shandra had the answer.

"Thunder Press," she told the woman.

"Does that include the collectible vehicles they had?" asked Jo with a smile at the information.

"Of course," replied Shandra.

They got in the vans, and as they looked back, the warehouse also was gone. Scratch that concern.

"Next?"

"What this gang had here was extensive. By the time the felons were in law enforcement custody, things had changed. The businesses awarded to us via the court were sold. The court records were amended, showing what the gang purchased in its place."

"The first one was a race track. Those are difficult to move, and I thought perhaps you would rather not own a gambling track. We held the racer stock that was there, for each was a champion, complete with full pedigree, and remind me of those you have at home. I put them under your corporation name. The property sold while we were moving the horses in trucks that came with the property. In its place was a string of restaurants. We kept one of those and checked out the employees. You will want to look at that one. However, the rest sold," laughed Jo at the look on Mara's face.

"So what you are saying is you have time to claim what you want, then follow the money to the next place?" Mara asked as she began to understand the magnitude of what was going on.

"Something like that, yes."

"Okay, lead on."

"Have you eaten?" Jo asked.

"A few hours ago," responded Mara.

"Granddaughter, that was hours ago. Hopefully, you plan on eating more often than that," Granda said, and they all heard her. Everyone laughed and drove to the restaurant.

When they saw it, Mara thought it was just a typical restaurant. The outside was not at all impressive. Once inside, she saw the difference. It was a vast buffet with every kind of food one could want. Mara paid the fee for everyone, and they moved to an empty conference, and there the group had space to eat. There were other such rooms nearby, and Jo advised that all of them were electronically secure.

"Are you saying we own this one?" asked Mara.

"Yes, it was the best of the lot and will have the best resale value," explained Jo.

"I think you have a different idea as well," commented Mara.

"This location would cover all the craftsmen and women at this end of the country. It is central on the eastern side of the states. You could have them meet you here to show their wares and not do as much traveling as you would otherwise. You would have access to fresh nuts, maple sugar, lobster, bagels, to name a few things that would not be cost-eff ective to purchase on the open market in our area. That would also give you an available place to land if you need to work on the east coast. The motel we are staying at goes with it," Joe told her.

"What makes you think we would want to travel this far to keep track of employees and such?" asked Mara with a grin.

"Oh, it comes with a manager who has made this place what it is. She asked to remain as Manager since she knows the area, the market, the employees, and the business. Just a moment, and I will locate her," said Jo, who got up to do just that.

Soon she returned with a woman of about thirty, at a guess.

"This is Rebecca, called Becky. She ran this establishment and asked for continued employment."

Mara noted that Shandra had risen and had one hand in the air, no doubt using Thunder to check the feasibility of keeping the woman. A nod showed approval.

"We would like to keep you in the position you now hold. Your employees will need to meet with us, though you first need to take an oath," said Mara.

The woman laughed with joy.

"Finally, an honest owner knew sooner or later I would get one," Becky told them.

Mara introduced her group once she heard the oaths.

"What education do you have?" asked Granda.

"I'm a school trained Restauranteur. Have college degrees in business, marketing, and management. Now can cut up most foods we serve and know the right way to do it due to taking a course in being a butcher. I have an account in several major businesses where we get the products you saw served. Took some of the profit and invested in each of those businesses. Try to keep costs down and products up. I have been here for six years, and we have been in the black the whole way, I'm glad to say."

"Did the former owners support you in your decisions?" asked Granda.

"Let me see, Mom did. Then she died, and the merry-go-round began. She left the property to Jason, my brother. He gambled it away. The guy who bought it just wanted to seem legit and didn't care how I ran it as long as he could say he owned it and that it was profitable. That was where we were when he got shipped to a prison, and you folks inherited the property. You can't imagine how thrilled I was when Jo and Shandra told me that the new owners were honest and might be willing to let me continue as manager. One thing that will be different is this time; you get the financial base that I have kept hidden as I waited for an honest owner. I told the last guy that we were breaking even. Supporting illegal business is not something I am going to do. I will quit first; therefore, refused to furnish money to aid him in his endeavors. Have a draftsman's rendering of what I would like to see done outside the building, pending owner approval. With a crook in charge, I put the folder in a hidden place. Advertising is ready to be placed, though didn't want to do that without owner input," Becky told them.

Chapter 7

Just one more

"Perhaps you should be the one owning this establishment," replied Granda.

"No, I do not want to be the owner, which is why Mom left it to my brother, who is now in prison. I like running it. My preference is not to be the owner. You can adopt me if you want and keep it in the family, though please make me the manager. I am even willing to manage more than one such place," responded Becky.

"You have the job. One added requirement is you have to report to our leader once a week until she is sure she knows the business, then it will be once a month," Granda advised.

"Who is your leader? I prefer to deal with them directly."

"I am. You see, I am the one adopting, and this is my family or at least part of it. We could use this location as a base to locate craft items we need for a few events planned for the west. We will need Real Estate to have a craft show open to the public with us having the first call. We can purchase or order what we require then leave the shops open to the public. They have to be useful items, not junk, and the craftsperson needs to know what they are doing and be willing to keep us supplied with their products. If they decide to quit doing what they are, someone else must have the training to keep the products coming as needed. We will also look at new products as they come available. We have a manager for that area," Mara explained.

"If you ever want an overall Restaurant Manager, let me know. I love to travel and know the business well. It would require a new vehicle if I'm to drive all over. I use a vehicle a year, about. Can't fly a plane or would ask for that," she told them.

"Becky, you are hired to run this Restaurant and to oversee any others we finally own. You will have the training to fly; however, I think it will have to be west of the Mississippi before a plane is needed. We have a hangar at the airport you could use, plus units on hand. Your name has changed. I need your birth date, age, and education. When we are out this way, we will let you know, and you can go home with us to see who we are if you are to be part of my family"

"I'm twenty-seven years old, born November 4, and would like to keep the name Rebecca as it was a family name and also the name of a dear friend who is now gone. Becky is fine for call name. What is my last name?"

"N-Sign and you spell it N *dash* S I G N. I am Mara N-Sign, and this is:…" she introduced each of the people with her, including Kelly and Joey.

Shandra was handed a passport to Becky to let her think it had been there all the time.

"Do you know of someone knowledgeable who is honest and willing to manage a motel for us?" asked Mara.

"Yes, I do. Give me an hour, and the woman will be on-site," responded Becky just as one of the servers asked her to take care of an issue.

She gave the new owners time to enjoy their meals before returning, and when she did, it was with another woman at her side.

"This is Hilda Hungerford, who was born in Germany. She has lived here since she was one year old. She went to college to learn motel management; however, they won't hire her due to her age and lack of experience. She grew up in that business even as I did in this one."

"Hilda, I need your age, birth date, education, and

passport. Would you be willing to work for us as manager of a motel near here?" asked Mara once she saw the nod from Shandra.

"Which one and where?" she replied instantly, then handed over her passport showing her birth date, plus her resume, which listed her education.

Mara took time to read the resume and also looked at the woman's age. She was twenty-one; no wonder folks didn't want to hire her. Their loss was Mara's gain. According to her paperwork, she spoke seven languages and could live at the motel if the owners allowed. It would cut expenses for her and give on-site management for them.

"Meet us at the motel at four. Right now, we have other businesses needing attention. At that time, we will see that you get the position. What we would like to do is put you over any more motels that fall under our influence. They may be located out of the country as well as within. Those you see with me are part of my family. As you can understand, I do not have a lot of time to spare; however, I will do what I need to to the best of my ability."

"Hilda, didn't you say you wished someone would adopt you?" asked Becky.

"Yes, then will apply for citizenship in an American name and leave nightmares behind," responded the woman.

"What name would you like?" asked Mara. She looked at Jo and saw the woman had a very still face, yet Mara was sure she was taking it all in.

"Is Heidi an American name?" asked the woman.

"Let me see: Heidi N-Sign, has a nice ring to it, I think," laughed Mara.

"I will take it and thank you for a dream come true. Have three questions, if I may?"

"Go ahead."

"What is the pay, when do I start, and may I take my guard dog Benson with me to live there? Oops, make it four, is a vehicle included?"

"You start later today, yes to the guard dog, and you will have to give me time to research what the pay for that position is, for we wouldn't want to short you. Vehicles will be delivered later today or first thing tomorrow," replied Mara though the AI at home had given her the location information.

They finished their business at the Restaurant/Buff et, and the Quads took them to the next location.

The Quads asked Mara to wait as they explained the person who lived in the house, which sat before them.

Granda got out to stretch her legs, for she could hear what they said regardless.

The door of the house opened, and a woman on crutches came out.

"May I help you?" asked the woman with a smile.

"Oh, just getting some exercise due to a recent surgery. Do you live in this beautiful home?"

"For a few more hours, then have to leave. I'm out of funds and have to find someplace else to live. Rusker and I have lived here for both our lives. He came when I was sixteen. Until my injury, we made payments on this place. Now can't work, so we need to leave," the woman explained.

"What is wrong with your legs?"

"Fell down the basement steps, good thing that Rusker was here. He called nine one one."

"Who is Rusker?"

"A child who dropped on my doorstep the first year I lived here. He is five now. It makes me rather concerned about where we will be living. He was adopted as soon as they let me."

"Do you have much to take with you?" asked Granda.

"No, what money we had was to pay for rent and food. The place came furnished. Medical bills are rather large, so I quit going. I want Rusker taken care of first of all," replied the woman.

"Hello, Melissa, these are the folks I wanted you to meet," said Shandra.

"So good to see you again Shandra, didn't think you would return."

"My word is good. Where is Rusker?" the Guard didn't show any concern over the comment.

"He is playing in the front room. I told him not to come out as I wasn't sure who was here."

"May I bring him out to meet these ladies?" asked Shandra.

"Why not bring everyone inside since I know you and have met this wonderful lady?"

Everyone departed the vans and moved inside. The inside of the home was neat and orderly. There was plenty of room for everyone to sit and visit.

"It is nap time for those littles; why don't you put them in this room and let them rest while you folks tell me what I can do for you?"

The two with small children did as directed, and soon the little ones were asleep.

"Would you be willing to leave this area? I know somebody who can repair people if that is ultimately the problem. We have some wonderful surgeons that have done wonders for others we have taken to them," said Randy at a nod from Mara.

"Only if Rusker can go as well and be taken care of while I get fixed, plus you need to tell me how I'm to pay for it," said Melissa.

"There won't be a charge. You have met our youngest children though we do have others who are in school at the moment. He will be our first five years old though there are four eight-year-olds. You would both be welcome," Granda advised.

"Really and truly? You would take us where they can fix me? With a place for Rusker while I mend?" asked the woman in shock.

"What type of work did you do before you were injured?"

"I always wanted to keep house for someone with a nice big home. I like taking care of pretty things. Those folks where I grew up said I was too dumb to have that kind of job. I wasn't real good at schooling, and that is why I left there. They said no one could stay past sixteen, so when the time was up, I walked away. Going to make sure Rusker gets educated, though."

"Why don't you gather up what you want to keep and come with us? Yes, Rusker too. We have some business to take care of, and you will be staying in a motel tonight. Tomorrow we leave for France. However, we will only be gone about a week then return home to take care of business and family there. Would you like a plane ride? We will have to get you a passport, so please give me the birthdates and full names for both of you," advised Granda, for Mara was speaking with someone on her com.

Shandra had been watching the rental vehicles outside from where she was checking out the new people. She gave a sign to Jo, and the Quads left the room. Pat went with them.

"Stay put, folks; we will be back soon," said Mara as she, Shandra, and Kennet followed Pat.

"What can we do for you folks?" asked Mara, and as soon as she spoke, the team moved from where they were to slightly behind her, except for Pat, who matched steps with Mara.

"These are our rental vehicles, and we are taking them back," said one of the men.

"Not today, you aren't. We paid for these vehicles, and they will remain with us," responded Mara. Pat shut up as soon as Mara joined them; therefore, none of the Quads said a word as they watched.

"Those are our orders, and we will follow them," said the same man.

"Your choice, however, these vehicles are not going anyplace unless we are the ones taking them," said Mara as she stood relaxed before the men.

Shandra moved a little to get the newest Quads' attention, who then proceeded to be where they should be, which was slightly behind Mara. Pat stood next to her Twin, and Kennet was behind and between the women.

The man raised his arm, and two dozen men came instantly.

"I still say no," said Mara.

"Get this over with," said the man to his group.

Mara turned as if to walk away though she was allowing space to use the swords. Her group backed up as she moved.

"Twins down," shouted Kennet, and the group of women dropped to their heels.

As Mara turned, she was facing a bullet that had stopped less than a foot from her. She drew Lightning and went to work. The Quads watched as Mara and Pat took care of the incoming. Mara asked for a silence bubble when all the men were down, and Thunder Court began. Mara's person would record in a small recorder for the authorities while their AI also kept a record.

"Empty their pockets and allow pictures," said Mara.

When the women finished following her orders, she again spoke.

"Man in charge, speak up."

"I'm Razer; what do you want?" he asked with a frown.

"You just attacked Thunder group. That will cost you your freedom. Give me your name, address, any property you own, do you have kids, and where are the ownership papers for the vehicles you have in your possession? What are you doing, and what is your intent?"

"Those vehicles are ours. They that had them didn't need them, and we do," the man replied though he tried to lie, it still came out the truth.

"You will not be taking possession today. Those vehicles go back to the ones known as owners. Now about the other items you own," continued Mara.

By the time they finished, a rather long list was in their possession, and to their amazement, it was in the states though not all in the same ones.

"Pat, take over," said Mara.

Pat called for local law, and when they came, she presented the court's documentation and the judge's decision. To her amazement, no one questioned either of them, just loaded up the felons and signed a receipt for them. Pat put on gloves, then checked the vehicles they were using. The team remained outside to keep an eye on things until Rusker and his Mom were ready to depart.

Pat was not surprised when she found the vehicles bugged. She checked for the under-seat release, and it came as no surprise when the floor opened in each of the vans. She added that to the recording and paperwork that the officers took with them.

In a matter of minutes, two officers returned.

"You wished to speak with us?" asked one of the men with a smile though it was not threatening in any way.

"We busted a ring that is moving contraband. Here is the release location. These vehicles need to go to your cop shop and new vehicles brought here to replace these. Please make sure the ones you bring are clean," said Pat.

The man she had spoken with made a call, and soon new vans arrived. Pat did a sweep and found them clean.

"You also have about forty vehicles that need identifying. They belonged to those we sent to prison about an hour ago. The judge gave us the vehicles; however, they will need checked out by your folks and replaced. Thank you for your assistance. We always abide by the laws of the area," said Pat.

"I wish everyone did. Okay, have drivers on the way. Will you point out the suspect vehicles?" he asked.

Pat did as directed with aid from Lightening. Some vehicle movers came, and those designated as belonging to the men were loaded up then the contract drivers left with the trucks. Any that belonged to people living in the area returned to them.

"Okay, we are ready to depart. Let's go before anyone else urgently decides to be put in a prison cell," Mara said.

The team entered the vans and gave places to Melissa and Rusker. Their small suitcases were in the back of the vehicle assigned.

Still, the Quad said nothing. In silence, the vehicles moved to the motel, where they had another appointment. The twins went inside, and the rest remained in the passenger vans.

A young man was at the front desk watching over the area.

"Is your owner or manager available?" asked Pat.

"I will check and see," he replied.

When he returned, he had a frown on his face.

"The bookkeeper says we are getting a new one this afternoon. I asked new what, and she said both positions. Guess that means a new owner and a new manager. Works for me, as long as I keep my job because I have to pay for my schooling," he told her.

"What are you studying to be?" asked Mara.

"Want to be a program manager and work on and with computers. Like making robots work and finding ways to help disabled folks," he replied.

"When you get that degree, give me a call. Might have a job for you," said Mara as she handed him a card that said M. N-Sign. He wrote a note on the back and put it in his shirt pocket.

"Since we don't have an owner or manager at the moment, who would be next to speak with?" he asked.

"How about whoever you spoke to?"

"Okay, her name is Myra, and I will see if she is busy," he replied with a smile.

When he returned, he had an older woman with him.

"Myra, I don't know their names. However, they wanted to speak with whoever is in charge. For now, I think that is you if we don't have an owner or manager," he told the Accountant.

"Would you be willing to take an oath? Both of you?" asked Pat, who then led them in the oaths.

"I represent the corporation that now owns this business, and one of the women coming in the door is your new manager. We have the necessary paperwork to show ownership. Heidi will be in control and have access to us whenever needed. Currently, we are staying here overnight. Part of our group will depart in the morning; however, the eight you also have booked will remain until their work is also done," Mara advised.

"That will be fine, Ma'am. We were advised by legal that you were coming. Just as a bit of information, I retire in five days. Would you also hire an accountant to fill my slot?" said the woman.

"It has been done, and thank you for your service. Do you have a retirement fund in place?" asked Mara, for Granda was asking.

"No, they didn't pay one here. I will have to go to work someplace else that is not as stressful," the woman replied.

"Give me your bank account number, your name, and home address. Your retirement will be there within a week. It will take a little while to get the paperwork done. What would we do without paperwork?" asked Mari with a laugh.

"There are days when I would like to find out," said the woman, although she was pleasantly surprised.

A young woman entered the door and stopped to allow them to finish their conversation before starting her business.

"An accountant, they need an accountant? I am one if they won't hold my age against me," said the woman though she spoke with Shandra, who was near where she entered.

"Stand right there for the count of five. Now, wait a minute. Mom, your applicant is here," said Shandra.

"Did you check her?" asked Mara.

"Yes, she is good to go and has her resume with her."

"Oath then we put her to work with this woman to learn the ropes," responded Mara, before telling Heidi she had a new employee.

When done, Mara asked the young man for another room for her group. They needed to put the last two in it. She ordered a passport for the two new family members, and it was at the desk when they had everything resolved. Until then, the desk clerk had no idea who they were for the reservation was made by their home computer, and he did not hear any names in the conversation with the accountant.

"Now, it is five PM. What would the girls like to do for a meal? Do you have any other plans for us," Mara asked Shandra, who was in charge of the mission though Jo led it.

"There is a good show at the auditorium, and we thought this might be a time for Jero to talk to performers here. It would allow her to get some contacts for home. Do you want us to continue with chasing this 'we sold it' story? Otherwise, the new Quad needed the training you have now given. We can continue from here if you have to be on your way."

"Tonight, we are all yours. Tomorrow at six AM we depart, so get all your answers before then. You need to know there is another jet in the hangar. It is for our Restaurant Manager, and on a guess, she will probably share with the Motel Manager. The airplane cannot move until Becky is authorized a pilot's license. The show sounds wonderful, and I agree that Jero will probably be elated at the possibility. Book all of us if you will."

"How many is all, since our numbers have a habit of changing," said Shandra.

"You are not wrong. We currently have. Please wait a minute; we forget the men. If you want to include the two we just adopted, twenty-three for tickets, though three of them are ages one, two, and five. Since we are only going to France, would you and Cherry mind flying for us while Michelle and Gretch can fly with Jo? Pat and I will meet your qualifications for backup."

"That is my preference, as well. I volunteered my Quad for this mission due to Jo's lack of training. Now, they are trained and see no problem in turning it over to Jo. Let me advise her of the change," Shandra told her second Mother before going to fill Jo in.

"Granda, we are going to go eat, then a concert and a night of sleep. We leave early again to miss most of the commercial traffic. Shandra will be pilot with Cherry for backup. The rest of the other team will continue with Jo in charge," Mara explained.

"I want you to go to your motel room and remain there for now," said Granda.

Mara was surprised yet did as directed.

"Randy, I need you. Everyone else can check out their rooms. Melissa, if you want to remain in the lobby until we leave for dinner, it probably won't be a long wait. They have an elevator, so you should have no problem getting around," Granda advised.

Most went to freshen up before dinner. Pat used Granda's room as she would be with Mara and Randy. The rooms didn't accommodate more than two unless one asked for a suite.

The Doctor had a puzzled look on her face as she met with the two women in Mara's room.

"We have a problem, and hopefully, you have the answers. Here is what is happening: Mara keeps getting more and more tired. She is exhausted from taking care of that small group at Melissa's. If she is to continue with her duties, you have to find a solution. We knew that putting some book gold in her clothing would rejuvenate her for a time. Now that no longer works. What would you suggest?" asked Granda with concern.

Randy began with the usual doctor type questions: any illnesses, allergies, surgeries, etc.

"I want to check something out." She raised her hand, and an instrument landed there.

She took a blood sample from Mara and checked it. She spoke with the AI at home and got the previous sample information.

"I want to try something. Have you ever had a B-twelve shot?" Randy asked.

"No, yes, I know what they are, yet no need. Why? What did you find?" asked Mara with a tired yawn.

"You need some vitamins. Somehow they are being depleted in your system. I'm going to give you a B-twelve shot with vitamin D in it. You are to lie down for thirty minutes while everyone gets ready for dinner. Then will see how you are doing," said Randy. She knew it would do no good to beat around the bush, for Mara had the knowledge and training to identify her symptoms.

Without comment, Mara did as directed and was instantly asleep.

"How long has this been going on?" asked Randy.

"I didn't notice it until we got back from the hospital. I do not have a time frame of how long, although I heard the comment about being tired a time or two before that. We need Mara far more than she realizes. She is our foundation, and without her, it could all crumble around us," said Granda.

"We can't let that happen. Too many would-bes affected if that came to pass and us most of all. Will see how she is in thirty minutes, then go from there," replied Randy.

They departed the room and returned to their own. Granda found Pat waiting for her.

"How is she? What can I do to help?" asked Pat.

"You knew?"

"Yes, for what she feels, so do I. We are identical twins in every way. Randy, bring your kit to Granda's room, please," Pat told the doctor. A tap at the door, and she was there.

"If you treat one twin, you have to treat them all. If you treat a Quad member, you need to cover all those that make up the quad. It would be best if you gave me the same shots you gave Mara," requested Pat.

"Then let's take you to your room, for you too will have to rest for thirty minutes to allow the medicine to move through your veins," advised Randy, who didn't hesitate at all.

Once the twins were asleep, Randy and Granda had a visit. Neither of them ever shared what was said, although the AI shut off all communications for five minutes.

"What time is it?" asked Randy with a frown.

"About four, I would guess," replied Granda.

"More like three, and we only got here at four. Thunder has entered the picture, and the twins will sleep until five, then we will go out to eat. With the shots and good food, I hope to take care of the problem. I do know that Mara asked Shandra to pilot the plane from here and Cherry to ride second. That does not sound like anyone I know," said Randy.

She sat thinking for a moment, then told Granda to roll up her sleeve. She promptly did as directed.

"Shandra come to room two-two-seven and bring Cherry," directed Randy.

When the two women arrived, each received the same

shot that the twins got.

"On a bet, Shandra and Cherry have become part of Mara while the other two have split and will join C Quad. Not intentionally, just the way it is working, it looks like," directed the doctor, who then had Granda explain.

"Good catch, we missed that one," said Shandra.

"Now you two go catch a nap," directed Randy, and they departed immediately to do just that.

As it turned out, the entire group took a nap. They awakened at five minutes to five and went to eat. Only Granda and Randy knew about the actual two hours they had slept. Besides, knowing Thunder, it could have been days instead of hours if that was what was needed.

They enjoyed their meal then went for a walk in the area of the restaurant. The neighborhood was peaceful, and no one was bothering any of the vehicles. Pat noticed that the parking lot had cameras all over, and the security crew watched those areas regularly.

When they reached the place the concert was they were met by four security people.

"We have had a security breach, and so your vehicles will be occupied by officers until the show is over," said the man in charge. They thought he looked familiar then realized it was Chester from home.

They enjoyed the program, and when it was over, they went to a snack bar around the corner. Then it was time to go back to the motel. Their vehicles were waiting.

"May I hitch a ride?" asked Chester.

"Yes, get in," replied Mara with a smile.

"They told me that you need a guard for your vehicles," he explained.

"Truth," replied Mara.

When they reached the motel, the clerk told them of another reservation. It was for Chester.

"So where are Gary and Jerry?" asked Mara with a smile.

"In the room next to mine," he replied.

"That makes three; where is the fourth one?" asked Mara.

"He was driving the other van."

"I see one jet stays here, and we will take the larger unit for the rest of the trip," Mara chuckled, for she was feeling a great deal better.

"You said we were not to travel with funds, so put the charges we made on the Corp account."

"Thank you; Granda will pay the bill. Now we will sleep so we can be in the air at six-thirty tomorrow morning. Good thing I have your passports," said Mara.

"So that's where they are. Tried to find the documents; however, we departed so fast wasn't time to do much looking," said Chester.

"How did you get here?" asked Mara as it began to dawn.

"In the big airplane, we didn't pilot it, just rode in it."

"Then who was the pilot?"

"Understand it was Thunder," he replied.

"Ah, now things begin to make sense. Okay, thank you. Now get some sleep, and we will be on our way to Paris tomorrow. We are meeting the other team for breakfast," Mara explained.

He departed, and so did she.

She was amazed that he had that much faith, yet he was from the book; maybe that had some bearing on it.

"You are in room two-zero-eight. Here is your key; I will see you in the morning. Some of us need some sleep," Pat said though she was laughing.

"Wasn't my fault you lost two of your Quad; now you have one Quad and a set of twins," Mara laughed.

"I know, but seriously, with you fielding all calls, we better have separate rooms. One of us has to be awake for the flight, especially if they turn out to be the pilot."

"Won't happen."

"And why not?"

"There have been a few changes while we were napping. Chester, Gary, Jerry, and Price are here. We will be taking the large plane they arrived in and leaving the Restaurant Manager's jet, who will share with the Motel Manager. I understand from Chester that there are still two of the smaller jets in the hanger at home. I have sent the funds that the enterprise team collected to the vault at home. Pi and Shira are aboard the big plane. Also, Shandra and Cherry now fall under me, for they will pilot us. Gretch and Michelle are piloting the Military, making them a sextet though I am betting they will move back to me and remain a Quad once things settle. The four men will fall under Pat, that's you, isn't it?" asked Mara with a chuckle.

"Ask me again in the morning; right now, I'm not sure," replied Pat, who instantly went to sleep.

Mara laughed and took the other bed with a silence bubble over her twin.

Chapter 8

Was it worth the trip

The following morning found everyone up, rested, and ready to eat. The manager was waiting for them at the restaurant.

"Good morning, folks. Ready for breakfast, lunch, or dinner?" she asked.

"Anything with pie or my son will revolt. The rest of us probably eat normally; however, never know if you aren't the cook."

Mara was feeling great. Now that she knew why she was so drained, she could let the medication fill her and get back to work. Being in two places simultaneously and piloting an aircraft the size of the large one had truly drained her. She flew solo in a plane that should have had a pilot and copilot. What little energy she had left was used to take on the felons at Melissa's home. The plus was that all her adults had now received training. The mothers got an outing, Merry was on her way to school, and the four men were now with them to serve as guards. She had learned it was okay to split the group; however, her part had to have guards at all times that were not part of the lead force. The group in Tennessee would finish up there then move to Texas to cover that area.

The flight was a beautiful one. The sky was blue, the water calm, and those not flying had time to relax and rest for the next adventure. Mara knew one was waiting. As she told them, they would never know all she knew.

"Doc, I want to thank you for taking care of us. You are much-loved daughter mine,' said Mara when she located the woman.

"You are not going anyplace ever again without a full backup and all trained," said Randy.

"They are all trained that were told to be. The men will be with us on any future trips. We have a Chef getting trained that can even travel with us, a housekeeper onboard, a watch guard at home, kids getting trained, all adults qualified, new vehicles headed home, as well as a full warehouse that will need sorting. It is probably on that empty lot at Riser and Fifteenth, or it could be in our backyard. Who knows? It should be fairly close to the properties we purchased for a dollar, which will make it easy to move stock from one place to the other. There were some pretty expensive trinkets in the one pod I opened."

"We, as the leaders, should check them out and see what is in the pods. Then we need to liquidate some on the net. Also, they could use some of the items at the stadium. We get the first choice if something is needed. I have some collectible weapons in the vault along with some other valuables that we can add to that batch."

"I should have gotten my weapons from you," Randy said, for she could never stay upset with her Mom.

"Not really; they are in sealed boxes and have never seen use. It just dawned on me I forgot to check the date of manufacture," Mara explained.

"Just being able to say my seventeen-year-old Mom gave it to me would be a wonderful conversation piece," laughed Randy.

"It would be at that," replied Mara, who was also laughing.

"No one would believe this family unless part of it," said Randy.

"And even some of those haven't," the girl replied with sadness.

"Mom, never have regrets. Those who didn't believe are in the minority. Do the best you can with what you receive, then move on. Don't second guess yourself, for it is a waste of valuable time; if you are always honest, you never have to remember what you said. Love those who are family, no matter how you got them, and trust only those who have earned that trust," Randy advised.

"Good mottos to keep in mind," Mara told her daughter.

"That's the hard part, keeping them in mind," responded Randy.

"When I was fifteen, I knew that something wonderful was going to happen—no idea what just that it would happen. Before sixteen was looking at College and thought that might be it; however, Mom wanted me at University. That wasn't it either, as I never got there. The day I read a book and found myself inside it was the beginning of my adventure, and it seems new every day."

"Have you any regrets?" asked Randy.

"Yes, I should have never brought Star here. On the other hand, had I not gone, become Thunder, and brought them all back, their dreams would never have come true. Nor would I have the wonderful family I have. For all positives, there are also negatives. It is up to each of us which we keep track of," replied Mara.

"Ah, such wisdom from one so young," replied her daughter.

Suddenly their conversation was interrupted.

"Mom, where are you," called Kennet.

"I'm here talking to Randy."

"Shandra wants to know if you have a minute to talk to her before she has tower contact," he told her.

"On my way, and thank you," she told him. He went below, and she knew he was talking to the animals.

"You wanted to talk to me?" asked Mara.

Cherry got out of the copilot seat and gave it to Mara.

"I'll be back in a few," she told the two women.

"She says I need to talk to you. No doubt she is right. She knows me well after all these years. You made me the lead guard. Now over half of them are on the other team. You made me a pilot and moved two of my backup to the other team. What is it you wish of me?" Shandra asked as she was getting concerned that perhaps she had done something she shouldn't have.

"Well, first off , you are still head of the guards and the two groups of people. The thing that changed is your insistence is that I will be your Mom for the request was recognized, and you have moved to where I can be your Mom, though your duties didn't change much. You fly for me, not for Jo, which is about all that happened. The other two will probably return to me as well once this flight finishes. Since I am the leader, the board said I should not be doing any more flying. I suppose my flying an airplane at the same time I was fighting some felons and rescuing a few businesses might have had something to do with it," replied Mara matter of factually.

"You did what???" Shandra almost shouted though she made sure no one else heard it over the headpiece.

"It seems that as Thunder, I decided that I needed the men here. None of them fly, so I went back and got the plane and the men. It was the same time we were checking out the restaurant and motel, then the battle at Melissa's was as the plane landed. That is why I was so tired. Now I have eaten, rested, and been given some vitamins, so I'm good to go only have to watch those kinds of stunts they tell me. Use them only in an emergency, I understand," Mara filled her in.

"Mom, you are now and always plus a magician at times, along with a lot of other titles. I'm glad we are under you, and Cherry agrees. However, if you take any long trips, like the one Jo is on, would you please make sure we all go?"

"That's a promise I had to make to your sister Randy as well as Granda and Pat. Yes, I promise we will all go, though that is not a good idea in case of an accident of any kind. When Jo returns, she will be hiring a team to do what they are doing now. Without having done it, she would have no idea how to train. Now she has the training. I desire to keep us all busy and enjoying life together. When duty calls, we have the training to handle it. When time allows, there is a family to love and a lot of work to get done," said Mara.

"I will help any way I can. Thank you for explaining, and please don't split your personality unless it is a life or death thing. Consider yourself as receiving a hug, and I will give it after we land and clear customs."

Mara chuckled and departed for Cherry was back.

The pilot notified the passengers to resume seats for landing. Everyone hurried to do so. The babies were taking naps and had been strapped in during that time. Their Moms had seats nearby.

Everyone noted the Eiffel Tower, Arch de Triumph, and Seine River as they flew to the airport. Once safely on the ground, they waited for the escorts to check out the plane, check the animals' records, look at all weapon permits and review all passports. They secured the Jet in a hangar while they caught a bus to take them where they wanted to go. The first stop was to get Merry situated; then, she could walk around with them if she liked before settling in.

She said she just wanted to get settled. She would tour later though she gave Pat and Mara big hugs and a thank you for the ride. Her class started in three days, with the fee paid. She had a private room, which was a luxury in her life.

They next took care of Randy's requests. All of them got a picture at those three locations. Two men remained with the plane while Shira and Pi stayed hidden as they were with the women. Only Mara knew where they hid hidden, and that was on the buttons of her blouse.

They took tours to see England, Germany, and France. One of the ranches was in England, requiring another stop. The horses were hunters, and according to the display case in the house, they were champions. Mara discussed with her leaders, and they said the management should remain in place. It would be up to Jo who to keep and who not. They rented a bus to go to Spain for that was a business trip. When in the town nearest their destinations, they stopped at a motel. Mara selected the rooms for everyone in the group. She would cover the bill. The lead group and guards departed for the destination while two male guards stayed with those remaining behind.

The place they had the address for was a large ranch. According to the paperwork, it covered thousands of acres. Those in residence welcomed them. It was a good thing that the lead group all spoke the language.

"Welcome, welcome. You are the new owners?" said a woman who ran out of the house to meet them when the bus stopped.

"Yes, we have that blessing. Can you tell me about your family, the ranch, and the horses it holds?" Mara directed.

"Come we see, I am Seniorita Conswella," replied the woman.

When she entered the house, she spoke one word, and people came from all over. Mara introduced her group, and each took a seat after introductions. Conswellia offered them food, and Mara accepted the offer, for it had been a long drive though they enjoyed the beautiful countryside. After the meal, they were offered rooms for a siesta. Mara explained that they had to return to their family left behind and could not stay the whole day. They saw the buildings on the property, all of which were in good repair and appeared freshly painted.

A bell called in the horses. They entered corrals and waited for the reason for the summons. Soon a Stallion trumpeted. The team remained in place except for Mara and Shandra, who moved to where the stallion was.

"Hello, fellow. We are the new owners and would like to see a show of these horses, so we know what they do and whether or not we want to take a pair to the states with us," Mara explained.

He asked her to release him, and she complied. He walked with them back to the rest. His step was high, and his tail flagged. Stopping at one of the corrals, he waited for entry.

"No, don't do that. The big boy will create mischief," warned the woman in charge.

"By his oath, he will not," replied Mara, who then entered the corral where the stud was, and with his permission, she mounted and rode him in the corral.

"Pi, tell him that I am going to let them all out and want them to put on a show for us. We need to know about this breed. When finished, I will ride him wherever he wants to go and for me to see. We will make some decisions afterward," Mara advised.

The horses were at the corral gates as Shandra opened each. They moved out of the holding pen and into the pasture, where they waited for orders. The stallion trumpeted, and the horses quickly lined up as if at a show. They ran, jumped, danced, and showed the discipline under which they trained.

The woman who was their guide stood in open-mouthed amazement, watching the horses perform. Never had she seen such a show, and she had been in charge of ranches since in her teens.

"The horses from the field may return. Stud you will have to return to your holding station. We will discuss and let you know what we plan on doing before we leave," Mara advised once he gave her the tour she agreed to.

He walked to his area and waited while she dismounted, then nuzzled her neck.

She laughed and hugged him.

"Yes, it was a good ride. Thank you. Are you the only stud here?" Mara asked him.

He shook his head.

"Please show me the others before we put you away."

Again he did as directed. They approached the first location and saw an old stallion who looked longingly at the pasture.

"You have until time for me to leave to enjoy the pasture, then, will have to return you to your station," she advised him.

He stood at the gate to the pasture, and one of the ranch hands opened it for him at a nod from Mara. The stud walked into the field and began munching grass before he rolled on the ground and shook off the dirt. He ran and drank from the nearby water trough. Not once did he move toward where the mares were watching. He looked upward as if thanking a higher power then returned to the gate. Mara opened it, and he returned to his pen. He, too, hugged her with his head and neck. There was a sparkle in his eyes that had been missing.

She saw two other studs. One was a fiery two-year-old, and the other a settled nine-year-old. In each case, they showed her their talents. After returning them to their pens, she spoke with the woman.

"We are going to make some decisions before we leave. If you don't mind, we will go to the bus to discuss," said Mara.

The woman said to send the driver to the house while they did that. They thanked her and did so.

"Jo, how are things going where you are?" asked Mara over the microphone she wore.

"We are in Texas though we picked up three ranches on the way here. We have located a ranch manager/foreman. He has two horses he would like to bring with him for he wants to move and prefers Montana. He will explain when you meet him. His family will also make a move. He has a wife and two daughters, twins. They need your aid," said Jo.

"That is very interesting; thank you for letting me know. We are in Spain and trying to decide if we should take some of the stock homes or leave them here and decide after checking on some land we own. The ranch in England is on hold though we did accept it. It has champion hunt stock. We own it; however, you will have to decide if it remains under you or if you prefer to sell."

"Leave them, we did. Once you have sound buildings and caregivers, you could move them; however, I don't see how you will have time to take care of forty ranches. Wouldn't it be better to leave them where they are if they get proper care? You can always go there and see them if that is your desire," replied her enterprise manager.

"Good suggestion. We will be staying in a town near the ranches. Afterward, we return to France and fly to your location. Since we have four pilots, we can stop in Tennessee and have a meal before flying to Texas. I committed to pick up the two I adopted there and take them home. We should be there around ten tomorrow to avoid the heat."

"Oh, you won't avoid the heat even if you come in the middle of the night," laughed Jo.

"We could fly home and drop off the extras and then come your way. Don't want the little ones to have problems," said Mara with concern.

"You go from air-conditioned plane to air-conditioned vehicle to air-conditioned lodging. Doubt you will notice it much," laughed Jo.

"You seem to be in high spirits; what is going on?" asked Mara.

"Will fill you in when you get here. Is Shandra there?"

"I am here," replied the woman.

"Fly to Dallas and stay at the Crossroads Inn on Sixteenth and Confederate if we are late. They are holding your rooms. Give a call when in the area, and we will meet you at the airport with transportation, if traffic allows," Jo advised.

Mara was puzzled, yet she had a decision to give the woman who showed them around. She thought it best to advise the studs first, so that is what she did. They seemed to agree with the directive, so she told the woman that the horses would remain in her care for now. They might take a pair to the states; however, not at this time as they were out taking care of some newly acquired businesses and were quite busy. Pat led the resident family in taking the oaths, and the driver returned to the bus to take them to their night's lodging.

Upon their return to the motel, they found a note saying the group had moved with a new address given. Mara put her hand on the sword and asked some questions. Then she lowered her hand and again loaded the bus after leaving a tip for the people in the motel they were at and returned the keys. She also paid the minimal charges.

The driver knew the area, which is why they chose him. He drove to a large home and stopped.

"Where are we?" asked Mara.

"This is the address you told me," the man responded.

"Then best I knock on the door," she said.

When Mara exited the bus, Pat did as well then Kennet and Shandra followed. Mara chuckled yet knew it was as it should be and knocked on the door.

"Welcome home, Mom," said Joy, who opened the door.

Now Mara was puzzled.

"Home is a long way from here, my dear," responded Mara.

"We were at the motel when the Police Chief came and asked if we were the N-Sign group due to visit the Morrison and Shaffer Ranches. Since I am senior, I was the one who spoke with him. He said that the records on file at the courthouse showed someone missed this house on the list about what you now own. Rather than run up a bill at the motel, we moved immediately, and I am so glad we did. He had a bus bring us here. Come, I wish to show you. The babies are with Keri," said Joy.

The driver sat on a lounge in the back of the house where there was shade. He seemed content to wait on everyone.

The lead group moved behind Joy as she explained the various areas and the property itself. It had fifty suites, a restaurant with seating, and an indoor swimming pool. The floors had Spanish tiles that were shining.

"This is Prina, the housekeeper. She wishes to remain here and in your employ. Jobs are scarce, and she grew up in this home as a domestic," Joy told her Mother.

Mara walked around the home, not saying a word, yet her family knew she was asking higher authority questions. Only Shandra walked with her as her guard. She covered the main floor then moved upstairs, where she walked in and out of every room. The twins were asleep in one room, and she tiptoed in and out not to disturb them or the sleeping Mom.

Mara's steps hesitated in one room, which caused her to note where she was before moving on. The basement would be next if this place had one.

Suddenly she turned around and returned to the room she had noted after asking Shandra to return downstairs. She crossed the floor and looked at the fi replace. It didn't look it had seen any use.

How strange, she thought.

Next was checking out the ornamentation on the fi replace. To her eyes, it looked like precious stones. Then she laughed and pushed on some of the rocks in a newly disclosed order, and the fi replace moved to allow her a stairway to the hidden basement.

When she reached the bottom step, she stopped, shocked. The room contained many things of value. The entire basement was a vault.

"Granda, would you please go to the upper level?" Mara asked while keeping her excitement covered.

The woman rose from her chair and walked through the home as if inspecting it. When she reached the upstairs, she told Mara she was on that level.

"Go to the fourth suite on the right. See the open door, use those stairs and join me, please. Lock the suite door fi rst, however," Mara directed.

Soon Granda joined her.

"What on earth is this?" asked Granda in shocked surprise.

"A vault, and from the looks of it, I'm the first to enter it in many years. There are no footprints, and the combination upstairs was stiff with age. Saw no watermarks or rodent tracks. There is a stack of gold bricks in the back at least six feet to the side. There is also currency kept along with some other precious metals like silver, copper, and platinum. The currency is American and is redeemable in gold. In this corner are handmade saddles and bridles in the old Spanish style. There are stacks of pictures in frames in this area. It looks like they put all their valuables away and locked the door never to return," said Mara.

"A Tiffany lamp, my goodness, I haven't seen one that fancy before; it must be one of a kind. I always wanted one of them; however, the money went to raise my kids."

"Not this time; it is yours and will be home when we get there. Look at these serving dishes; they look like someone made them of gold. My goodness, they are! I think they must have hidden this at the beginning of World War One. I will have Pat install an AI in this home to watch over what is here and keep an inventory."

"Why? I'm not saying don't do that, just wondering why you are keeping a ranch and home so far from where our base is," Granda said.

"It is never wise to have all your eggs in one basket. If a state government collapses, we can come here or any special homes we now own. If a state or country we live in has problems, we can move to places where we have homes and property, if we so desire, for the family needs protecting at all costs. That means people and animals."

"Our next trip will be to Switzerland and maybe Holland with a trip to Ireland to follow. Jo will oversee our various enterprises with her team. We have plenty to do with your books, family, ranch, training, and backup, to say nothing of the enterprises we seem to acquire. My bet is Pat will hire a computer tech she trusts and send them to put an AI and link in every property we kept."

"Our on-hand funds also need spread out more. My understanding is that we are going to be on the go until all bases get covered. Instead of waiting a year to do the other tours, we will check in at home then go again until it is all done. It seems to me like a ranch in various places might be advantageous for it allows Pi and Shira to be out, us to keep up on our riding skills, plus a place for the whole family to stay and be secure," Mara explained.

"Okay, I agree. How are you going to move all these animals you care for?"

"Via a book?" asked Mara.

"That might be doable. It will also have to be used to move the planes, vehicles, and people unless you plan on putting planes in each location. The next ranch you keep should have a plane runway to accommodate all the craft you own."

Once she saw it the way Mara did, she realized it might be an excellent idea.

"Now you begin to see it my way. You are correct; we don't want anyone catching us away from a way to escape if things go wrong, though, we will have to deal with what is wrong. It will allow the family to be elsewhere and secure. When the bottom falls out of the housing market, we will begin using some of our funds to purchase as much as we can, for we will restore the property to its full value once the market settles. The properties we picked up for a dollar have each grown in value to a huge amount. Jero found several people willing to put on shows at the University Stadium."

"I had the opportunity to hire a group of people who lost their jobs through no fault of their own. Jo made me aware of them. They are called Logisticians by the Military, and their job is to keep track of anything put in their care. When their particular branch disbanded, they found themselves without jobs. I hired all of them and sent twelve to the warehouse; they are making a list of everything we have acquired. They will stay at the Hilton until we get back. We own it; why not make use of that fact? Pat did something or other that resulted in an AI being in place at the warehouse, each of the ranches we kept, and the homes we are gradually adding to our inventory. As a result, we can check on those areas any time we wish to."

"I'm glad you are hiring those who are losing their jobs in

the Military. They have to eat and feed their families, plus have skills you need in what you oversee. They have put their lives on the line for us, and it is time to aid them," Granda said approvingly.

"Very true. We have designated who is considered family and Thunder approved. All adults in the lead group have their Master's Degrees to include Gwen and Dan. Randy will take care of Melissa and see that she gets the repair she needs. Joy said she would watch over Rusker while the surgery gets done though she too needs to be tested, so she went with those who did the tests on Friday. Randy took on the babysitting duties for the littles."

"Let's not borrow tomorrow's cares. You will have to get this property filed in your business name. You are timing it again, and thus, so is everyone else, though they don't know it. We need to eat a good meal, go for a walk, allow Pi and Shira a good run, then go to bed," directed Granda, who was still concerned about how tired Mara was.

"Pi and Shira are out back in the pasture, running to their heart's content. It is fenced, and they are the only ones there. There is a building in good repair for them to be in during the night hours," Mara advised.

"Are you at peace, Granddaughter?" asked Granda.

"Yes, unbelievably so, my dreams are coming true, as are those of others. You are healthy and with us. Shandra and Cherry are now under me, which I didn't think could happen though I believe that Gretch and Michelle will return to me when this trip for Jo is over. Randy has finally accepted me as her Mother. All who now know are ready unless we pick up others who will be part of the lead group. I believe that the tutors are with us for as long as we have littles coming into the home. Yes, Grandmother, I am at peace. We have a lot of work to do, and that also is needed," she replied.

"Then I am at peace as well," Granda said.

They then returned upstairs and out to the patio. When

Mara and Granda entered, the driver moved elsewhere.

The two of them sat on the back patio, watching Shira and Pi playing. Everyone again went to bed early, for all admitted to being tired. They slept until daybreak when they heard a disturbance at the front of the building. The leaders immediately dressed and were on their way to the front door. Pi and Shira joined the group once Mara was outside.

"What can we do for you?" asked Mara of those before them.

"What are you doing in our home?" asked the man before her.

"Your home? I think not. We have the title, and legally filed," responded Mara in the man's language. He rocked back on his heels.

"They said you were a foreigner," he replied.

"So are you," Mara countered.

"Why do you say that?" he asked.

"Because your tongue gives you away, you are not as fluent as you should be. Also, you don't have the law with you, yet you knew we were here. It looks to me like you don't want the law involved this time. You broke the rules and are looking at Judges and lawyers. We hold legal title to the property we are sitting on," Mara told him.

"You do not; we have the title," said the man in anger.

"Granda, call for backup, please," whispered Shandra into her speaker.

Randy, the men, and Cherry showed up to join the show. They spread out in Thunder formation and waited.

Kennet stood between Pat and Mara, though back a pace. The N-Sign men stayed in the third row, where they guarded the backs of their leaders. Shira and Pi remained in the shadows. Therefore, the men trying to enter the house didn't know they were there.

Mara saw the lights yet gave no sign of it. She turned to speak to Shandra, and a weapon flashed in the night. By the time the lights reached them, Thunder Court had formed, and the men were down. Confessions were signed, and it was all recorded.

Pat met the incoming officers and, using their language, explained that the men were breaking the law, and she had proof of their actions. A copy of the original confessions and recordings went to those who came. One of the men said he was the Captain of the Guard and wanted to see her ID. She showed no expression as she presented her information as Thunder Two. He read the inscription and then handed it back to her.

"Thank you for considering us worthy of having a visit from the great Thunder. We have heard of you. These will be processed, and you will know when the transfer finishes," he told her, then saluted and left with the prisoners.

Once inside the home, Mara called together those who had joined her outside.

"I have secured this location. It now has an operating AI that will only allow the housekeeper and those of us with the proper ID onto the premises," Pat told them.

"Scratch one concern. I doubt that anyone slept through all that noise," said Granda, who had heard what was happening.

"You heard it through your speaker from Mara. No one else in the house heard a thing. I know the women are up for saw one of them in the kitchen fixing a bottle, and another was chasing her son down the hall. Think we have one more concern to handle, however," said Shandra.

"And that is?" asked Mara.

"The bus driver, for who else knew we were here? He set

us up and will have to meet Thunder. You see, we gave the address to him and no other."

Mara rose from her seat and walked to the room assigned to the driver. She knocked on the door but getting no response; she opened the door, which she heard unlock as she touched it. He was spread across the bed, fully clothed and snoring away. With a flick of her wrist, he was moving out of the room and out of the front door. Mara requested a sound barrier, and another trial went into session after he awakened.

The Judge asked him why he sent for those who would steal from the group.

His response was he worked for those who came.

In the course of his testimony, they gained more information as to what was going on. The bus company was involved, as was the driver. It was a scheme they had perfected, they felt. It paid them well with little effort.

Again the police visited the residence.

Chapter 9

Changes in the offing

The Police Chief took one look at the driver and loaded him in his sedan with cuffs on.

"This one we know though we have not been able to prove his involvement in what was going on."

"You now have court testimony with six witnesses. You also have the confessions of the first group. Now you have another person that we tried. The Judge heard his testimony, and this man is to see your Judge for his crimes. Thunder Judge has given you her judgment. You have what you need to process him this time," Thunder advised.

"Will you be remaining?" asked the Chief.

"We first need our transportation replaced. Since you have the driver, we will drive ourselves. We still have a business to finish. However, no one is to enter this property in any way except the housekeeper who will keep things in order until our next visit," replied Thunder Press.

"We will make sure of that," replied the man who then departed.

"Okay, folks, we have a bus and own the company; however, what do we do about a driver's license?" asked Mara when the new bus arrived.

"Yours should be the same as mine, and mine says I can drive here," replied Pat.

Mara looked, and sure enough, she too was qualified to drive wherever they happened to be.

"We have taken care of the first ranch now have to look at the second one. The lead team of Pat, me, Granda,

Randy, Shandra, and Cherry will be going. Everyone else can remain here until our return."

Everyone went to do as bid. Joy went looking for the housekeeper. They needed some breakfast, and Mara supplied the funds; the woman was on her way to take care of that requirement. They ate and those designated departed for the second ranch.

When they entered the bus, they found two maps. One was for Spain and the other for France. The Spain one showed the two ranches and also showed where the new home remained. It wasn't long before they found the horse ranch they still needed to check.

They found that a ranch needed some help. There was a lot of damage to the buildings, and the fence needed repair in places. Mara removed Shira and Pi from her blouse and full-sized them. Pi gave directions to the horses who entered a door that formed on the property. As soon as all had entered, the door closed.

The women moved to the house and knocked on the

door. "Enter," was all they heard.

They moved inside cautiously, quickly moving to opposite sides of the door. On the couch was a woman who tried to rise and could not.

"How may we help?" asked Randy immediately.

"I thought everyone forgot about us," said the woman.

"You are not forgotten. What has happened to you?"

"I heard a loud noise and went outside to see what was going on. When I woke up, the place was in shambles, and me in the condition you see me. I tried to take care of the stock however can't stand up. Will you feed them for me please," asked the woman with tears in her eyes.

"They are being fed. Now let's see what we can do for

you," responded Randy.

The woman had to have a thorough check-up though they didn't have an x-ray machine until Mara raised her hand and one showed up. The x-rays were made available, and the Doctors huddled to decide what course to follow.

"We can't leave her here this way. Why not remove her entire ranch with the horses. We can then set them up at home when we get back. Right now, she needs some surgical intervention. She has a broken collarbone, a dislocated hip, broken leg, and skull fracture. I can handle those if two of you will scrub to help me with instruments and anesthesia," said Randy.

"Got it covered," said Mara, and they found themselves in a surgical room with the patient sedated and ready for repair.

Sterilized garments appeared on each of those who would do the procedures.

Mara aided Randy in the repair while Pat watched over the machines, and Shandra kept the instruments handy at need. When Randy and Mara had the woman repaired, they discussed how to get her to the house where the rest were.

"Come on, folks, you ask that due to her condition, she have a Thunder move to the house. The rest of us have to get the ranch moved, again via Thunder and Granda, so that it will be available when we return to Montana," commented Randy.

Thunder 1 laughed and made it happen. The ranch disappeared, with fences, buildings, and all. There was plenty of food on hand for the horses, and it too went.

"I will check it when we get home," Mara whispered, for the house would have to be carefully gone through. Something was wrong with all this. The ranch would not leave the book until she made sure it was safe to do so.

When the Ranch, woman, and animals were given care and removed, they returned to the rest of the family. Randy checked on the woman who said her name was Connie. More groceries would have to be purchased to replace what was used earlier and not leave the housekeeper without necessary food items.

The following morning found everyone up and ready for departure after another meal. Pat climbed into the bus; the rest took their seats, and they began the journey back to Paris. They intended to stop for food; however, instead, they drove to the city.

The newest patient was lying on a mattress at the back of the bus.

They found the motel where they had stayed before, and since it was evening, they ate then rested though the woman received care first.

Granda was the one to request the break.

Mara suddenly realized she had taken three people from the hospital, from one continent to another, then across a country, and all within a day of their release. She was ashamed. It was her duty to look out for her family, and Mara hadn't been. The flight to get the men she forgot was another example. No one was moving tonight, period!

When they got up the next morning, the phone said that Mara had a message at the front desk. She went down to retrieve it not to disturb Pat, who was still asleep.

"I understand you have a message for me?" asked Mara.

"May I have your room number?" the young woman asked.

"Two-twenty-two," she replied.

"Yes, it says it is for Mara. Is that you?"

"Yes, I have an ID if you need it," replied Mara in flawless

French.

"Do you also speak English?"

"Yes, is there a problem," she said in the requested language.

"The message is yours then. A student at the Chef's school said she needed to reach her Mom and wondered if she might still be here. Found you were registered and held the message," the woman told her.

Mara moved away from the desk and sat in a lounge chair to read the message.

"Hello Mom, you said you would be returning here and hope this might be the time. I have completed Chef's School and wondered if it would be alright to ride back with you. I passed with flying colors and learned a great deal. I am now a certified Chef." Merry signed it.

"Oh dear girl, you did it. Come to the motel, and you can go home with us," replied Mara to the air.

In minutes Merry walked in the front door with her luggage in hand and a box. She later explained the box was books of recipes and training aids plus tricks of the trade. She was relaxed, and her eyes sparkled.

"I'm so proud of you," said Mara as she hugged the young woman.

"Thanks, Mom, it is nice to have someone proud of me," Merry replied, for she had realized her dream, and she was amazed.

"Pat, we have a surprise in the lobby," sent Mara.

"How did you know we would be here?" asked Pat as soon as she spotted the young woman, for she had awakened soon after her twin departed the room.

"Mom said I should check here when class was over to see if the family was in the area," replied Merry.

"We have a flight to leave this morning for Tennessee where we pick up two passengers then have some folks to talk to in Texas before we go home," explained Mara though she wondered why the women in the group were deciding that she was Mom to all of them. Not that she minded, only why were they leaving Pat? She didn't want her twin left out.

"Sister mine, I can hear your thoughts. Don't worry about it. If Merry wants to stay under you, that is fine, and there is probably an excellent reason. It seems to me that the rest of Quad-A will probably go your way as soon as the Military learns to fly, or all of them might move to you. Neither of us knows where we are going, so go with the flow. I have no problem with it, don't you have one either. The adults should have some say in who they call Mom. If you are their preference, then that is the way it should be. As long as you and I are doing our jobs, it doesn't matter who calls us Mom or anything else for that matter," laughed Pat.

"Pat, I want you to know I have never regretted adopting you as my sister. We make quite a pair as twins. Since we will always be the same age, I picked mine as the one to use," Mara explained.

"Oh, you did? So that is why I'm once again athletic and on the go," laughed Pat, for she was wondering.

"Yes, I would say so."

"Our group is growing. Now we have a Chef named Merry, and a housekeeper, which is Melissa - once repaired. Doctor Randy, Restaurant Manager Becky, Motel Manager Heidi, and Enterprise Manager Jo. A Foreman Mike, his wife, the twins, and two horses. An Inheritance Enterprise Manager in Jo, guards, pilots, tutors, Director of Events, and a makeup artist. A leather craftsman, Goldsmith, some guards, people of all ages."

"To me, that is what a family should be. I'm so proud of

all of them. Oh forgot Jero has the properties we bought and the event schedule. Now let's get some breakfast and get on the plane. I'm ready to go to Tennessee for lunch," commented Mara.

The three of them were arm in arm as they returned to the twin's room. By then, they could hear the rest moving around.

Soon luggage was packed and placed on a luggage carrier to move to the bus. The hotel said they served breakfast; therefore, the group had a continental breakfast in a room off the foyer. There was fresh fruit; waffles, pancakes; juices, coffee, tea, milk; eggs, potatoes, ham, sausage; cereal – both hot and cold; an assortment of bread type products including bagels, rolls, croissants; yogurt, and everyone was full when they loaded the bus. Mara handled the bill with Shandra at her side then they were on the way to the airport.

The men left on guard at the airport remained inside. When the Jetplane moved into a hangar, the men were already in the Jet. They were to guard, and that is what they did. They found meals waiting at the door of the unit when mealtime. There was a bathroom in the hangar, and they slept in the plane. When Mara asked about it at the entry desk, the contact said others could not enter there since she owned the hangar. The bus was taken into the hangar and parked. It would be there for the next time they needed it. They rather liked the new one that even had a bench at the back that allowed Connie to rest and not be on the floor. Mara set up the bus company to be run by French personnel under her ownership. Thunder checked all out.

Once on the plane, x-rays were taken of the woman they had done surgery on, and as anticipated, they found her fully healed. Randy removed the casts, and Connie was allowed to take a seat.

She had a passport, and Mara had furnished a list of her family, so there was no reason for concern when questioned by inspectors who monitored those who came and went by air.

The Jet airplane taxied down the runway, and they were headed home, with a few stops along the way.

Shandra was pilot and enjoying it though she split the duties with Cherry. Pi and Shira were again on-board, and the smaller children were sleeping during the flight to Tennessee. There they found Becky waiting for them with transportation and her luggage as well as Heidi's. Luggage went into the aircraft basement, the aircraft was locked, and they went to eat once again.

They ate at the buffet, and when done, they picked up Heidi, then they returned to the interrupted flight. The next stop was Texas, where Shandra had the location and instructions.

The Texas airport was bustling, and they remained in a landing que for what seemed a very long time though the team learned they were overhead. They asked for access to the runway for private aircraft and received the go-ahead. They were going to park the plane and look for transportation; however, the sign over a hangar that was opening said it belonged to Mara's group, so they put the large plane inside, where they met their group waiting for them.

Jo walked over to Mara, for she had something she wanted to say. In truth a few somethings, to share. Mara asked that the AI close all other circuits Jo and her discussed.

"I would have never believed that a week away from you folks would make us miss you so much. Welcome to where we are. We have visited the ranches and, for now, will keep them. Have a family that you should meet. Next is a question. I realize that you have a time frame to claim the rest of the properties you inherited, though you did that by special courier, am I correct?"

"Yes," said Mara with a smile.

"Then there isn't a rush to check things out?"

"I suppose not; why do you ask?"

"We have received word from some folks we know that none of this family should head south at this time. Forces are building to meet you and or those you send in that direction. Also, some things are happening at home that you need to be aware of," replied Jo and hoped she had not overstepped what her duties required.

"Jo, you are fully trusted. Yes, I put you over all enterprises, including the two in Tennessee though the managers of those locations will take care of them and report to you regularly. That puts you in control of the event stadium and arena at home. That is why you received a call with whatever is going on there. Since Jero is handling events, she reports to you. She long wanted to do it yet didn't have hands-on training, although she does have the degrees. Thus you who have the training were put over her. She does the work, and you see it gets done right," explained Mara.

"Thank you. I didn't want to do something you had not approved. I also spoke with the Logistics folks you hired, for they were under me in command. They have some information for you when you reach them. I put them under oath to make sure no information gets out. You already had my oath; therefore, no one will learn any of what I know from me unless you consent. Each of us checked with our contacts, and that is how we know that going south would not be a healthy move at this time. We planned on taking you to the ranches here. The man who wants to go home with us, to serve as Foreman on the home place, is waiting with his family to meet you," Jo explained.

"Appreciate you using your contacts on our behalf. I know that there are some huge changes in the offing, yet not sure what they are. I see you have transportation available. Where do you want to start?" asked Mara with her signature smile.

"Before I forget, some vehicle movers showed up at the warehouse, and they have been stored inside by my direction. Pander, our specialist in that area, says they are new, both the trucks and their cargo. The drivers of those trucks are also people we know and ones you might have a use for; therefore, they are waiting at the motel to ask for employment. If this is not what you want me to do, I will cover the motel rooms," offered Jo.

"Not necessary; however, thank you for the offer. For your information only, we own that motel. It is one of those we hired Heidi to oversee. At the same time, you will be watching over her as she is just twenty-one and might need some training. When we bought it everything was new. No one had stayed in the facility. We have not opened it to the public as yet for was advised we would need it for a while. You have done well," Mara advised.

"A voice told me what to do, and I felt inclined to follow the directions; however, at the same time, you are overall and didn't want to cause problems," Jo told her.

Mara laughed with joy and surprise.

"Good you have now heard from Thunder. In case you haven't figured it out yet, I am Thunder Press as well as Mara. We both have the same education, and if a problem comes up, I have to make the decisions according to what part of who I am is the one in the hot seat," explained Mara.

"I trusted that was the case. It seems we now work under different rules yet honest ones, which I can adapt. How you take care of all this and keep it straight amazes me," Jo replied.

"You are doing the same. By the way, your former command will not recognize you until some adjustments get made to those who remain in our employ. I requested Thunder to have the entire lead group become my age. To those around you, your body will grow older until you reach the age you were. However, your mind and physical abilities will remain my age. When you reach your current age, you will again become my age until we all retire from public view though we will continue to be overall as long as we are comfortable doing so."

"Mara, you have made my day. Thank you for all the benefits you have sent our way. I speak for all of the Military personnel you have hired. So far, you have hired the cream of the crop. I will see that continues, although I do not want to overload you," Jo responded.

"Would you object if I left all former Military under you at this time unless someone outranks you? You know their talents and what can and cannot be shared. Those that I adopted will remain in the family. The ranking member will adopt the new ones under a new family name if you agree unless someone that outranks you is coming. I just had thought. How does Fredrickson sound? That new branch will show a connection to us. We do not want others to know where we acquired our workforce from."

"No objection at all. When you get it figured out, let me know, and I will take it from there," said Jo with a huge smile. The mere fact that she appreciated the offer yet seemed to be asking for time alerted Mara not to push the issue.

The Major had promised her unit that she would help any of them if she could. She didn't change that promise when an entire Brigade disbanded though her Company had only been a small part of it. Now it would happen. They had saved her life when the Command was overrun. The Company assigned to guard were all killed. Those in her Company seemed like her kids, and she would give any needed support. Most of them were in their twenties. Her command had received many awards both in and out of the battle zone. Although they had met the enemy, she had not lost a single person while overseas. They had many awards as a unit and more as individuals. What they received so had she for where they went, Jo would lead. She managed to select people from the Brigade to keep in touch with her due to their unique skills.

Mara was allowed to hear the Major's thoughts and was overwhelmed that this well-trained person was willing to remain under her and her family.

"You need to build your organization, not just family. You will need those who are being sent to you for your duties will expand once they have the training," said a voice Mara knew well.

"We put in a reservation at a nice eating place not far from here. Would you be willing to call it a day after that? We will be on the move by five AM to show you the ranches. Your appointment with Mike Menser is at ten. Then it will be lunch and rest, for no one goes out in this heat that doesn't have to. That evening we are invited to an event that I thought you might enjoy. You are invited as our family, not by name," advised Jo.

"That sounds good to me. Do we have motel rooms?" asked Mara.

"No, though I don't think you will be disappointed," responded Jo.

"Okay, I'll accept that. We do need the rest, it seems," Mara told her, for she knew they had timed it again.

When they reached Tennessee, she asked Becky the date and time. It was two days after they left the states originally and noon of the day. That told her they needed the rest, for duties were awaiting all of them at home.

"Granda, Randy, and Pat, we have our orders. Load everyone up for we are going to eat then see where we are staying. No guards needed this time, for we own the

Hangar, which means the planes left here will be fully secure."

Everyone did as directed. The group they met was intermingled with the rest of the group so that everyone had a navigator to reach where they needed to go.

Mara wasn't the only one glad to see it was a Texas Buff et. According to the advertising, not the kinds of food they had in Tennessee, however equally good. The ad said it was a mile-long buff et. While the rest were eating, Jo took Mara and Becky out of the room.

"Becky, this is one of ours now; therefore, you will need to take charge while we are here. I continue to be over you, though the duty is yours," Jo explained before taking her to meet the local manager who answered to Pensor. Her full name was Bonnie Pensor, and she had been a Staff Sergeant under the Major.

Mara signed as the new owner putting the enterprise under Becky for control, then froze all in that room except her and Pensor.

"I have accepted the position as leader and Commander of the Lost Brigade. If you wish to remain part of that group, you need to be under Jo or Shandra, who is part of the lead group. What is your desire?" Mara asked.

"I took this job to make me easy to find. The woman I replaced is the one that Jo swore in, and she is not Military however wants to continue working here. She will make a good manager, which was her job before allowing me to take her place for the contact. If you have space, I would prefer to go where the rest are," replied the woman.

"Get your replacement here and leave when we do. If you need something from where you are staying, let me know, and it will be on the plane," Mara offered.

They then returned to their meal. Mara was sure that Jo had already sworn the woman in though she checked and found out for sure. When everyone finished eating, they loaded into the vans for the next stop on their visit, and included in the load was Bonnie.

The convoy moved to a nice area of town that had several residences. As they entered the site, they saw a vast apartment building.

"Jo, why would they have an apartment right next to private residences?" asked Mara, for usually, they were each in a different location.

"The man who owned the area wanted a place for his group to stay while he was at his home. You could stay there if you so desired, though you might prefer to live in a house where you have full privacy," explained Jo.

They stopped in front of a modest home. It had a two-door garage, which, when Jo opened it, was empty. Once their vehicles were inside, the door was closed. She pushed another button, and the group drove the units downward. The underground garage would hold one hundred automobiles like the one at home, and she found a dozen new vehicles stored there.

"Josephine is here to turn over the property to Mara N-Sign of TX Corp. She will name those to have access," Jo spoke to the air.

"I am Pat, the computer tech who will keep you operating as required. Please admit me to the property," began Pat, who then looked at Granda.

As each person identified themselves, they moved to one side until the computer knew them all, except the small ones, and their Mothers introduced them when their turn came.

"N-Sign family welcome, please name me," said the AI.

"Erase all former access and allow only those you just met," directed Pat.

"Pat, you are the tech, name the AI and let's go look over the new property," directed Mara.

Before Pat could do that, the rest of the family need to move into the building. They moved around looking at what was there and were amazed. It seemed new and as if no one had ever entered it except them.

Merry went to check out the kitchen. Her report said she could fix meals any time they wanted any. The place came fully furnished, and the larder was full.

Mara advised they had a reservation for the evening meal; then everyone would rest for the following day would be busy.

Once all had done what they wished in looking the place over, the babies went down for naps, and their Mothers did the same. Once again, Shandra was at Mara's side as she wandered through the large home though everyone else was resting. It was the only free time Mara had; therefore, she used it to catch up.

"Shandra, you are oathsworn, are you not?"

"Yes, Mom, why do you ask?"

"Because I'm about to ask some questions that it would be best not to remember," said Mara with a smile.

"I won't say a word, as you know," replied the woman though she was puzzled as to why the question.

"Computer request secure room to speak with you," said Mara though due to Shandra's age, she sometimes forgot who she was speaking with and the wisdom the woman carried.

"Follow the lights on the floor."

They did as directed and found they were in an office of some kind. Shandra looked a bit puzzled yet went where Mara did.

"Are we secure?" asked Mara.

"Yes."

"This place is new, it appears. Did the previous owner live someplace within this home space? Was he or she aware of the spaces you are showing us?"

"Yes, he lived in one room in the basement. No, he was not aware of what you are asking to see. He never entered the main floor of the unit."

"Show us," directed Mara.

A wall panel opened in one wall, and a set of lights came on. As they walked into the opening, they entered an elevator. In the slot for a key were three sets of keys. Mara took them all. Mara asked if anyone was in the location they had reached when the elevator stopped, and the answer was no. The door opened, and they entered a large room. It looked a lot like the house they just left.

"Is this home a duplicate of what is above?"

"Yes."

"Come on, Shandra, we have some checking to do," though Mara had shut off her speaker before entering the private office. As long as she had a guard with her, she could do that.

The house below had everything the one above did with one exception, for they found a bedroom had been used and still had personal items of the former resident. There were weapons, electronics, and maps. They also found a stash of precious metals. Only the one bedroom and bathroom appeared to have been used or even entered. There were two large closets, and one of them was where they found the precious metals and weapons.

"How did he manage to come and go while using only one room?" asked Mara.

"He was convinced he found a hidden location that only he knew how to enter. Said entry led to the one-room he occupied. The rest remained hidden from his view," replied the AI.

"AI, is there a vault in this area?"

"Yes."

"Show us."

Again lights came on, and Mara followed them to a blank wall.

"Require entry," she directed for the AI need explicit directions to comply.

A wall began to move, and they got out of the way until it quit moving. They then entered the hall before them. Once inside, the AI spoke.

"This is your vault and arms range. No one has been in this area since the builders left. To your right is the vaulted entry, which you have authority to enter any time you so desire. Your computer Tech says to not hide anything from you. Directly ahead on the left is the qualification range for any weapons known. There is also a room that was for martial arts. Where would you like to enter?"

"Let's start with the vault."

Again a door materialized and opened for them.

Shandra blinked her eyes and then raised an eyebrow in question as she looked at all the room contained.

"This is not the first one found," Mara advised.

"Don't tell me."

So, she did not.

They looked over the items in that room. There were new weapons of many different kinds in one area to include bullets for each that required them. Not just handguns, there were also rifles of every type known. Another had bladed weapons – swords, knives of many different kinds. Mara was amazed at the full armory they had found. Handguns were in cases with capsules to keep moisture from getting in. They even found some lasers, and all were new in their containers. Each style was in mesh stacked to the ceiling in flexible wire mesh controlled columns and carried a label showing what kind of weapons were in that stack.

Then another door opened, and they moved inside the second room. It carried items of value such as precious metals. Mara opened a cabinet drawer and found it filled with silver and gold dollars in rolls and bills in bundles labeled with the amount. They looked like they had come direct from the printing house and showed payable in gold. A second cabinet the same size had what appeared to be a coin collection encompassing several nations. Each carried a label as to what country they applied to and were also rolled or bundled.

"Are there weapons in here that you know how to use yet do not have on your person?" asked Mara of her guard/daughter.

"Yes, though they are assassin blades and weapons for hiding. I can use every weapon in here. You have my oath of no harm if you require I be so armed. I will only use them upon your order," responded Shandra, who had not told anyone of her skills. The only ones who knew were the one who ordered it and her trainer, until now. Since her former instructor was also a Commander now deceased, only Mara would know of her skills.

"You are to arm under those limitations and maintain your proficiency," Mara told her guard and daughter, then watched as she selected additional weapons and quickly placed them in accustomed places on her body. Mara stepped up and chose the same.

"Please advise AI Zulu Alpha one-two-forty of the contents

of this space and have it put in sealed file for MEO. Thank you for allowing us in. Now we need to look at the other room here. Decrease your inventory by what we have removed."

Thunder froze the area and guard for this was a location that Shandra would not be aware of at this time.

Chapter 10

A Grand Assembly

"Lead me," directed Mira.

Her guard was unaware yet led her Mother by following the AI's lights for ahead of them was something that the Mother would have to make a decision about before anyone else was allowed access.

Another panel opened in the corridor, and they were in an office setting that held banks of computers that she would bet linked to satellites around the world. She noted that the area had all the electronics Pat had learned.

Mara knew what each was for and was amazed. There were clocks for the time all over the world. Listening, she heard many different languages spoken. It was the secure nets from other countries she learned. In a short period, she knew as much, and more, than Jo did about the danger in the south. She soon discovered what they knew about the Military that she now claimed as part of her; according to what she heard, the entire Brigade had disappeared. Then the conversation was as if no one ever heard of that bunch and found no reason to try to locate them. She chuckled at the confused report. When she felt she had the information she needed to know, the AI had some questions to answer.

"Thank you, now that I know what is here and how to use it, has anyone else been here since installed?"

"No."

"Do you know if anyone knows of this location?"

"Not to my knowledge."

"That is good enough for me. If the young woman with

me ever asks for entry, please grant it."

"Yes, Commander."

They departed the room they were in, and the panel closed. Upon leaving the vault, it too closed. Again in the hall, another door opened, and they walked to it and inside.

"Show me how to use this room," Mara directed, though Shandra was now aware of all around her.

As the first test came up, Shandra stepped up and began using the weapons she had just picked up. Mara stood in total amazement at her daughter in action. Once all except two weapons, were used Shandra stepped back and waited.

"Recover and keep the last two," said Mara with a smile, for she then stepped up and repeated what her daughter had done. This time, Shandra looked astonished on her face though she now knew Mara was fully qualified to oversee and direct her actions.

A video appeared showing how there were various means for testing a person with unique skills. Once she had placed that information in her mind, they departed for the lower level's main house. At a prompting, she returned to the bedroom the man had occupied.

"AI, can you hear me?" asked Mara.

"Yes."

"Please remove all valuables from this room and put them in the vault. Also, request all personal items be removed and placed in a case by the elevator on the main floor. I will retrieve them later. Secure this area from anyone except those who now have clearance. Thank you. I will call you MSthree."

"I will answer."

The two women returned to the office they departed from on the upper floor.

"Now we need to know what information this room contains," directed Mara.

"Mom, I can catalog and record all that is here if you direct it," said Shandra with a smile, for the more she was with Mara, the more she felt like the young woman she had become.

"In other words, you were an undercover agent and now work for me?" Mara questioned.

"You could say that," replied Shandra.

"Were you a double?"

"Only if requested or directed of me," she responded, for she had been so directed a time or two in her younger days.

"Thank you. I feel like I just opened a huge vault, and the value is knowledge. From here on, you will be my personal guard, for Pat will find herself overseeing other things. What I know you may find out, and what you know I must learn," Mara advised.

"Yes, I am willing," replied her daughter.

"That is why you insisted you needed to be under me direct, isn't it?"

"Yes, however, I could not give you the information unless you first knew to ask for it. I had to be in your branch of the family, which put me fully under your control. I would suggest that you do the same with all Military personnel or at least those you put in leadership positions."

"You Military folks have disappeared by joining me, am I correct?"

"Yes, as a result, there is no reason to look for what no longer exists, for our records have now disappeared and become yours. There is no longer any record to show that the Battalion I Commanded ever existed. What amazes me is we all still receive an income as retirees, yet instead of a name, we have a number. The finance group considers us Special Ops, meaning operatives."

"When we get home, these records will be in a secure room where I have items of information on each of you. Not to harm, to protect each of you. Never will it be used to harm you. I will destroy it first," Mara explained.

"Yes, I know. I'm glad it is now in your hands, for we are oath sworn to you, and therefore you are the same to each of us. Thank you, Mom, I love you," said Shandra.

"You have been worried about that information, have you not?"

"Yes, not due to your having it, due to who might get their hands on it before you did, for it could be deadly and detrimental if in the wrong hands. The special skills of each member of this group you are getting, are in some cases are the only a copy if you will, of them as in what you now know of me. The records disappeared as soon as I received a discharge."

"We were scattered all over the nation when discharged to keep anyone from realizing what was happening. The rank we held at the time of discharge has nothing to do with the rank we held. Some of the officers departed as enlisted and vice versa. I was the key to give you first contact, and the others came at my command. My actual rank was, and I guess still is, Brig General. By now, you have figured out that of the Military you have coming, I am ranking. Cherry was my Executive Officer and held Colonel's rank, and she will watch over the Military people you employ. My highest rank was BG though I wore the rank of Colonel or LTC when Commanding. I was Brigade Commander while Jo was a Battalion Commander and a Lieutenant Commander with her Executive Officer Chris as a Major though their discharges were as a Major and a Captain. It was to sever any links to us by name, rank, location, and any other way. None of us will compromise you. If you have questions, you

Sharron L Ensign P.O. Box 583 Helena, MT 59624
Mara Trains Randy
406-458-7091

may now ask them, and I will answer as the only General headed your way. I designed and initiated the system that made us available. Jo has some of the answers though not all, due to security set up by the Military and special training only open to one of my rank or higher. Knowing that our records are all secure was the second key. The third key will be when we call the roll after all who are coming are with you. There will be a roll when we get home. However, that will not be the final one. It will require that you select those you wish to utilize from the ones in reserve."

"Won't flags go up someplace when they see how many we now employ?" asked Mara.

"No, you and your family were in place before the first one of us received a discharge. What I did was take the woman you call Cherry and work for a firm in DC. When it folded a month later, we took the two planes and headed west as directed. What I told you from that point was true. As soon as the new planes came, we could change our ID from the civilian occupation, and the fact that you adopted us broke the last link to our former occupations, for we used different names all along. Example: My birth name was Shandra; however, I never used it during my Military career. We lived under what we thought of as our aka or a user name. None of us knew that you had so many Master Degrees and that each of us had to pass those same exams, which is a good thing. It makes us appear exceptional people, and since the Military is a volunteer force. Most ranking personnel in the Military did not want to hire anyone with so much knowledge. We are members of your family, which means there is nothing to question there besides which you have a large number of businesses that belong to Thunder Press with you in charge. As you can see, it covers everyone," laughed Shandra.

"Thank goodness you know what is going on. I thought I was the only one," Mara replied.

"When you made us, the adults, twenty-one years of age,

your age also had to be raised to leave you in command. You are now a full Colonel by rank. You are at least six months older than any of us. I have activated your Military record, and you now get a retirement that goes to a number, not a name that is needed to hold the rank you now carry. The record is a copy of my own. When you have all the information needed, you will become Major General over the Military you control. Granda holds Lt. General rank though you will be ranking, and she is your age. I understand that Pat and Randy are as well. As I see it, that makes those two and me the same rank. New names, new skills, new ages, new relations, so as layer after layer gets put in place, we become Thunder Press, and no one can break into that code."

"Jo is required to report to me for when this began; we did not know your identity. Now I will report to you though she could not tell you that. If you were to know, you had to ask me. The warning she gave you was legitimate. There are armies in place to stop you from taking possession of the properties that she was to secure for you. Your command now secures all such places," Shandra advised.

"Do you know why we have all been so tired?"

"No, wasn't a requirement. Following your orders is."

Mara then explained the timing they had to do to stay ahead of those looking for those from the disbanded company and her personally. The motel at home had all those seeking Shandra waiting for the return of the leaders. They were to report by a code that Jo gave each for only she had the contact information for everyone. No one would have all the pieces of the puzzle, except Shandra, who set it up.

"Thank you, now we are on the same page, and it will be easier to accomplish whatever you so desire," said Shandra, who had joined the Military at eighteen and was immediately on the fast track to Command due to having completed college at sixteen.

"I feel the same. May I have a hug?" asked Mara.

"Anytime you want one," replied Shandra with a grin. She found it interesting to be twenty-one yet retaining all her knowledge, which included what Mara had.

The records were recorded by the AI there and placed in a secure file for Mara only. Thunder was the only one who knew where they were until Mara. Even the AI at the last location had no idea what was in that section of the property. His programing was to guard the area, yet it was not to be used by anyone else without authority. Mara was the authority, and she would designate who would be allowed entry. Thus it was safer to send the records to Montana, where no one had any idea about who she was.

When they reached home, all Military records could be secured and researched. It turned out to be the ones missing from the Military that pertained to people now in Mara's employ and family. Everything was there from orders they had been given, pay records, medical reports, shot records, and all in their birth names with the original documentation. Now Mara would need to cross-reference who they were previously to who they were now. She would be the only one, other than Jo and Shandra, who held that information. Mara and Shandra would use those records only to certify a talent, check on shots, or check blood so that they didn't marry someone who was in too close a bloodline to any of those under her.

No one except Mara and Shandra ever knew what happened to them, and they conveniently forgot until they needed the information.

When the brief with Shandra ended, it was time for the evening meal and some rest as they continued to revitalize their systems.

Everyone went to sleep with the AI on guard.

Even Shira and Pi were inside a building resting, which turned out to be fortuitous.

When Mara got up, she released Pi and Shira; then she discovered from the AI that they had again had visitors.

Once all were up and breakfast covered in the main house, Mara directed her team to hold a Thunder Court. Those who had entered the area returned to appear in the house's main hall. Those to be judged were unable to refuse, and the assembled group numbered one hundred fifty-four suspects.

All children and their mothers moved into a secured room in case of problems with the court.

According to the testimony given, the group received orders from the man who had owned the place: that if anyone, other than him, was to enter the area which he defined, they were to stop them. During Thunder Court, testimonies were in recorded form, plus the confessions were in written form as well, and the men signed them.

Pat called for law enforcement and gave her ID. The felons were standing in rows outside on the pavement when the officers arrived and were immediately taken to prison and locked up. Their vehicles went to the police vehicle checking point.

"Jo, you will have a new batch of property under you. If in the states, go ahead and check it out, if you wish, or wait until we are free to go with you. If anyplace else, ignore it for now. I will get the paperwork off claiming the property; however, none of this family will be leaving unless we fly to Europe or Canada. All other areas are off-limits at the moment," Mara advised.

At ten AM, one of the drivers brought in the man, who was applying for Foreman's job for the two ranches at home. The Leaders met with him to see if he would be their home ranch foreman, which included an interview with his wife. Jo introduced him as Mike Menser. His wife and twin daughters were with them. Shandra took the watch during the interview; Jo stayed to watch over the twins in a side room while Mara interviewed the parents.

"Mike, I need an idea of what you can do, what you want to do, and what your family requires," began Mara.

"I was in the Military. My daughters became ill, and as a result, the Military gave me a hardship discharge. One of the doctors we saw said to get the twins to a cooler climate. I always wanted to see Montana, so that is where we have been looking. Jo stopped in to say hello just as I arrived home from a recent trip there, and we mentioned that there was a need for help and a job. Jo told us to give her a day or two, and we would meet with you, though she didn't elaborate on who you were. I was raised on a ranch and ran one until the Military came calling. Been in for about eighteen years, which means I missed my retirement by two. However, the hardship is like getting a clean discharge. I get a retirement, although it is not enough to pay for two sick children's care. All my siblings learned to ride from the time any of us were walking. At eighteen, each of my siblings went their separate way. Have no idea where the rest of the tribe is.

"The Commander said that you are honest, will provide housing, and that my home will be near where my wife and kids are, so she doesn't have the whole burden anymore. My wife Mary and I have two horses we would like to bring with us. We put our house up for sale, and as soon as it sells, we can leave," he responded.

"Randy would you join me please?" asked Mara.

"Shandra, we need some oaths," directed Thunder.

By the time Randy found them, Mara had a fair idea of what was going on with the twins, though Randy would have to do the official exams.

"Mike, you will be working for me. To know what you will be overseeing, you will need to make the trip home with us. There is a hospital there that will have their doctors help you find the answers you need. Meet Randy, who is our Doctor, and she will take care of the process. Pack a small suitcase for each of you and one for private papers you might need where you are going. Suggest you liquidate any funds you have and pass them to me for securing. They will be in an account that no one except my group can locate though you will have access anytime you wish. The rest will follow you. Randy, they are all yours. This is Mike, his wife Mary, and their daughters Shanny and Sherry," said Mara, who then departed. She asked Thunder to load the two horses, feed, and gear onto the plane where Pi and Shira were.

"You have an appointment scheduled for the day we return. If we get in too late, it will be for the following day. You will be living in a housing complex, which is the family home on the ranch. Your accommodation will be a four-bedroom suite. We have a chef who will cook meals and a housekeeper who does the general use areas. Your suite is to be maintained by you. Currently, we have about five hundred full-sized horses. Some are racers; some are Quarters, some are Arabians, and some are little horses with twelve diff erent breeds. They are a wide variety, and housing will be available for them by winter. We only recently acquired them. If you have questions, please bring them to me as you will fall under me as long as you have medical concerns. Should I not know the answers, I will get them soon," Randy informed them. At each bit of information, the couple seemed to relax.

"We wanted so very much to be part of the group that no longer exists; however, our daughters have to be taken care of first. My duty was as Brigade 1SG. My wife and I are both former Military. Both Mary and I wanted to retire to a ranch though her Military duty was as an MP with SFC's rank, making her their 1SG. When the twins were born, she got out because we found out they had medical issues and asked for discharge. That is how the Commander and Colonel knew how to find us," Mike explained.

"You are welcome. Why don't you let me take care of the girls for now so that you and your wife can clear up any loose ends before you come here to prepare for the flight home? That way, you will be nearby when the flight is ready?" Randy told them.

"They can't be in the sun at all. That is why they were fully covered to get here," explained Mary.

"Yes, I know, however here they are out of the sun, you are free to close bank accounts, turn in rental keys, and all that stuff. I will remain with them until your return," advised Randy.

"Oh, thank you, it is much appreciated. I have not been away for more than a potty break and sleeping in five years," replied the woman.

"Do you have transportation?" asked Randy.

"We came with the Colonel," Mike responded.

"Not a problem. Jo, would you be willing to send one of the quads as chauffers for this couple so they can take care of some business before we fly out? I will have their twins while they do that," Randy advised.

"Rae will cover it. She is on her way," replied Jo.

The couple departed with Rae to get the errands done. Randy was already researching the problem the twins had.

"Mom, we will have to have a dark area for the twins. If at all possible, could we land at night? They cannot be in the sun. The following morning we will get them into the hospital before the sun is up. It appears there is some help available at home," Randy advised though Mara knew the twins needed admitting as soon as possible, so she put in a call to the Hospital Administrator.

"I will get it set up. Thank you for advising me. I doubt those two have had a day off since the twins were born. We will factor in a nursery both at home and at the hospital, I think so that all our Mothers get a day off when they need one," commented Mara.

"I will take these due to their problems, for now. However, I agree that is a good idea," responded Randy,

Mara chuckled, knowing her daughter did not want to become the nursery caregiver.

She added that to her to-do list and went to ask Shandra some questions.

"Mom, if you are looking for me, how about looking behind you," Shandra chuckled when she heard Mara muttering to herself.

"There you are. Come with me," directed Mara with a smile, and they once again departed for the hidden office and the basement.

Once they were at a secure location, namely the radio room, Mara directed Shandra to have a seat. They had some chatting to do.

"You know I like your way of calling a meeting much better than the way some called them in the Military," laughed Shandra.

"Why put folks on the defensive if you don't have to?"

"For many, it was to show their authority and to make those under them squirm. Not good tactics in my book," replied the resident Commander.

"I like your way best," Mara laughed.

"I like yours best. Now, what can I do for you, Mother mine?"

"You don't have any problem with my being younger than you?" asked Mara, for she had been wondering.

"Mom, you have far more education than I did. We have joined your show, and you are the ringmaster; I just came along to help and keep a promise. Now you can't get rid of me. I am here for the long haul and with you as my Mom. Not too many in their fifties can claim they have a seventeen-year-old Mom. I love it," Shandra continued to laugh.

"Agreed, and Randy feels the same way; she said she wanted a gift from me to use as a conversation piece. She will say this is from my seventeen-year-old Mom."

Mara found Shandra to be knowledgeable, willing to work with her, and a definite asset. Here was someone who could oversee a thousand people or more and have no problem with it. Mara would get there. However, it might take her a day or two. Well, unless you counted the hospital, clinic, stadium, ranches, etc., for ultimately, it was all under her.

"Now we have some information to exchange. I recently was given access to this room. You need to know it is here, for you need to make sure all your folks are in place when we get home. Some items have come to my attention. This room will be moved to the home base when we leave. Scan your folks and give me two people who are fully trustworthy and can monitor this room. It cannot be anyone in the main Lead group, for we need the information from this room even if we are traveling."

When Shandra continued to listen, Mara quit stopping and just talked.

"Next on the list, we need a daycare for all those under five. We need for the Moms to work during the day yet have competent care for their children. I found out the need, which was brought to light by Mike's situation. We will have to set up a dark room and play area just for his twins until the Medical Doctors find some answers."

"Next, we have a formation to call when we get home. You and Jo should do it first to be sure everyone is there before I speak with them unless you want to take over."

"Oh no, you don't! I'm willing to keep track of everyone, even find if all are here. I will hold the formation; however, you need to make them aware that you are now the person in charge, and we work for you. It would be best if you swore them in, not me. It could split their loyalties otherwise. They need to know I can give orders from those in the lead group, although they are not our, meaning Military, orders. They originate with you. This ship has one Commander, and that is you. I'm not going to be taking over your job. It is all yours, and you have earned it. I'm willing to be Brigade Commander for now. However, once you set things up the way you want them, you will no longer need me as the former Commander. Then the force will see me as your daughter and guard. That is enough and my chosen duties. That does not mean putting someone else in my place. You won't get the cooperation you need if you do that. I do believe that my position will dissolve as time goes on. Jo feels the same way; until then, we will support you in every way we can during this transition. We want to be part of the working force, leaders if you allow, and part of the action. Life would be very boring otherwise."

It was easy to see Shandra had not finished though she paused to put her thoughts in order.

"Now you mentioned this radio room. What is here? Is it encrypted or open text? Does it operate by satellite, and if it does, who controls said equipment? Do you have personal lines that only you and I can use, or is it all here for anyone working that shift? How many hours a day do you want it operational? Where will the monitors, meaning people, sleep? Have you thought about Mary, an MP, and probably knows more about maintaining this setup than anyone other than me? If you had a daycare, she could work one shift or oversee those who do take the duty. She needs to be needed and not just by her kids. You will need two on and two off plus a backup shift in case of a day off or illness. They will need to know who to report to and that you are the only person they will report to."

"This is why I ask for your input. I didn't know all that stuff . My thought was to have the AI monitor and let me know if something comes in I need to know. At the same time, your way would probably work best, especially if that person knew what to watch for, and it sounds like Mary might. We will find out in time what all of this is; however, a starting place is needed, and you are it."

"What I think would work best is: you have a suite and are the only one in it presently. I have quite a few kids and will get more, making my suite not a good choice. Could we place the part of the information net that you and I monitor in your suite, or would it be better to have it hidden on the first floor where only the cook lives and she is oathsworn? Many suites are on the cooking floor, and we could convert one to the radio room with the AI keeping it hidden except for those who are authorized to enter. The rest will be in the secure room monitored by whoever you designate, and with bedrooms available in a normal suite, there would be room for any monitors to sleep in their off-duty time. If that turns out to be Mary, she could have her kids with her in that area though I think she needs some time away"

"Shandra, you are going to be my Commander as long as there is me. How else can I learn?"

"Mom, I do not want your job. I thought I had a tough job until I saw you in action. I will back you, watch your back, be Commander, keep track of those who are coming and help any way I can. The rest of the job is all yours. All I can do is help, and that you have my word I will do. I'm beginning to see what you meant by you needed my knowledge even as you gave me yours. I was concerned at first; however, now that I know you, ask anything, and I will answer. Thank you, by the way, for your knowledge and the degrees. I will do what you require, make home a secure base, and see that you have a second one to monitor this one and have those lines of information that you do not want anyone else having access to, except me. That is within my capabilities, for those were duties I had at the comm center. What else did you need?" asked Shandra with a loving smile.

"You were in the group that took Star back, were you not?"

"Yes."

"So you know what I can do and what life required of me. Maybe now, if I tell you what is going on, you will believe me. Will you listen, or will you tell me again, not to tell you?"

"Seriously, Mom, at that time, that was how I felt. Now you may tell me whatever you like, and it will remain secure within my mind."

"I am the owner of five mines that produce gold in the book format. Therefore it is necessary to pick up the nuggets and flakes from time to time. A person mines it, then leaves it where I have immediate access, for it comes from properties I own. Recently we acquired several properties that the state of Montana does not want to monitor anymore. Thunder moved those mines to some of that property, and a few of the ranches may also get moved. Both ranch and mines came with their a support force. If I can catch them in time, maybe those folks can stay where they are, and we will take just the property. I have a Goldsmith that will refine the raw gold for me. There will be mines still in the book realm; however, we will no longer have to go there to pick up the sacks. We have finally reached a place where we are self-supporting without the book. They will be in the mines I own here."

"At the same time, I still need to furnish law enforcement within the book until Thunder says not to do it anymore. You met the woman who has taken over one area. Is that all of them? I don't know. Sometimes I need a runner to move the end product. That is where you will determine if you have someone to trust with that kind of duty or if you and I need to do it. Only someone who believes they can ride into a book and come out at another location would work. Not everyone can do that. Only Granda knows of the funds available to us, and she cannot enter the book realm. Never again will someone think she is the one in charge and nearly kill her as a result. I will admit who I am and take the lumps that go with it. You have the skills to protect yourself and me; therefore, she won't be the target. Thank you for increasing my knowledge, for we can now fully protect one another. Pat has new duties headed her way. She will still be my twin and work as Thunder Two; however, she will be taking over all AIs that we now control for her original degree was in electronics and communication. Every private home we have has one, as does a number of the ranches. Pat has to see they all operate as they should and that someone monitors in case of problems in those areas. If I decide to liquidate that property, we will remove the extra hidden areas and any funds on site. If Pat wants monitors, she will ask you."

"I'm glad she has that duty, for it is not one I trained for."

"They are also in many of the ranches we acquired. The homes we have acquired stateside we will keep, and only a housekeeper will live there. The home in Spain is the same. Due to the traps set for me, it might be best to bring all ranches here. We could put them in a book world, I suppose. However, Granda found out the state was liquidating some property, and she picked up all she could while she continues to watch for any more such properties that become available. The Ranches from South America might get moved to some new property; please note I said I could, not will be. I do need them here while we check them out without endangering any of our people. If some of your group desires to run ranches, let me know, and we will look at it. I have one foreman for two or more ranches at the home place. He will do the miniatures and the racers until all others are covered. If he has too much, someone can take on the miniatures, for they come with the property ready to be setup. Also, the main ranch has more than one breed of horse and could result in additional ranches. One woman with four kids, which translates to two sets of twins aged twelve and fourteen, controls another for me. She made the comment that she wished that ranch was closer to where we are. Six ranches have foremen in the states, and you were at two of those. That leaves about thirty-some that need checking by you and me. You entered a vault with me. That is why I have to have a firsthand look at them."

"The next area of concern: What happens if the government here has problems, then what? I will not abandon what has been loaned to me for my use as long as I hold the duties I do. People and property both need to be secure. Are you with me so far?" asked Mara with a straight face.

"Yes, I am with you all the way. Let me know what you want me to do, and I will find the person or persons who are willing to cover that area for you. If it is super sensitive, you and I will cover it. How are you going to pay all these people until things are up and running?" asked Shandra.

"It has been covered. Now we need to purchase or build a bank that the Federal does not know exists. I think that underground would be best. Granda pays all bills from those funds. We will operate off our funds and leave no trails. I do not think it a good idea to have all collateral in one place. Thus, we have some in Tennessee, Texas, Spain, England, and a few other places we can access. There are few states where we do not own property. Bringing all the ranches here and going through them will give us an idea about what to keep and what to send back. If we don't want the ranch we need to look at, though we prefer some of the purebred horseflesh, it could happen during that transfer. What is the reason behind that decision? We now own a riding arena and can have horse shows, riding events, etc. Since we own it, it wouldn't be a problem to put our own on display. If we can't trust the area where the various businesses and ranches are, we might have to bring them here."

"The thought here is: the more people see us, the less they pay attention," Mara explained, for when people are always in a given area, others tended to ignore them or forget they were there.

"Do you see why I don't want your job? Mom, I need someone to tell me what they want me to do then let me do it. You are the kind of person who builds the whole thing from the bottom up and, with your mind, follows the thought to the end to locate problems. God did not make me that way. You do your part like normal, and I will do what I'm best at, or you can teach me as you did with the sword."

"You learned that quick enough," Mara laughed.

"I took fencing in one of my lives," Shandra responded immediately, then realized what she said.

Soon they were all but rolling on the floor in laughter.

Chapter 11

A barn-raising-hoedown

"Mara, Mom, you have given me back my youth, a job that I love, and a way to continue. You helped me fulfill a promise to some folks who had no place else to turn. Thank you: for all of it, the laughter, the joy, the fun, and still the time for work and seriousness. I'm with you for as long as we are," said Shandra.

"With that kind of help plus Thunder, Pat, Granda, Randy, and Jo, we will win. My daughter Joy would be in with both feet if it weren't for Joey, and I am trying to cover that base as well. Joy is sixteen and has the same education as the rest of us. Due to her having a son, I upped her age to a year under me though she will not age like the rest. Thunder has made that a gift to all of us that work directly with me. I did the same with Kennet though he has yet to realize it, and I'm not telling him. Let him find out himself."

"I appreciate the information you are giving me, for it will make it easier to understand what you want to happen and how best to do it. When and how do you plan on moving the ranches to Montana for inspection and determination?"

"Since they are opposite us in day/night, though it might work to freeze the location, bring the ranch to Montana and check it out. Put it on a property we own so we can keep part, all or none. Then what we don't want goes back, though that might decrease our overall value. Animals concern me because they may try to take out their anger at these tactics on them. The same goes for the people who run said ranch. That means we bring everything and everyone, check it out and return what will be a skeleton of what there was or nothing at all."

"Give me a time and tell me who you want to be checking. I will make sure those you request are available," replied Shandra.

"You, me, Randy, Granda, and Pat was my first choice. However, Randy had patients to keep track of, and Granda overseeing the kids under age five. That means we will be short some people. We need Mary for radio communication; Pat will cover all animals and electronics, for she owned and operated a ranch of her own, which she still owns though she will only install AIs in what remains. You and I will look for hidden funds, weapons, and the like. Afterward, we do that we will decide who to keep and who not. We can do about one ranch a night that way. My guess is we will be doing all of them once we start, or they will find out what is going on before we can finish. When that is covered, plan on a week of sleeping and doing nothing else. Randy will see that we have the vitamins we need to accomplish this. We need to take them before the mission."

"Joy can run the show until we wake up. The new Foreman will take over our home ranch, and we will freeze what we keep so we can get some sleep before putting anyone in charge of the various ranches."

"Tell me when and it will happen. You can use Jo as a backup for Joy during that time. It will keep her busy, and if I'm with you, she will know that we are doing something that is not for everyone to know."

"The more I think about this comm center, the more I think it should be where we can access it and no one else. What are your thoughts about it? This is an area I'm not sure about," said Mara.

"I know my people, and if they are oathsworn, they are not going to be able to tell anyone anything about what they do on your behalf. I believe that putting Mary over that area will serve two purposes. It will give her a break and allow her to make use of some skills she has. Which reminds me, where are we going to plug Mike into what is going on?"

"He has been adopted and wants to work with and for me. He is Military retired. Check him out if you will. Make sure he is who he says he is. If so, then and only then will we put him to work. Thunder has passed him; however one never knows," responded Mara.

"Will do, though I agree that Thunder has the best intel available. Also, all of us know Mike and fully trust him."

"Intel?"

"Intelligence."

"Agreed."

"Tell me when you are ready to start this change out, and I will be ready. When do we head home?" asked Shandra.

"Jo said she had some ranches and enterprises for us to look at; however, according to what I recall, we took care of that when we first got here; otherwise, that should take a day. When we finish that, we will depart the following day. Oh, that's right, you are the pilot."

Soon the two were laughing once again. It felt so good to Mara to be laughing.

"Now that you have given me the necessary brief, maybe we should return to the rest and see what they have been doing while we were visiting."

"Good idea, and thank you for listening. Sometimes just hearing things gives me ideas or confirmation as to what is going on. I do not want to keep all knowledge to just Pat and me because if anything should happen to one of us, it will affect us both. You wouldn't have the information needed to carry on. If we are both gone, you become me."

"Oh, what a thought! You stay here; we will guard you the best we can. I do not want your job, though. If something did happen, I would attempt to pick up where you left off ,"

Shandra responded, for she knew her Mom needed that confirmation.

"I know that, and this time has given me some time to relax and look at where we are and where we need to go. Yes, we will return. If we cut through the basement house, we can come up where Pi and Shira are. We could have been visiting with them," said Mara, almost more to herself though that is what they did.

"Mom, everyone is occupied. What do you think of you and me doing the first ranch from SA and seeing what snags need to be taken care of before the rest join us?" asked Shandra as they walked to the house.

"Agreed. However, it has to wait until we get home. Find out from Jo what ranches we need to look at here. I know we did two; however, I vaguely recall we ended up with more property in the US. Where are they? Will Jo and her team be checking them out while we continue home?

The leadership team decided they would eat at home then go to the event that Jo had booked them to attend. The meal would be lunch with enough leftovers on hand for whoever remained with the children and the children themselves.

Melissa felt that she and Rusker should remain at the house. One reason was her lack of mobility, and the other was she didn't feel she should be moving with the family. When Mara realized it was what Melissa wanted, they were allowed to remain home, and Mara asked her to also look after Joey and Kelly. She agreed for she loved kids.

The group moved outside to find a bus waiting for them. They boarded and laughed when Pat took over driving.

Jo directed her where to go, and they ended up at a barn-raising-hoedown. They laughed, danced, sang, and met many folks they would not have met otherwise. The folks who were already there put in the full weekend building the barn. Now they were celebrating the finishing of the task.

Someone asked Mara if she played an instrument. She said yes, and they asked which one.

"All of them," Mara replied, then looked at her family. She had an idea of what was about to happen.

"No one can play them all," said the person asking.

"Right hands," she said to her family.

As they raised them, into each hand, fell an instrument. As each person joined the concert, the family members used their devices by exchanging them as they moved.

"Want to bet?" she asked with a smile.

"I'll just take you up on that one," replied the person pushing.

"May I use your stage?" she asked.

"Certainly, go ahead. Hey, Moe, empty the stage, will you? I got a bet going; this young lady says she can play all instruments," hollered the man.

Mara moved to the stage with Shandra. Mara sat at the piano and began playing. When she finished with the piano, she moved to a saxophone, and Shandra took the piano changing the tune, and so it went. Then one by one, the entire family took the instruments in the same order until the whole group had played all.

"Never bet on a sure thing," said Mara as she walked over to the man and asked that the area around them be frozen.

"You win, and what do you want for winning?" he asked.

"Hopefully, something that won't cost you a thing. If you know of a performer or three who has a date open in September or October, have them contact Jero, and we will book them with the standard terms they expect for a concert in Montana. Should you decide to attend, we might even have a ticket for you at that time," Mara responded.

"You are on. By the way, some funds come with this one as well, when you perform. You may collect at the door and thank you for the wonderful music. We do not often get to hear such amazing professionals out here in the country," he told her.

"On a guess, I would say someone set you up, my friend," Mara advised.

"You bet, and I'm the one who set it up. That gal you sent down here on business said that some relatives were coming to visit. I asked what kind of music they would like, and Jo said their own. I knew I had to find out what that was," he responded.

"Are you disappointed?" she asked.

"No, definitely not; as you said, you have mastered all of them. You do not just play the instruments, you have mastered them, and I have never heard of that happening before. Thank you for showing us the possible although, to most of us, it still seems impossible."

"Nothing is impossible if you believe," replied Mara.

"Guess I better learn to do that," he said with a smile.

"It has a price if done through me," Mara told him.

"I'm willing," he responded.

"You have to take an oath to me." She wanted to be sure he knew what he was asking.

He frowned a little, then smiled.

She led him in the oath and then told him the only way to receive the faith he would need. He followed every step she showed him.

"I am Thunder Press, and this is my family, of which you

are now a member. We will be here for a few days. When we are getting ready to depart, Jo will notify you. Pack one bag only and meet us at the private side of the airport. Hanger two-twelve is ours. She will give you the times when they are known. Thank you for the wonderful time. Glad you liked the music. You see, my kids begin training as soon as they can hold an instrument. They also are taught to ride at that young age. Tutors teach them until they are ready for University and the exams there," she told him.

"That was always something I wanted to do, go to University. There wasn't any money available, so instead, I began building a fortune a little at a time. Now I know it is not the money so much as the road that led here. When you get home, we will meet again so that what is in my name becomes yours. I noticed something different in the oath you gave and the one that Jo gave. Why is that?" he asked.

"First off , you are Military, and you were known as Jonas. Your transition made you James, called Jimmy, and far from the Military. The Brigade is assembling, and you need to be part of it. The rest of the story is not written yet though giving me your oath makes you part of my family and the lead group. See you when we leave," Mara/ Thunder told him.

"I look forward to it. This barn is not mine. I'm here as a favor to a friend and to get my orders. See you soon. Have only one request. I travel with a guard dog who rescued me," he told her, then called for Gigot.

Mara directed it to happen, and a large German Shepherd rose from behind one of the tables. It moved to where Jimmy stood with Mara.

"Hello Gigot, I am Mara and head of the family where you will be going. Those who train you will be Pi, a mare, Shira, a wolf, and three studs. Listen to them as they have been there quite some time. There is no time to train you myself, though I don't want either of you left out of what is going on. There are other guard dogs with us so ask them any of your questions if you like though only Shira, who is Thunder's guard wolf, has what you need, and I do require that everyone get along. Now I must take my family home as the young woman taking care of the children needs some rest too," Mara told the pair.

Time resumed, and Mara was in the parking lot with her family. She found a rather hefty purse sitting on her seat in the van though it had her name on it, to be sure. She placed it in a hidden pocket without checking the contents, for it was heavy.

The group enjoyed the sights and sounds of the area they were in as Pat drove them to their temporary residence. It was the night of a full moon, and the country area where the event took place gave them a chance to enjoy the moon and stars on their way back to where they were staying. They also saw a lot of neon signs advertising various events in the area.

Mara looked at her group and found most were asleep. It was time for another night of rest. When they reached the garage, everyone that was asleep was placed in bed while the last two, Mara and Pat, got there on their own though it was quite late.

The following morning everyone was up and packing what they had used. The area was cleaned and made ready for the next time.

"How are things going?" asked Granda when Mara located her.

She put a silence bubble over where they were and silenced her speaker.

"I have learned a great deal. When we get home, there is a lot that needs doing. Some of us will be processing the properties from South America. Before that happens, would you please fill all of us with the necessary vitamins as this could be a weeklong no stop duty? We will fly home at night to protect Mike and Mary's twins. They cannot be in any sunlight. They will be admitted to the hospital as soon as we land, for there is a darkened room being made ready."

"Randy put the Hospital Admin on alert for an ambulance to meet us at the hangar. We are taking back a few new people cleared to be with us. Melissa is scheduled for surgery as well. A guard dog called Gigot is going back with us, and Jimmy is the handler. Our new foreman Mike will go to work once his twins receive help. His wife was an MP and will be working directly with Shandra and me. We needed to sleep well last night and tonight for duties ahead could make for long days. Do you feel up to this? You don't have to do it, you know. Us younger ones can handle it if you want some time to rest," said Mara.

"Now that I am your age, why should I want to rest? I am going to get into anything and everything I can," Granda laughed.

"I'm glad. We need you to keep us in line."

"I never intended to put you in this position. At the same time, I am glad it is you and that you have the knowledge needed to get the job done."

"Couldn't have done it any other way, and now that we have experts in all areas, we are winning. Hopefully, I will do things unexpected to get the job done. The courts are over for now, and we will handle the transition when we reach home. I understand that most of the property they released to you is in one county. That will aid in keeping control and having access to the herds. I don't want to spend all that time figuring out how to move all the vehicles, including trucks that will be going that way. Then there are the enterprises that the managers will have to sort. They will be busy with that stuff while I handle other things." Mara wanted to make sure that Granda got included though some, she would keep control over so that no one would again injure Granda to get even or gain information Granda didn't have.

"Did you find someone to watch over the little ones when we get home?" asked Granda.

"No, are you volunteering?" asked Mara with a smile.

"Yes, I believe I am. Would you mind?" responded Granda.

"Not in the least. I am going to be busy getting everyone sworn in, duties assigned, and questions answered. The adults need to take on their various duties, and your taking on the littles would free them up for the duties they have agreed to work at for us. Yes, that would be ideal," Mara told Granda as she hugged her. She knew it would happen, just not when.

Shandra confirmed the ranches were done in Texas, although some needed finished in other areas. Jo wanted to go home for the assembly and check-in, then she could leave with the rest of her Quad to finish what she started.

They left for Montana in a time frame that would put them home after the sun went down. The family flew to Montana using two jets, one large, one small. Randy notified Hospital Admin that they were in the air and gave landing time. When they arrived, the ambulance was standing by. Once the planes were inside the hanger, the ambulance drove in, and the doors were closed. Medical personnel moved the twins into the ambulance, which had blackened windows and a divider to keep light out of the back. The parents departed with their kids. Everyone else loaded into the vans and went looking for some food.

Merry offered to cook at home. However, this would be her last night off for a while, Mara felt, so they ate out, besides which the girl had no idea what, if any, groceries they had on hand. She had a few days and then would leave for the second course in becoming a certified chef. After that, she would be the full-time chef at their home with at least one day a week off.

Mara usually made a Sunday meal in advance. That way, she could bring people to her home for a meal. Since they now had a Chef, she wondered if they could have a BBQ or some such event so that the new group could mingle with the rest of her family. Maybe do that on a Saturday while having the premade meal for Sunday, and everything would be ready. It was a way to get to know one another without anyone being nosy.

Randy ate with everyone then drove herself to the hospital to check on the family left there when they flew in. She had called to find out what anyone ate and ordered meals for the parents. She also took Melissa to get her set for surgery

A full night's rest would be necessary for those who were going to be working with the ranches they had to check out, as well as various enterprises.

Mara had left her eight-passenger unit in the hanger, which Randy would use.

They no sooner received meals at their table than Gwen and Dan walked in the door how they had grown. Dan was close to six feet, and Gwen had shot up though not quite as tall as Dan yet. Their ages were now twenty. They heard the family was back, and the pair thought they might need more transportation. Therefore they brought two more vans in case.

"My goodness, how you two have grown!" Mara told her children.

"Wondered if anyone would notice," said Dan with a wide grin.

"How could we not?" asked Shandra.

The kids were beaming.

"So what have you two been up to?" asked Mara.

"We have been looking at the professions represented

at home and what we would like to learn to do. Just daydreaming, I guess. We can do so much in the family that we don't want to work anyplace else. Just looking for a slot that will help within Family," said Dan.

Mara was pleasantly surprised. She didn't want to push anyone to do anything. She preferred they chose their way, although it would be a joy to her if her kids decided to follow in her footsteps, regardless of age or rank.

"Dan did you notice how Kennet has grown?" asked Cherry with a smile, for she was used to making sure no one was left out.

Since Kennet and Gwen were close in age, they would continue to grow for a few years yet.

"Yes, he has, and he too is taller," said Gwen to tease her other brother though she was very proud of how Dan worked to help her and, therefore, the family.

They both knew that Kennet had to travel with the Twins, though they weren't concerned about why. Their main focus was on how to help their Mom and the Clan.

Dan had helped every day with the horses, and they even gave riding lessons for the younger members, plus kept up with music practice and study. Both hoped that Mara would be proud of them.

She was so proud she was almost in tears. They had to want what she had to offer, or they would have left with Star. Both got a motherly hug and sat down to have a treat with the group.

The new people met the youngsters.

"When we finish eating, if nothing happens, we will head for home. I need to make a call and see how those in the hospital are doing first," Mara rose from her seat, and when she did, Shandra also stood up. They moved to a corner that had no customers and called for a silence bubble.

"Randy?"

"Yes, Mom, what's up?"

"Since you have transportation, do whatever you want. Did you remember to take a guard with you? We were getting ready to head home and thought we would see if you need us first," advised Mara.

"The kids are quite tired from the trip; therefore, they are asleep. Mike and Mary might as well go home. I can remain here, however, see no purpose. I think I will take them home if you don't mind. Melissa has been checked in and will get seen by the Ortho folks in the morning. We can come back in the morning after breakfast, which will give Mike a chance to look at the ranch. You will be busy tomorrow. Therefore, I will handle this part of what is going on. Didn't you say that Granda had offered to babysit the littles to free up some adults?"

"Yes."

"Are you going to have formation and roll call early to get it done? Then you can do what you have to, yet have everyone busy with something to do," suggested Randy.

"That is my intent. See you at the house, in case anything else comes up," replied Mara.

While the bubble was still up, Mara spoke with her daughter Shandra.

"Shan, how are we going to cover the assembly, swearing-in, getting everyone doing something and still have time to take care of these properties?"

"We don't; that is what the enlisted do. Cherry and I will get people assigned to have everyone given the oath and accounted for while you and I are busy. Jo can put them to work at the places she oversees. You know she is so thrilled to be working at what she knows, and now that our knowledge has increased, we can do more, which is amazing. Gwen is willing to show Mike around and advise him of the two in one ranch. Dan is covering the riding and music lessons. Then the students go to school. Merry will handle the meals for she just returned from the second school. With Granda taking on the five and under group, everyone will be taken care of," Shandra advised, which told Mara that Thunder had it covered.

"The closer we get to getting everything working that way, the better. I will leave that to you. You and I particularly have to get some sleep tonight. Anyone going to work with us must do the same. Randy can give us the vitamins we need tonight. We need to let the horses know we have not forgotten them as well. Also, the guard dogs and new people need introducing to one another. That has to be done by Pat or me, for that is the only way anyone can get access," advised Mara.

"I am sending Cherry to help out Jo in getting things organized at the motel. Chris will also give a hand. Cherry knows all those coming, as does Jo, who has to give the codes that should unlock security for the roll; we can let the two of them cover that issue. Then too, there is Jero to work with them as she learns. The Logistics people have asked to meet with you to share some information. I think that can wait until we get these ranches and enterprises done if you agree."

"We have to meet with them first. I need to know what requires sharing. At that time, I will personally give the oaths. Some vehicles need issuing to those needing them. I understand there is a vault under the property that the warehouse is on. Quite possibly, that is something that we need a person or persons with clearance to control. We could do that while the rest are doing riding and music drills and then returning for breakfast before beginning the other duties. Once we take on the first property, we will not stop until it is all done. At that time, we will need to call for drivers and go home to rest."

"Why not have Michelle and Gretch cover to and from for

us? We might need them to move livestock, keep track of people and the like?" offered Shandra.

"That works for me. Are both sets of Quads, officers?"

"Yes, I'm still ranking; however, we have Majors, Lieutenant Colonels, and Colonels with me ranking of the Military and you over me with Granda retired and over us all. They have the highest security clearances ever issued, which includes you and Granda."

"I suggest Rae as your accountant. She has that kind of background and is good with numbers. We call her the bean counter. When you get to the point where you want your funds set up in differnt locations or need some banking in place, she was Commander of a Fiscal group, which is funds. Her second was Spicer. Since they are oath sworn and adopted, would that work? Having activated my A duties and personal guard status, that would be your best solution, I believe, keeping it within the Family with those having the talent. Use Gretch and Michelle as runners to get messages back and forth without anything compromised. If you have other concerns, let me know, and I will see that it has coverage by people you trust. For now, I think we are needed," said Shandra as she looked at the table.

Kennet was looking outside. Mara moved to him and looked where he was. It was time to get to work, by the looks of things. She nodded at Pat, and they led the way outside with the remainder of the leadership team following, though the others were to remain where they were. Any lessons needed would be taken care of at home.

After the lead team departed, Granda directed the new members to move outside and remain by the entry door. The guard dogs remained inside with Granda, though Shira moved when the lead team did and was always near Mara in case of trouble.

As soon as they departed the restaurant door, people began leaving vehicles and forming a ring around the group, trying to destroy units belonging to Mara.

"Go ahead, pay no attention. These are mine," said Shandra in a whisper.

"Why are you damaging our vehicles?" asked Thunder One.

"We do what we want, and no women are going to make us do otherwise," replied one of them.

"I think you are wrong; however, we shall see," replied Mara.

Dan and Gwen were standing well back and cautioned the others to stay behind the women, though they were also watching to see no one got behind Mara and Pat.

Pat and Mara waited for something to happen that would allow them to draw Lightening. The pair always allowed a felon to fire first; then, they would eliminate the bullet aimed at them before taking care of the rest.

Shandra sent signs to a couple of the people, and the entire group returned to their cars, leaving just the women though they made sure they were behind the twins. If their vehicle was in the line of fire, they stood by the building.

"Granda?"

"Yes."

"We need to be in a safer zone. This bunch needs to meet with us; however, do not want to endanger those under Shan," replied Mara.

"Done."

The area around them became an open pasture. The Military climbed the risers to take seats before being hidden. That way, they could see what was going on yet not partake in it. There was a force shield between that group and the Thunder group. The adversary was ahead of the twins.

"Since you seem to think this is a game, perhaps you would prefer to meet me one on one," said Mara.

"This should be a short meeting," replied the smart mouth as he stepped up.

"Pat, stay put and watch those behind him."

When a second man stepped up, so did Shandra. Pat didn't move, for her directions were to stay put. The two men moved toward the two women he still thought of as Twins.

The first man pulled out steel knuckles, and the second man reached for numb chucks. The women did the same.

"Don't lose your concentration. Pat has the rest covered. Focus on these two," Shandra cautioned, for she saw that the second man was an assassin, and he would be trying for Mara, who now had her daughter's memories in that particular area.

As soon as the men switched places, they tried to lead the fight. Neither of the women moved until the men were close then the battle was on. It took about one minute, and the entire group was down. Shandra's sisters and Pat returned gunshots, and they countered fists, regardless of the weapons used.

Thunder Court came to order, and a trial began. Was the judge Jo? And the lawyer was Chris. Mara just managed to keep her smile hidden.

The Thunder's gave testimony and, using sign language, prompted those who needed to do something. When the court was over, the prisoners and council signed the documents, and recorded confessions were ready to be given to the officers waiting at the restaurant.

"Take care of what you need to. I will stand watch," said Thunder One to Shandra in private send.

"Thank you," replied her guard. She moved to where the

Military was and asked for a speakerphone for them alone.

"Friends, this is how Thunder Press does what is required. You wanted to know what this mission included. You have now seen Thunder in action. These men have been investigated and charged, exactly as you saw. They will be turned over to law enforcement now, for that is who carries out the sentence. Never get in front of the women when they are in Thunder formation. Do not interfere with those who move when the Twins do. Dray, Gena, Tyler, George, front and center, here are your orders for tomorrow," she told them exactly who to contact, what orders to give, and what the order of business was to be.

Shandra also asked that Mara speak the oath from where she was so that they could repeat it after her. The Military learned who would be overall in this organization and who would be in charge of the following day's duties. Then she moved again to where Thunder stood waiting.

"They are ready," Shandra told Thunder One.

"I'm advised that there are two thousand people there and that they are now ready to go to work. As my family, I release you," Thunder One replied.

Once the former Military returned to their starting points, to include the new ones they had picked up along the way, the prisoners were placed in the hands of the law enforcement group who was waiting, for Pat had called them.

The newest members would always recall seeing their Bosses in action and were honored to work under such talented people.

Any damaged vehicles showed as tagged for replacement. When duties were over, Mara's family departed for home. The Military had been summoned and left as soon as the action was complete.

When they got home, Mara laughed for the time there was

the same time that they had called the tower for landing. Now they could sleep themselves out to be ready for the activities of the following day. She agreed with Thunder that this was the best way to get to know her enterprise's new additions.

"Would you advise Jo to put the new ones in housing, please? When she finishes, could you send them to the stables? We will be there to get them introduced to the herds. Mike will be working at the Ranch tomorrow to figure out what needs doing where. A plan will be submitted when I am again available. Randy will serve as support for Melissa and the twins. Granda will oversee all age five or under while the students will go to the Tutors."

The new people followed the pair to the stables. The twins mounted the studs, and the ride began. The studs ran, jumped, backed up, and did many other things that the new people had never seen. The new hires then met the horses, for they would not be allowed on the ranch unless known by the horses. Then it was time to depart for their suites.

Chapter 12

Who can answer

"Mom, you have a lot of new people within these walls. I suggest that for the first week at least, you let me move to your quarters for you need a guard. I am it," said Shandra with a smile.

Mara nodded acceptance and smiled in return.

"Randy, do you have the vitamins we need to take? We depart right after breakfast tomorrow," asked Mara.

"You will have them and the shots at breakfast," responded the Doctor, for she was going to make sure they all ate. She knew they were prone to skipping breakfast unless they had a reason to be there.

In a short time, all were asleep, and none awakened until everyone had rested. The clock showed five AM, which was the standard time for them, yet they got up fully rested.

All except Merry, Mara, and Shandra raced to the stables. Pat received a warning that the new people would fall under Pat for Mara and Shandra had to be elsewhere. Gwen was to see that Merry was trained for music and riding though it would have to be different since she was the cook.

Mara shook her head and moved to a black sedan sitting further into the garage, allowing Randy to take the red van. Shandra took a passenger seat, for she did not know where they were going.

A short drive of about forty miles took them to the lot that had been empty the last time Mara saw it. Now it had a large parking lot and a series of warehouses. One held collectible vehicles, one had new ones, and one contained empty pods only. Next was a stack of pods that still needed sorting. Everything was fully secure.

Shandra took the lead, for she was known to the workers inside. The door opened immediately, and a smiling woman met them.

"Hello Commander, thank you for coming. Those inside have clearance for the duty they are doing. Hello boss lady," said the woman who was one of the Logisticians.

"I am Mara if you wish it," responded the leader.

"Not to me, you aren't. Hello Mom. That was quite the display last night. It is always nice to know who is guarding your back. We have begun to sort the pods. We emptied the pods of anything except the gold. In this row is where the gold is sitting. Due to weight, silver, copper, and platinum are in separate pods rather than with gold. We were discussing ideas on why someone packed it that way. We thought maybe it was being readied for a shipment out of the country. Then we watched as the pods tripled, so I guess it was what we were supposed to do. I said it would be nice to have someplace secure to put the items of value. A door opened in the floor, which led to a vault that must be as large as this whole lot. There are towering stacks wrapped with wire fencing to hold them in place. The people who work with me are inventorying and putting value items in the vault, though the precious metals were in the new vault when it opened. Upon checking the pods that were storing gold, I found that the pods are now empty, for the gold is underground, and none of us put it there. There have been questions as to where they will live now that everyone is here. The motel is fine for the short term; however, some have families that will be coming and would like to have a permanent home if possible," said Rae, who was in charge of the Logistics folks and had just returned from putting some people to work.

The woman who opened the door returned to her duties at a nod from Rae.

"Have them remain where they are until we finish some other business. As soon as we can, we will give you other options. At the moment, we don't have the answer though we are working on it. I recently purchased some property, and it needs checking out before deciding," Mara told her daughter Rae.

"Works for me, and I will fill in everyone else if it pertains to them. For some reason, there seems to be pressure to get this stuff put away as quickly as possible. There are a couple of trucks that can move the pods. As soon as they are empty, we put them in an empty warehouse. Is that where you want them? They can become housing, used for storage, can even make stables out of them if you have horses small enough," laughed Rae.

"We may need to use them for that exact purpose. We need about," When Mara halted, Shandra picked up the conversation.

"You will need twelve different ones if you are thinking stables. They can be whatever size you want. We have people who know how to weld and can do the finishing work. They are insulated and should work well for the small ones. If you allow them to report to Pat at the house, she can show them where the units need to go. Also, it will allow them to see the craftsmanship you already have in the buildings. There must be a reason the former residence for them was in a hole in the ground," replied Shandra.

"True. However, we have one foreman presently, and we might want the miniatures closer to the racers to take care of them in winter. Also, we have the two horses that belong to Mike and Mary," Mara commented.

"Agreed, however, since you planned tunnels to connect with the main stables, would distance have that much bearing?" asked Shandra.

"Thank you," replied Mara with a smile. She had her mind on the places coming and appreciated Shan keeping her on track.

"Mom, I have no idea how you keep track of all you do. Shandra is a good guard to have and will help you any way she can. We are delighted that you have welcomed us and given us useful things to do that we know. I was worried you would have us doing something in which we had no knowledge or tried to use our training against those who trained us. I'm having a grand time sorting things and finding homes for them. While this is my training, the Military used very little of it, and now it can all be put to use," Rae replied, for she had to have a college degree to be an officer.

"I'm so thankful for every one of you. A task that was far beyond me has now become doable with everyone's help. It is amazing to have such high ranking help. I never thought I would see a General in my family, let alone so many other high ranks. I never dreamed I would meet a General, let alone be one. On special holidays like Veteran's Day, Fourth of July, and such, you need to pull out your uniforms and go in style," laughed Mara.

"If we did that, they would find us," Shandra said, for she knew that was what Rae was thinking.

"Not really, you see only one wearing a uniform will note the uniforms are those who are family. The rest will think you are in your usual Sunday clothing," Mara told them, then laughed again.

She had not thought about the information she heard earlier. She would be in an issued uniform as well, and her fund account received pay for her retired rank.

"That we can and will gladly do," replied Rae, who was proud of the uniform she was authorized to wear.

Mara was always surprised when they took her at her word and did whatever she asked of them. She wanted to see her Family in full uniform, even if only once.

"Remember that arena you own? Why not call for a formation there? Everyone can participate, and you will see us with all our lettuce, then we can pack it away once again. We could pull them out whenever you want to have a formation of your family Military," suggested Shandra, who had been with Mara so much she was picking up on her thinking and knew something was up.

"That would be best then no chance of making an error," replied Mara, who looked at her watch and smiled. They had plenty of time to make breakfast. She would have skipped it; however, Randy specified she had to be there for the vitamins and shot so that she ate before doing the tasks before her.

"Mom, would you come with me please?" asked Rae.

They followed her to the vaulted entry, then down the stairs and to a back room. Rae gave the codes at each door, and Mara heard the information, plus the AI would let her in anyplace she needed to be. The room they were now in had a lot of computer equipment in it.

"This is your new bank. Everyone will have a number or numbers, and that is how they access their funds. They can write checks and pay for items. The businesses will have a bank where they can submit those checks for cash if that is what they require. All checks belonging to us will come to this location and go into the accounts of those they belong to for deduction or addition, depending. I will be your banker if that is agreeable," explained Rae.

"Yes, that is agreeable. I just don't have time to cover this area. Please make it work for you. Thank goodness, my daughters are the ones controlling the funds," replied Mara with a smile of relief.

"Mom, when this all began, for us, we wondered what was going on. We were each to find the best-qualified personnel in all areas. We did that, and it took a bit over a year to be in contact and advise them to stay silent about what was going on. Little by little, we weeded out the ones who wouldn't do as directed. When we got to five thousand, we wondered why so many. Yet the directions were explicit, and we kept those already approved then kept checking the new enlistments, both officer and enlisted, to see if there were others to capture. When we reached ten thousand, we set those aside and erased all others, then started over. That is how you ended up with those you now have. If there is a need, advise Shandra, and she will activate others. We have about ten thousand more that we can call. The day we contact them, they will take their discharge and disappear. There was no reason to keep that many standing around, so they are available, just not here," advised Rae.

"What amazes me is you were able to do this, and no one except me seems to know what is going on. My family sees this as people I hired who needed jobs. They do not see you as Military. The best-trained people available when the Military downsized now are a part of who I am. I am humbled, shocked, and amazed. Your willingness to work with and for me is what made all these wonderful things happen. This mission began for me when I was fifteen. The school I attended said I should not graduate at fifteen, so I waited for a year. That must have been the time you were identifying the ones to come my way. I graduated at sixteen, and by seventeen was Thunder Press. Now I am twenty-two and in charge of thousands of people who do whatever I ask and know what they are doing. Who could ask for more? I was worried about how to get them paid and cared for medically. Those are the last things I'm concerned about now."

"From our side, we knew we were getting downsized. It was just a matter of time. That would put thousands of people out of work that needed a steady income to support a family. A dozen women agreed to put their lives on hold and get this done in a way that would benefit those that would fall through the cracks otherwise. Your force could easily triple if you have the need and funds. We still have a few people in the force who are keeping an eye out for exceptional people. When we finish, the armed forces will have dropped by three-quarters or more, which could mean hundreds of thousands of persons. That is a lot of folks with no place to go. Their talents are as varied as one could want."

"All have security clearances according to what they do. Many have families they are supporting here in the states. For example, a young woman came to me a couple of weeks ago and said that she had to move her children from her Mom's care as there were some strange goings on that had her kids worried."

"I issued a week's leave, and she went to take care of things. When she returned, she had a few kids with her. Come to find out, a man went on the rampage and killed all the parents while the kids were at daycare. Among those killed was her Mom. Sherry has now received permission from the court to care for ten of them. She has no way to do that and still serve in the Military. Her mind wants to stay while her heart says she can't abandon those children."

"Get them here any way you can. Send trustworthy adults to serve as caregivers to get them here. I will take on their care until she retires. Then she can take over if that is her desire," said Mara without a second thought.

"I did that, and they are here. I'll pay the bills for them; however, you have more than enough to handle as it is," replied Rae with tears in her eyes.

"I did not realize you weren't aware that I have nine kids in school, as well as five that are under age five, some of which are my grandkids or great-grandkids. We have nine tutors and graduated three kids since you came. Gwen, Dan, and Kennet have graduated. Oh forgot, all adults have graduated except for Melissa, Connie, and Shandra's family. Merry has to finish a Chef's course for Restaurants, and she becomes our Chef. As I recall, she starts this weekend. Dan and Gwen are training the young ones in riding, music, and how to care for the horses."

"Now Randy is trying to get Mike and Mary's twins the care they need. Gary and Jerry had surgery a week ago, as did Granda, so they are fine. Little by little, we're getting it all done."

"Melissa will not try to learn anymore as those who watched over her until sixteen convinced her she was too stupid even to keep a house. I'm working on that one. I don't think I have ever seen a cleaner house than the one where she lived."

"Rusker is a sharp little guy left on Melissa's doorstep as a newborn. At the time, she was sixteen. Rusker will be in the five and under group until his Mom returns. Melissa is the one you saw using crutches. Randy put her in the hospital, where surgeons will deal with some leg and back issues to get her walking again."

"Add those you have to the group. Bring them to the house, and we will add them to what I have. If I am not there, Joy will see that they get in the group they need to be. Tell your young woman that they are in good hands until she gets her discharge and can again take over their care, or I can adopt them and do it myself," Mara told them.

"You are one amazing person Mom. Thank you for allowing us to be part of this wonderful family led by you," Rae and Shandra nodded in agreement.

"Is there anything else you need to make me aware of?" asked Mara with a smile.

"We have breakfast scheduled in an hour. Are the kids here so they could go with us? You are going to be plenty busy just doing the stuff here," Shandra advised, for she spotted something that her Mom hadn't.

"Well, yes, they are here. Just a minute, " Rae ran through the rooms and up the stairs to the main floor.

"Ole, Ole oxy free," she called, and kids came from all directions.

"You are all going to school with some other kids that are related to these wonderful women. This is my Mom and my sister," said Rae proudly.

Soon ten kids under age five, some were still a little unsteady on their feet while others ran freely. Granda was going to be busy.

The kids crammed themselves into the car, and Mara took the back road home as quickly as she dared. Once the vehicle was in the garage, Mara took them to her suite and assigned them rooms. Rooms seemed to materialize according to the need, with no more than four to a room. One space would always be open for Shandra as well.

Mara was surprised when she returned from an errand one day to find that an entire wing now held her, Granda, and Shandra's suites. Kennet also moved; however, it was to a suite of his own in the building's same wing.

Breakfast was ready when they got there, and Rae was present with the rest of the family. The adults made sure that all those under five had someone to help them.

"Granda?" asked Mara.

"Yes, dear."

"You just acquired ten under five. We have a week-long duty that will have us tied up. Please watch over that group until we finish. You have a bedroom in my suite if you wish, for they have rooms. That is where the school-age ones reside as well. Then will get you some help," commented Mara.

"Not necessary they will do fine. I heard your conversation with Rae, and we will love them like all the rest," smiled Granda from her place at the table. No one else heard the conversation, for everyone remained frozen while the two spoke.

When the meal was over, Granda showed the kids the routine for the house. They learned how the other kids kept their rooms clean and beds made as best they could. They would ride before breakfast and play musical instruments. Whenever someone needed a stringed instrument, it appeared. Wind and percussion instruments came from a store in town by making a phone call as there wasn't time to go there at the moment. The young ones seemed thrilled. Granda explained not today, for it was too late though they would get to do that the following day. Dishes had to be washed and put away. Then the tables were set for the next meal. The children's clothing and toys appeared in their assigned rooms.

Mara and Shandra grabbed some clean clothes for themselves, then departed for the property that Granda had managed to acquire. They arrived to start their day at eight AM. Michelle and Gretch were waiting in the Garage when the two women arrived. It was time to get to work.

Mara explained to the last two what their part would be. They could sit in the shade until needed; however, if they heard a call to be ready to grab horses, people, or whatever.

The first was a ranch. No one was home; therefore, they looked over the stock, checked out the house and stables. Mara asked that the horse ranch be small-sized and a force bubble placed around it while they handled the next one for that one might need keeping if only to get it operational.

The next one to arrive was a bank. Mara laughed and looked it over.

"Rae, didn't you say something about needing a bank in town that you could use as an exchange point for checks written by our bank? I happen to have one if you are interested and was thinking it might fit on that vacant lot across from the warehouse," advised Mara via the AI at home, which could communicate with all the AIs in their network.

"Yes, there is a property at Seventh and Orange that is vacant. A building burned down, and they leveled the ground. That means there could be a hidden vault as well as a means to transfer the checks without anyone being aware of where they are going, for it is close yet not part of the group of enterprises you purchased."

Mara received word that the bank had to be returned, to where it was from though the bank they needed was now in place. Rae would now monitor the bank.

The next ranch had a hundred head of horses, and the young couple who ran it was thrilled at the possibility of moving elsewhere. They wanted to raise a family, yet children in that area were kidnapped, made into slaves, or killed. Mara granted their request and placed them with the miniaturized ranch already nearby.

Next up was a huge ranch. Mara knew that by the size of the stables and home. Gretch and Michelle heard the call to watch their backs on this one. The four women inspected the ranch buildings. Next, they had the main building to look over.

The people were asleep and remained that way while the home received an inspection bottom to top, then the basement. They were not disappointed, for they found a vault.

Mara wondered where they got all the wealth, and it appeared that none of them had anyone enter since they were initially built and filled.

"This one has not been entered in years. It is a lot like the first one we did."

Michelle and Gretch had gone back to their shade once they realized everyone was asleep.

"Look at the condition of this ranch. It is immaculate, and the animals in excellent condition. That is the kind of people I want to control any of the ranches we keep. The only way I will remove people is if they agree to it," Mara commented.

"Then perhaps you should ask him," said Shandra with a nod at a man standing in the doorway of the room where they were.

"Sir, we own this ranch, and since forces in this nation have made it dangerous to my family to check out the various locations am doing it another way. The ranch you oversee is one of the best we have seen. Would you be willing to move to one of the states with your family and the ranch with all it contains?" asked Mara in the language of his area.

"You will have answered a dream for all of us. What would be required to do that?" the man asked.

"You will need to take an oath first," said Shandra.

He agreed, and at Mara's request, Shandra spoke the oath.

"Everyone in our employ has to take that oath," warned Mara.

"Awaken them, and they will speak," he replied.

Shandra called for her sisters, and the people assembled outside the Ranchero.

"Is this everyone?" asked Shandra.

"It is all that must take the oath," the man told her.

"No, I want all that are on this property to approach me and give the oath. Not some, all," said Thunder in a firm voice.

"Very well, although I do not know how you are going to know they have," he replied.

He gave a sharp whistle, then two more, with each call being different. Four children ran to the gates and opened them. Dogs, horses, and even stallions came on the run.

Mara walked up to one of the stallions and asked him if he would give an oath and swear in all those under him. He knelt with one leg set for her to step up and reach his back. Another did the same for Shandra.

When human oaths finished, Mara looked at one of the dogs and asked if they were willing to swear the promise to her. The Alpha dogs came forward and bowed low to her. Then an eagle came from the skies, and after giving warning, it landed on Mara's outstretched arm.

"Sir, does that answer your questions?" she asked the man.

"As the prediction said, we move," he replied.

As Mara and Shandra rode around the group, Cherry led them in the oaths.

"Eagle, we are north of where you have always lived. Will you join us for the rest of our lives?" asked Mara quietly of the immense bird standing on her shoulder.

He cocked his head at her, rolled his eyes, and bent his body forward, for he could not nod.

"You have all been moved with what belongs to you. If you have any young ones, they will be here as well. I need your services. None will be treated poorly by my family or me. Will you come?" Mara asked once again.

When she looked around, she saw everyone with a saddled horse ready to go.

"Thunder, please give them a prime spot the same size as the area they left, that they may have what they consider as home. Also, please give them the language of the area and citizenship under an American name so that they feel at home here," directed Mara.

The ranch materialized in an enclosed valley over which

eagles flew all the time.

"Thank you for joining us. We still have a long way to go before we complete everything. We will meet again. If you wish, you can be part of my family. The choice is yours," she told the man.

"I do wish it. What name do we use?" the man once called Petro, and now Peter asked excitedly.

"Shandra, are you willing to put them under you? You will also have your sisters who fall under you as guards, though they are under me in the lineage. You will have a family of about two hundred under you as Mom with the name of your choice," Mara advised.

"What would you think of Valleyshan? Helps us keep track of who is related to who," Shandra laughed.

The man had been listening and began to chuckle.

"Valeshan would work and is close," he advised.

"That means that your entire family has now become the generation under me. I become your Mother, and the rest fall into order accordingly if that works for you," replied Shandra.

"We will be related to Thunder?" he asked in surprise, for in his oath, he swore to Thunder, the N-Sign Clan, and those in Leadership positions.

"Yes, however, that might not be a thought to share. Men hunt us for they wish to kill us. My legal name is Shandra N-Sign, while my Mother is Mara N-Sign if that works for you," Shandra explained.

"We are honored," he told her.

"Now, we must return to duty. We will talk another time. Enjoy your new location," Shandra advised though to the man he had always lived there, and the only thing different was their name and adoption, which also seemed as it had ever been.

They then returned to where they were checking out the ranches and businesses.

Of the rest of the day's work, the personnel that Shandra adopted were the best of the lot. The ranch was in excellent condition, the horses were well trained, as were the dogs, and the family was thrilled to be where they were.

The ranch that had been in Spain, with the injured caregiver, was kept. They had removed the caregiver as a member of the family, and therefore she would care for the ranch once Mara inspected to see why it was such an obvious catch. Mara had a disquiet about that one for the location had no people on the property. That one would have to have an inspection before it was allowed in Mara's home state.

When Mara explained her concerns, Shandra called for her sisters, and they thoroughly inspected the ranches. They found electronics in both of them that had to be quickly removed and disabled. The horse ranches became part of the land where new people would manage the one, and Connie would be allowed to take over the one if that was her desire. When asked, she agreed immediately.

The house vaults were left with the ranches they kept, for as Mara said, she didn't want everything in one location. A few of the relocated horse ranches received new caregivers from folks that Shandra recommended from the Military if those designated as caregivers were not doing the job.

They continued to handle what came as quickly as they could.

By the time they finished, they had good stock for twelve ranches, and each one would have a hidden vault within it. A lot of products were retained and sent to Rae for accountability.

Mara learned from Thunder which personnel she was to

retain with the stock. She did as directed.

When they reached home at the end of their day, they were exhausted.

Mara was amazed to find, when she woke up, that she no longer owned property in South America. However, she received the value of the properties in gold. From the properties sold, all hidden room contents were placed in the warehouse for Rae to inventory. Pat had installed an AI to oversee the entire area though she was unaware of the bank and vault.

Every week Granda checked with the Secretary of State to find out what was up for sale. She purchased any that she felt might fill a need. Of particular interest to her were ranches, large pieces of land, and forested areas. Granda set up corporations to cover who owned a given property or properties, and for that, she tried to get buildings that were in good condition yet empty. Her only qualification on what she purchased was it had to be within Montana's borders though she saw the holdings move to more than one county.

The first ranch they had acquired had the woman, and two sets of twins moved closer to the home base, yet it encompassed the same amount of land as it had.

"Shandra, we have an issue. We need to have someone initiate a number system to keep track of what we own without anyone, except that person, knowing who owns what. Especially if it belongs to me," said Mara.

"How soon do you want them?" asked Shandra.

"Would now be too soon?" asked Mara.

"Not if you are willing to go for a ride," her daughter laughed.

"Let's do it," replied Mara.

They went to the warehouse and located Rae.

"Hello Mom, what can I do for you?" asked the woman.

"Need a private meeting," said Shandra with a smile.

"I certainly agree to that," replied their numbers woman.

She led them to the underground vault where they were. They could hardly get in for the stuff that the area now held.

"Pat, I need you here at the warehouse as soon as you are free. Bring your kit, please," said Mara into her mic.

"I'm on my way."

"Don't forget your guard," cautioned Mara.

"I'm never without one or two, sister mine."

Mara and the two women moved to the main floor to wait on Pat.

She came in pulling a large wagon, and her guard was at the other end.

"This is not going to work. Shandra, who do we have that can make things? We need a vehicle with all of Pat's special tools in it. It has to be made as suitcases so that when she needs something for a specific need, she can grab that case and go to work. The vehicle needs to be as secure as it can be. Bulletproof windows, armor-plated exterior, yet don't want it to stand out in traffic. It has to be tall enough to stand up in with no windows from the front behind the drivers. The panels in the exterior should appear whatever color the van is yet needed to let in light and view, although only one way. Pat needs six such units and as many people to know what they are for, plus how to use the equipment. They will be working under Pat. If they appear to be regular vans, that would be fine, yet they do need building as requested," Mara directed.

Pat turned around and left, taking her wagon with her. By the time she got to the door, it was gone.

"Now see what you have done, Mom; you scared the help," said Shandra with barely suppressed laughter.

"You are right. Every unit is as you said, and all six are here," Pat commented as she entered the room again.

The wagon was gone, and instead, Pat carried a small tool kit.

"You know Rae, she is our banker, and some areas have to be changed. I took care of the property in South America with Shandra's aid. Now we have a real mess. Bring your team and swear them to secrecy, especially in this case and make it a Thunder pledge. We have work to do," advised Mara.

Pat did as directed, and soon twelve people were on site that dealt with electronics only. The other twelve were already inventorying as they had been all along; only their area of concentration was the warehouse itself. They knew nothing of the rest.

Rae looked around at the busy folks and moved to the bank area. There she had twelve people setting up the number system for banking accounts. By the end of the day, those tasks were complete. All N-Sign property was under a number only, and it was that way throughout the state for the State Treasurer kept her appraised. Next would be recording the Real Estate they had out of state, for it too had to be put under a number system. It would be up to Rae to coordinate with the other State Treasurers to get it done.

"Mom, have you looked at this area? You own the county seat and all the ranch and farmland. Drought happened in the area, and no one has operated in that area for ten years," said Rae, for one of her employees had pointed it out to her.

"Yes, I know. We purchased the empty buildings from the state and county. As soon as we have people taking care of an area, it is rejuvenated and stocked with whatever animals are needed. You need to call for a few more of the extras. We need a Country Treasurer sworn to us in that area. When we have reliable people in those areas, I will own the property and lease it to those who work and live there. It will be a reasonable amount, and once they prove competence in running what is under their control, they may gain a clear title. We also have a few ghost towns in our inventory," Mara explained.

Chapter 13

How many is all

"Why do that? Why not continue to lease what you own to have a consistent income? They will take better care of the property or have to leave. With monitors to be sure the value is not lost, even those with limited funds will live in a decent unit. Charge them according to what their income is by percentage," Rea suggested.

"Those counties are test sites. Yes, I own the ranches and farms; however, the towns are still operated by those who live there unless their places come up for sale. Then I may purchase if it shows the possibility of an increase in value, which it will once I own the whole area," explained Mara.

"Why do you want so much land? However, not finding fault, think I need to know to better support your intent," said Rea.

"I intend to sell the properties to those who were once Military. However, they have to prove they are willing and capable of maintaining what they control. It is not a blank check; it is a test to see if they are honest, reliable, and ready to become full citizens. I want ranches that take care of their stock and the tools it takes to be a ranch. The farms require the same. This state should be self-sufficient, and it isn't. I also want our extended family to be the same. We will keep enough that the family will never be hungry, and we aid those who need it within this state, as long as it is the truth, and they are doing their best. It might require education to get them started. The ranches will furnish stock for horse shows and entertainment; therefore, the new ones will be kept, beyond that, let others run their ranches. I hope to get Peter to give classes at the U in care and maintenance of a ranch. That way, everyone will know the right way to do it. They will enjoy it more if they know how the right way. If the manager cannot afford to own the ranch, I will own it and will let them manage it. That gets them a secure income and me a reliable person to care for the stock and buildings."

"Now it makes sense. Thank you," responded Rae.

"I only want what we can use; however, for now, we take it all then sort and make decisions as to what to do with whatever. You are on the board, so think about how you would use it if in your care," replied Mara with a smile.

"Had a feeling you have headed that direction. You said that the A and C Quads would be part of the lead group with the T Twins. You know we will help you in any way possible. When we knew of our discharge, we were afraid we would be on the streets with many other people who have a high value. It is wonderful to be put to work doing things we know how to do and having a family to feel loved and cared about," said Shandra.

"You have a family to get doing things our way. We will have to take a few lessons from them then add a few of our own. By the way, you two need to know that once things settle, some of us may even get married and have natural children. Kennet will always and in every way remain my son, as will all of you that I adopted personally. I think that you ladies should be allowed to have as large a family as you want. When you reach a hundred in your family, you might want to build a ranch, farm, or home. Just stay within a hundred miles or so of us if you please," Mara told them.

"To be honest, I never gave that a thought. We have been too busy to think that way," replied Shandra in surprise.

"Don't have more than you can afford; love, train, and take give care. Otherwise, the sky is the limit. That does not mean you have to count in all those you adopt, for many will be adults, and they can take care of the afford and take care of part on their own," laughed Mara.

"Or they may come with a full family structure, and all they want is to know that there is someone someplace who cares and will jump in if needed," commented Shandra, for that was the way she saw her new additions.

"When a person has the loyalty of horses, eagles, dogs, women, and kids, what does it matter if the men want to revolt," laughed Mara.

The women laughed, although, at the same time, they were going over records and checking for errors, matching numbers, and names, double-checking properties.

At the same time, Pat was setting up an AI that was answerable only to the twins and Rae. Around her team were others inventorying the vault and putting things away after listing accountability. Liquidation would happen later. It was another long day for the women, yet the task showed as done when they stopped.

There had been some questions about what to do with a few items that they had never seen before. It turned out that Rae was an antique collector, and that was the store she still owned.

It gave Mara an option for liquidating some of what they had inherited. Jo still owned a car dealership, though she sold the one she had on the east coast and purchased one in the area where she lived. It seems that one of the Military officers wanted the one she owned previously, so she turned around and built a better one where she was. The car collection that Mara acquired went on display at one of their new properties, and Jo was the one in charge of it.

- - - - - - -

"Mom, where are you?"

Mara instantly recognized the voice.

"Thunder!" was all she said, and the Quads, Twins, and all departed a locked-down facility, and they were on their way to wherever Kennet was.

"I am here, my son," she whispered into her communicator.

"You left without me, and there was no other way to warn you," he apologized.

"It is okay. What is going on?" Mara asked.

He was standing on the porch of the home place. By turning slightly, he was facing the road coming into the area. Then he moved again and was facing the stables. They heard the AI secure all buildings. Each room within the complex was also locked.

Mara felt the Thunder formation filling. Still, she waited, wondering where the guards were so that they did not injure their people.

"Thunder split," Mara ordered, and half of the people went with one twin and half with the other as they moved to meet the two threats though they walked as a unit facing different directions. There were a twin and Quad in each group.

The women waited for the adversary to approach them, for they were not going to be separated. Mara began to notice a few things. The stallions were loose, Shira was moving, and when she saw the miniatures moving as well. It had to be only a glancing look, for she didn't want to give anyone away and needed to concentrate on those coming.

"Glad you have made it so easy to find you," said one of the men on the T1 side of the split.

"Why?" Mara replied.

"So we can eliminate all of you in one fell swoop and get on with life like it was before you decided to play heroine," he responded.

"Why?"

"How should I know why? You are making a shambles of our businesses. We get property coming our way cheap, and you grab it up. No matter what we do, you counter it. We have had enough. It all stops here," he told her.

"Why?"

"Because you cost us money, that's why. We even had a nice little trap set for you in South America, and somehow you found out and got around it. This time we have, you outnumbered, outgunned, and you won't leave here alive. Not you or any of those people you call family," the man said.

"Spenser, they are my family. However, you wouldn't understand that, would you? You stole your wives' fortunes, ran off the kids, and sued them for everything they had. Nice guy you are. Nice to know what kind of a person you are, and by the time this is over, you will know what kind of people we all are," responded T1.

Mara sensed rather than saw Randy join the formation, and with her were Joy, Sue, Keri, and Gwen. They took the west end of the location, with the house on the east and the other teams each facing north and south. The only ones missing were Merry and Granda, who always remained on guard as a backup to call in help if needed. Granda was also currently a caregiver for those under age five, which had freed Joy and Keri.

"That is true you will though it won't make any difference when you are no longer here," he told her.

He ordered his group to take her on just as the second group challenged T2.

"About time you met us in person. You keep sending other folks to do your dirty work," said another man.

"Hello Gus, we would be easy to find if you came in the open instead of skulking around. You will get your wish though it may not turn out quite the way you want," advised T2.

The animals departed for the stables, or so it seemed. Soon the area was empty except for those challenging Thunders. The house door opened, and another group exited. It was Jimmy, and with him were Gary, Jerry, Price, Dan, and Chester. They remained on the stairs as guards for the door with Jimmy in the middle.

Every member of the family wore the same clothing. They all wore boots, jeans, red blouses or shirts, and kerchief topped with cowboy hats. They had dark hair and were in their early twenties. They looked exactly alike, including the group's men, since in Thunder mode, they were all six foot in height.

"Thunder down," said Kennet, and all dropped where they were to be resting on their heels.

When the teams began to move, they had swords in their hands and met the incoming shells, with Lightning returning shots to the senders immediately. A third adversary group aimed at Randy, and she was ready with her group. She had been training those with her for just such an event. Something told her to wait before going to the hospital; therefore, she was ready for the call.

Once those incoming were disabled, the stallions appeared and began driving them to the corral used for court. Each of the leaders had one of the horses offer them a ride to the next location, which they gratefully accepted. The horses moved in a side by side row to not get ahead of the Lightening blade held in the open by each of the Thunder riders though the points were upward.

When they reached the corral, they found it packed full, and since it would hold a hundred horses, they knew there had to be at least twice that many people in it at the moment, and as the last group entered the corral, it expanded to accommodate them.

Mara dismounted by first swinging her right leg to the horse's left to keep the sword pointed in the right direction. All the riders did the same in the way and time.

"This court is now in session," directed Thunder Press.

"I serve as a council," said Jo.

"Who is in charge of this group?" Thunder asked.

"Mom, you have six groups here. The horses brought in one, you had three challenge you, then the littles brought in the ones coming from their side, and the last batch hid in the stable until Shira routed them out," whispered Kennet.

"Group facing Thunder one on the Southside, who is your leader?" asked Thunder

"I am. How do you manage always to be a step ahead of us?" the man asked in surprise.

"You will never find out, for you have broken the laws of this land. As Judge of this court, I require your names, your family, and a list of everything you own regardless of size. Then give me the reason you are here and what your intent was. Who has given you the information you are using to harass us?"

"My name is Spenser Wiseman. You are correct; I did take my wife's inheritance. She didn't need it, and I did, shouldn't be left in the hands of a woman anyhow. As for those kids, why should I support them for the rest of their natural lives? They need to develop a backbone and earn their way in life, as I have. I have four estates by four wives, and the same has happened to all their kids," he replied.

Without turning, Mara knew that the mentioned four wives were in attendance. Then a second group appeared, and she called on the Thunder group's male guards to stand watch over those two groups for the second group was probably the kids.

Mara's guards (Shandra and her three sisters) were two on each side of her, with Pat's group (Jo and her three sisters) on her left and Randy's group standing on the end to Mara's right. Each group had a leader in the middle. The young woman wondered when they had the time to be so well drilled, yet she was thankful for their precision.

The Thunder Judge gave a fair and impartial judgment once each prisoner gave their testimony, including each of the wives and their oldest child. Everything was certified and signed for the legal process to happen. They found the men all had the same opinion of women. The person who sent them was a woman, for she felt she would know how to counter Thunder and her group. Soon there were several women in with the men, and all charged with breaking laws.

"Granda, we are ready, and they will need trucks or buses," Thunder Press said softly.

The felons gained a great deal of knowledge related to their network, location, looks, gender, home, and formations. Now it was time to remove that information. The captives were judged guilty, with attempts on the lives of those in the Thunder Group.

"On their way," responded Granda, for with Pat helping keep an eye on the number of felons they had, she would be the best one to call law enforcement.

When the problems were gone, Mara moved around to thank all the teams, including the dogs, horses, and Shira.

"Jimmy, what possessed you to join us?" asked Mara when she finally caught up with him.

"I asked Granda how we could help, and she said to watch the door, so gathered up those not already outside, and we did as directed. Never will I sit and watch any of you getting massacred. That bunch was out for your heads. How can I ask you to marry me if that happened?" he responded.

"Took you long enough," laughed Mara. "Why me?" she added.

"Because you are the best of the best, and it will take that kind of person to whip this ole fool in shape. Besides, I love the music this bunch plays."

"Jimmy, you are wrong on a lot of accounts. You are not old or a fool, for you are my age. Next on your schedule is going to the University and taking some exams. Take the guys with you. It would help if you rode horses, as they never have any to use for testing. Dan has already taken the exams. However, he knows what you need to do and will serve as your escort. When you return, we will discuss that proposal," Mara continued to chuckle.

He immediately went in search of Dan and the rest of the guys.

"You know there is something we need. We need a preacher. Wonder if you can adopt one someplace?" commented Mara to Randy as the two were discussing recent events.

Pat had returned to the warehouse with those who were working there. Jo and Jero were setting up the schedule for the auditorium and had also departed.

Randy laughed and laughed.

"Mom, it seems you have the certification which comes from my memories. I was a JP before I went into medicine. I didn't want to be just a JP, so I took the full ministerial course. I also felt that if one of my patients was to die in an operating room, they had the right to have a preacher to aid them in the transition. You might want to brush up on being a Military chaplain, for many of your offspring are Military, and that might be the kind of wedding they prefer. Does that mean we are about to see some weddings?" asked Randy with a chuckle.

"We will have to be married as we joined. After Pat and

I are married, by you officiating, she and I can take vows from the rest by making it a mass wedding while each of the persons will think that it was just them and their guests. No doubt all of our family members will want to be present. That means that Shandra will have two hundred plus in her family group plus the Military, of which I have about twelve thousand, which is not for publication. Now might be a good time to bring out the rest of the reserve. Might as well get it all done and get back to business," Mara told her daughter.

"What makes you think that there will be any other than you and Pat?" asked Randy.

"Could be the proposals I'm hearing. None of the women told me that Jimmy was a Colonel. He moved up the hard way and built businesses in the area where he served overseas and stateside. Jimmy never sold unless there was a way to earn a hundred percent profit, and if they made that much, why sell them? When he got here, he signed over everything he owned to me. Knew he had an ulterior motive," Mara laughed.

"I prefer to remain single. One bad marriage is enough for me," Randy responded.

"No, that is not the case. You see, you learned without it doing permanent damage. There are no records anyplace that show you were ever married. Only Granda and I know what took place, and we forget such things unless brought up by you. As your Mother, the men have approached me to ask for your hand. Many admire you, and the choice is yours. Gary is a leather master; Price is a Goldsmith; Jerry and Chester serve as guards; however, once they return from the University, all of them will have the knowledge we do. It would be a bad marriage if we didn't do that. We also have tutors that might want to join us, and only one of them is male."

"You have got to be kidding! They all asked to marry me?" asked Randy in shock.

"Truth, however, you have a secret admirer that I think would fill the bill much better. He was a doctor in the Military, and yes, they did all ask. Russel did four tours in war zones. He is settled, ready to retire, and looking to start a new life so he can forget the one he left behind. Would you be at all interested?"

"Won't know until I meet this mystery man," responded Randy with interest.

"Merry has finished her last school and will be here today. She wants to put on a BBQ for everyone as a thank you for getting her dream education. I told her to expect to be cooking for anywhere from four to fourteen thousand folks. Her response was, that's alright. Merry had some folks at the school that were interested in joining her in working here. They told her they were headed this way anyhow for roll call. She will be head Chef while she has a dozen under her. A baker, a dessert maker, someone specializing in salads of all kinds, plus they can all help her in a case like this. That cattle ranch we inherited will be providing the beef, and Mitzer will furnish the pork. There will also be chickens for those who do not like the first two options. We can hold it in the riding arena as that is the only place I can think of that everyone will fit. Outriders will watch over the home place. Dan said he would see that they got some of the food if he could use my van. I agreed; however, what he doesn't know is that Jo has ordered a special vehicle for him. Everyone will have a personal vehicle so they can do what they need to."

"Mom, how long have you been doing this?" asked Randy.

"I graduated in June. By July, I had a full family, owned this place, worked as Thunder, and gained property. Which makes this what? August, isn't it?"

"Yes, it is the fourth, to be exact. You have trained and graduated all these folks?"

"Not exactly for the Military came trained as have some

of the others. I had to get all leaders on the same page; they needed to have the same education I have, plus I need their education. Thus we are the best educated in our family, for we reserved medical for Granda, Pat, you, and me," Mara told her.

"I think you should include Jo and Shandra, for they seem to be the layer right under me. Their Quad groups have more than earned that training; I would say," responded Randy after some thought.

Mara appeared to be thinking about it when she became Thunder Press to make sure it happened. While she was doing that, she froze the family and took care of a few other things that just weren't getting done. Items left for later often didn't get done at all.

"I recall you saying that you needed to winterize everything before winter. You commented on wanting an airport. How many planes do you have now?" Randy inquired.

"We have the two large ones for two hundred passengers each, the two smaller jets which hold twenty people each, and this last haul brought us a fleet of helicopters plus two transcontinental ships. We have several different kinds. It seems to me like we have around a hundred ships of which each different kind. That means we need a different sized runway for each, so I asked for the largest required and put them at our private airport. There they have indoor storage, mechanics, and hangars. That meant hiring those for the control tower and all the other support personnel," Mara told her eldest.

"Where did you get the mechanics?"

"They came with the planes; however, Shandra added an equal number of Military pilots and mechanics to even things out. Test pilots are needed if a plane needs service, and they can't have mine," Mara advised.

"What will you do if the lead group all marries?"

"Love them, teach them, and make room if they are willing to remain. If anyone wants to leave, not a problem, only that means ending up with the knowledge they came with, which means they forget us and all history of their Master degrees will be gone."

"I told you when I came that I was here for both our lives. That has not changed regardless of anything. You can't get rid of me," was the response.

"I am so glad. It will take all of us to retain what we now hold, and it will be needed to support the empire we now oversee. Everyone has to participate for it to work."

"Would you be open to some suggestions?" asked Randy.

"From you, I am always ready to listen."

"I know there is Military in our family, for I was around when the Quad's joined us. Why not use one of the twenty people planes and send that many to check out where you are going when you take a plane someplace? That way, you have a hangar ready for you, know the requirements, have guards in place, and you can have some of the men, who are married to those in the lead group, move with you. If you use the Military for the prep group, no one will blindside you, plus they can pick up intel as to what is going on in that particular nation. Once you are married, the planes might need remodeling. The other option would be to send the men ahead and keep all women in the Lead plane," Randy advised.

"I hear you and will take it under advisement. The lead group, meaning all who participated in today's little activity, are going out to eat. For Merry, it is a celebration of graduation; For the men, it is their graduation from University; For Joy, Jero, Keri, and Gwen, it was being baptized with armed fire; For the Quads and Twins, it is getting South America issues resolved. Now that Melissa is home, Jerry somehow convinced her to take the tests with the men. As they did, she passed, and she doesn't know whether to be mad at those who raised her or get to work with the new knowledge. We are getting ready to leave again, and before we do that, the rest of our force will be coming to watch over what we own and be the advance force on our flight to Switzerland. Now have to figure out someone to babysit who does not like to fly," said Mara with a smile at her daughter.

"I thought that Melissa was going to do that if we were gone. That is a country I have always wanted to visit, along with Holland and Ireland. Will we be going to any of those as well?" asked Randy.

"Yes, all of them though it might take more than one flight, we will also be going to Alaska."

"I thought about renting a cruise ship for that one since there are so many, and it will be a round trip. Or maybe take half at a time, not sure how many a ship that size carries," laughed Mara.

"Mom, you are so thoughtful," Randy chuckled then added, "Since that means that you, Pat, me, Granda, and the Quads, plus a few others, will be making both trips if there are two to Alaska."

"Well. There is a bit of truth in that," Mara grinned, then broke out in laughter though she was thinking how much fun it would be if her family became the on-board entertainment.

She would find the big ones carried between one hundred sixty and two hundred twenty-five thousand, which would mean one trip with everyone and space left over, maybe, unless everyone was married, then. They did have smaller units, which might work best if she wanted it to be all family and not give anyone their information. She chuckled to herself and changed the subject.

The two women chuckled when they heard Melissa cleaning the complex, and she was singing to herself. She was a different person with her new education. Some of the talents were reserved, like medical and languages; however, she had at least a dozen Master's Degrees.

Mara had given herself a few hours off for the things she had to do and where she went, so did Shandra.

"Shan, don't you ever have things you would like to do for yourself?" asked Mara.

"I oversee everyone else. Orders are left for them each evening to utilize the following day once I know your schedule. Since you don't require a gazillion meetings a day, I have the time and desire to do whatever you will allow. The more I work with you, the more I understand what you want me to do. However, on the other hand, if you prefer to have some time to yourself, say so, as long as it is in a secure location," advised Shandra.

Mara laughed and laughed. She admired and loved all her kids.

"Well, within two hours, this lead group is packing up and going to dinner. We are celebrating a lot of things accomplished by various members of this group. Dress in your finest, like maybe boots and jeans; you know the drill. We will reserve the restaurant for a private dinner for three hours from four to seven. Then we depart, and it will be like they had their regular customers during that time. The next question is: what do we use to move them? We have, just a minute, I'll find it," said Mara.

Shandra waited for the answer though she already knew what it was: Adults only: forty-four. The kids, twenty-one of them, would remain at the complex either controlled by the tutors or with someone volunteering to watch over them. She was quietly asking the computer if the tutors would take on twenty-one kids for four hours. They agreed.

"Okay, what is it?" asked Mara.

"What is what?" asked Shandra in surprise.

"You are supposed to have the answers I can't find," said

Mara with a grin.

"Oh, that, you have forty-four adults going to dinner and twenty-one kids being looked after by the tutors for four hours. That way, everyone's meal has time to digest before we go back to duty as usual, plus we have to factor in extra's since we are going to the restaurant," responded Shandra when she realized that her Mom was teasing her.

"Did you turn in the reservation while you were at it?" asked Mara.

"Yes, I did. Should I not have done so?"

Mara laughed and laughed, then realized what she was doing and did it again.

"Shandra, thank you, my laugh is back, you can take a teasing, and don't give in to me all the time. If I am wrong, say so, and we will make changes and move on. Look at our ages and know we may be together for a very long time. It is best to compromise and move on."

"Well, I debated then decided what I would do in your place. That was what I did. Glad I didn't upset the apple cart. What time do we begin loading the bus?" asked Shandra with a relieved smile.

"We are getting to know one another and finding out our strengths and weaknesses. Today showed that we have a lot more in the strength column. Did you notice those who joined us in battle? It looked like a well-drilled group. Not sure when anyone had the time though they sure shone today."

"Oh, we four helped Randy get them up to speed. I thought we were to be the trainers, so I went with it. Since they are related to you, it seemed to be necessary. I wasn't sure about the men, so I figured we could cover it later. Did you see Jimmy deck that man who tried to sneak in behind you? He flat nailed him," laughed Shandra.

"No, I didn't. It seems I was busy at the time," replied

Mara with surprise.

"The guy didn't wake up until the end of the court. Jimmy packed him to the corral."

"Shandra, what can you tell me about Jimmy? In case you didn't know, he asked me to marry him," Mara explained.

"Nothing slow about him," Shandra chuckled.

"When I asked him why me, he said 'because you are the best of the best and it will take that kind of person to whip this ole fool in shape. Besides, I love the music this bunch plays,' and that was all. When we first met, he made a strange comment, I thought. He said: 'When you get home, we will meet again so that what is in my name becomes yours.' I have said we will discuss it while I want to have my kids' blessing and know a bit about Jimmy that he might not tell me. Good or bad, then it can't hang me up later," Mara tried to make her daughter understand.

"Mom, I understand, truly I do. You see, I was married once. It lasted ten years, then he was sent overseas and never returned. We knew it could happen and planned for if it, doing the 'what then' drill. Now I know you don't plan for disaster; you live each day with what you have and make it what you want. All our pasts have changed due to joining you. You could say it is a clean slate for all of us, except for our education. Yes, we remember; however it is not the sharp ache it was for years. You have our full loyalty for giving us what we have never had, a family that honors us for who we are and loves us as part of them. I can't speak for others though we have talked about it and believe we all feel the same. You have been the missing link in our lives. A higher power created us to work with you. Your photographic memory gives you the answers you need when you need them. However, we need to be part of and feel we contribute, so you asked that any who work most closely with you have that kind of memory. All the things you have given us are those desires that we would never have seen fulfilled in any other way."

"I know the Military side of Jimmy, not a great deal of the human side. He is honest, for once saw him back out of a deal he had going after finding out the person he was dealing with had no idea what they had. Instead of buying the business, he went partners with the person, and when the business was paying its way and had a solid value, he offered to sell it for the owner first, then he walked away. He never told anyone what he did. I know because of my involvement in that particular business deal. If he gives his loyalty, it is all or nothing. To tell you that he would sign over all he owned to you told me it was already a done deal. Nothing is halfway with him. He has my loyalty, yet in a different way than you have it. He has mine because I was the woman he rescued, yet he never tried to be more than a help to a woman who suddenly found herself owning a business she had no skills in running for she was now a widow, and her husband had skills she did not. Never saw him start a fight though he wasn't at all opposed to finishing one. Jo asked me about his wanting to meet you. I gave it some thought and said, go ahead, for Mom can hold her own. I still feel that way; however, if there was any danger, any of us were aware of, we would have stopped it. We will guard your back to our dying breath, and that is not said lightly." Shandra stood straight and tall as she spoke, yet Mara could see the tears in her eyes.

"Thank you." Mara moved to her daughter and gave her a long close hug.

"It is all or nothing for you know my heart," replied Shandra, who returned that hug with interest.

"Now let me see, forty-four means two buses. We no longer fit in the vans, so those are going to the kids to run errands. Also gave them to the tutors to get around. When on personal errands, the lead group has regular vehicles. Someone is always at home to deliver a larger vehicle if one is needed."

"The buses are in the garage, as you well know. Quad A

will bring out the one for you, and Quad C will bring out Pat's unless you two want us to ride together. The men are qualified to drive buses, part of Military training. Therefore they can do the driving if you prefer. It won't hurt anyone's feelings; however, you do it. Just say what you want to happen, and it will," Shandra advised.

Chapter 14

An N-Sign Celebration

They loaded everyone up, and the men volunteered to drive. Therefore Mara let them and enjoyed relaxing with the rest of the group. She listened to those around her as they teased one another and repeated the day's activities. Then one conversation came to her attention.

"I wonder what Mom has up her sleeve now. It must be a special occasion for usually we aren't all included. Different ones at different times, yet this time we are all here, and the kids have caregivers for this time," she recognized Joy's voice.

"Don't matter, it will be fun, and we can enjoy family," replied Dan, who was sitting by her.

Kennet didn't say a word though she knew he was smiling, as was his Mom.

Mara had broken a couple of rules that day. She split herself and went shopping for gifts for those being honored. They went to the restaurant with Mara's name on them. There was no way to find the time otherwise, plus keep it a secret. Since she had orders not to split herself to fly a plane and she was on solid ground, it should work.

The group moved into the restaurant, where a waitress showed them a new room added at the front of the business where the group could keep an eye on their transportation. The restaurant had acquired some adjacent property, making it possible to enlarge the parking area and the business. Only Mara knew that Granda made the deal to allow the space for her family.

Once they were seated, there was still room for more

that might join them. Mara sat with Shira directly behind her chair.

"I want you to order drinks only at this time. Trust me, you will get to eat; only allow me a little of your time, please," said Mara with a chuckle.

They did as directed. When the drinks were at the table, Mara rose from her seat. After telling Shira to stay where she was, she had everyone's attention. She asked for a bubble of silence and began.

"This group has a few things to celebrate and think it time that we did that. We should celebrate: being family; Merry's graduation from her second Chef school with honors; the whole family having earned a certification of Master Degrees at the university; for the two groups of five who moved under fire today and those who have been in that position before; for getting some major challenges completed so we can move out in a day or so. I'm glad to see Melissa has finally decided to join us; thank you, Jerry. Because I head this family and Granda oversees it with me, I have some gifts I wish to bestow on each of you. Merry for you, there is a white Chef's coat and hat with your name on both plus that book you were looking at." The items were given to the blushing girl when she moved to Mara's place at the table.

"All of you have Master Degrees. You are a smart group, and I'm proud of every one of you. Keep learning and growing. There is much work to be done; however, it will be done with all of you helping. Every person in this group has a notebook that carries your degrees and licenses, which are a requirement in some cases, like as a pilot, for those who are one. They are at the house in your rooms for that is not information we want where the public can find them. The groups of five that activated today get acknowledged as well as thanked. Your gifts are also in your suites, same reason as previous. I will call a meeting when we get home. Now you may order for we are going to be very busy I understand. Not exactly the way I wanted to do this; however it works and fits the timetable. Love you all," said Mara, who then resumed her seat. She was surprised when everyone stood up and clapped their hands.

She removed the silence bubble, and everyone sat down.

"Way to go, Mom," said Randy, and others echoed the comment. When she got home, Randy was pleased and found a brand new antique pistol in a case sitting on her bed.

The family ordered meals and chatted about general things through the dinner. For once, there was no interruption during the meal. They were having dessert before a group walked in the door and seemed to be looking for someone specifically.

"Shira, move," whispered Mara when she saw the group of ten or twelve people, both males, and females entered the door of the business. They were a bit shabby yet polite as they held the door for an elderly patron who was leaving.

At her comment, everyone moved their chairs back from the table to allow easy rising. They continued to eat; however, they also kept an eye on the group without seeming to. When they turned toward the room where the family was, Mara rose and moved to the door. Shandra was at her elbow and Shira at her other side.

"May we help you?" asked Shandra.

"We are looking for someone that might be here," replied one of those in the group.

"Who might that be?"

"Not sure we should use her name," a woman said, then ducked her head as if she should not have spoken.

"Come in here, all of you. Now stand in this open area and don't move for five seconds. Now, give me the name of who you seek."

"Thunder," said a whisper.

"I am Thunder Press; why do you wish to find me?" asked Mira.

"We had never met before however were advised that we needed to contact you. There is a force on the way to try to destroy your family. Because you aided some of our family, we wished to aid you, if you will allow," said the woman who spoke before.

Thunder looked at Shandra and saw she had her hand raised to the left. Thunder spoke again.

"Who did we aid? Who are you, and in what way do you wish to be part of our lives?" asked Pat as she stood to join her twin.

"I made a search on the network for your name. Some people are causing an uprising in South America, saying they were going to get you. Shi, tell your story," said the first woman to speak.

"You got my Mom's inheritance back to her. She needed it to take care of her Mom, who is getting older, and my sister, who has a disabling disease. Geo," said the woman to another.

"You stopped my Mom from destroying anyone else's family like she did ours, Press," and so it went.

"It sounds like the Thunder justice may have aided you. Now you said people were coming to destroy us, and you wanted to help. Who is coming? In what way do you wish to help, and how qualified are you to do that?" asked Thunder.

"No one would help, believe or trust us. Strange as it might seem, we prefer to be on the side of Justice. All of us have charges against us someplace, yet we are trying to clean up our acts. We know we are not super fighters; can we learn? You give the orders, and we will do our best to follow them. Please, will you give us a chance? Everyone else feels we are worthless and incompetent," said one of the women with tears in her eyes, yet Thunder also saw sincerity.

"Sit down. What would you like to eat? We were having a celebration so join us. Shandra would you ask the waitress to return, please?" asked Thunder, who then became Mara once again.

"How did you meet up, and how did you know where to look for us?" asked Shandra when she returned, for Mara had gone silent.

"We found those who you had helped then asked those in this age group if any of them would be willing to try to find you and offer our services. We will wash dishes if it frees up someone trained to back you. Marsh said he heard someone tell him to come to this town, yet he didn't know why or who it was for he didn't see anyone. We did as he said. We walked some, hitchhiked some, hid some, ran some, and always hit the points where we were to go as soon as we could to meet up with the rest of us. There are more outside. We didn't want to upset the place by all coming in. Once we met in Texas, we happened on a man who said he thought he had met you. He suggested we might want to try Montana. A semi came by, and we asked if all of us could hitch a ride to Montana. He asked where in this state, and we told him what the man in Texas told us. He chuckled but didn't seem to be laughing at us as others had. We were let out in this town and told to find the hospital. None of us are sick; however, we tried to do whatever anyone told us. The woman at the hospital said if we were to find you, this was a place to look. That is how we got here," replied the woman who wanted to be on the side of Justice.

"Conversation over, for now, order your meals, please, as the waitress is here," said Mara.

"T2, would you be willing to move with guards and bring in the rest of this bunch? We need to order more transportation from home," commented Mara.

Pat tagged Jo, and they went outside. They found a group of young people sitting on the grass out of the way. All were in their early twenties and looked like they should be in school someplace though their clothing was ragged, and some looked like they had never seen a decent meal.

"Are you with Shi, Press, and Geo?" asked Pat.

"Yes, why do you ask?"

"You are invited inside for a meal. Would you care to join us?"

"You don't want a bunch of trash in there. We don't dress fancy cause we been on the road for a rather long time and didn't have much to start with," said one of the group.

"No one will notice for you will be joining my family, come on," Pat responded.

They got up and tried to brush the dust from their clothing, then followed her inside. Each removed their hat and stood at the back wall of the room where the family was.

"Gals, you need to follow me, and we will give you a chance to wash your face and hands. Kennet will you handle the guys, please?" asked Mara.

As she moved, so did Shandra, and Dan went with Kennet.

"Okay, folks, this is a bunch that Thunder has passed as needing us as much as we need them. There is more to this story; however, we will have to get home before we hear it and then only if they want to tell us. They asked for our trust, even as we would ask for theirs. Let's give them a chance. Thunder passed them after all, and one should never turn away a possible friend," commented Randy after asking Granda for silence.

"Okay, Doc, we will do our best. Space out, folks, so there is room for all of them to be intermingled with us. We need to take them to get some decent clothes at a store and tell them it is our uniform if you will. I will foot the bill.

While we are doing that would someone be willing to go get another bus so that we can take them shopping?" said Jimmy.

"We depart in a day or two and will need to take them along. Be thinking about what we will do with them on the next trip. They need protection for they have no training. As we are the trainers and won't be here, they will need training on the flight, I would imagine," added Rae.

"Wonder if they are going to become family or just additions? If family, we might have to take two planes. Put the men on one and the women on the other one. Mara will ask when we get home," commented Granda to get them thinking.

When the group returned, they had been given the oaths and noted the changed seating in the area. Some smiles came out, although tentative, as they each filled one of the empty seats.

Dan walked out the door with Gwen, and they were getting on the bus. Jo ran out and joined them. They pulled out of the lot and headed home.

"Kids, why not contact the tutors and ask them to bring a van and a bus to meet us? That way, one of you can drive the bus, or I can, and they won't be gone long, nor will we," offered Jo.

Dan stopped immediately and asked the computer to contact the tutors for him.

"This is Dan, Mara's son. Would a couple of you be willing to meet us on the road from town? We need another bus. Use one of your vans to take the driver back once we meet you. Can you get to the city limits? We will be sitting there. Yes, at Fourth and Washington of the Stanley exit. Thank you," Dan turned to Jo.

"You heard me; they will be there as soon as they can," he told his fellow passengers.

When they reached the location, a bus and van were waiting. Dan jumped out and thanked them for being so prompt. Gwen moved to the bus just delivered, and they found themselves again in the restaurant's parking lot.

"Mom needs to have backup vehicles in town. It takes too long to run home and get one," commented Dan.

Mara heard him and took care of the issue. From then on, there were always additional vehicles in town to get them where they had to go when more than expected arrived.

Once the combined group finished eating, Granda got up to pay the bill; however, Mara waved her back and did it herself. Shandra remained at her side.

"We need the full bill for our group. Thank you for your patience. Have included a gratuity for the cooks and all who made this a good experience for our guests. There may be others from time to time. Remember how you would feel in their situations," advised Mara with her signature smile.

She looked outside and saw that the buses were in place, and the group finished eating. Moving in the buses' direction, she did not notice the man watching from the corner of the building, for she focused on the vehicles in the lot.

Shandra, however, saw him and was ready. He ignored the two women yet was watching the door of the building.

"Granda, don't let anyone leave. We have an issue," said Shandra, for as Mara's guard, she had access.

Mara heard the call and watched her guard, then followed her lead.

Mara and Shandra walked to the restaurant's east side, away from where Shandra saw the man, then ran behind the building to get behind the man. He had a rifle in hand and was trying to hide it behind his leg.

"Watch my back," said Shandra, who moved forward and

clipped the man behind the ear, catching the rifle before it fell though she let him land as he would.

Both women had their normal going out gloves on, and though others did not see them, they kept them from things that would have been dangerous or to keep from putting fingerprints on anything.

Shandra unloaded the weapon and removed all weapons from the man. Then they removed the bandoliers that he wore with the shells for the rifle and pistols. They found a billfold in his pocket, giving them an ID. Jesrey Summers, it read home Madison, WI age forty-two. He had a money belt on that held two million in cash. The money went to their vault at home. It would be turned in to Rae for authentication before being added to the bank accounts.

"Now, what do we do with him?" asked Shandra.

"I am not going to let him destroy our evening. Put him in the basement, and I will freeze him until we get home. We can deal with him then," responded Mara.

Shandra did as directed and then called Granda to let her know it was safe to allow their group to come to the buses, for Pat had checked them out as that was her first request. Once everyone was loaded, it was time to go shopping. They had placed a call to the men's store for the male portion of their group, and the women said they were fine with shopping there for boots, hat, and jeans. Only jeans worked for the women. The rest they would have to get at a woman's store. Mara didn't mind. She could tell that they were a bit embarrassed even to ask; however, Mara didn't flinch at all, just told them to go ahead. They finished at the men's store and moved to the woman's store, down the hall.

"Mom, I am very proud of you. You are doing wonders in the lives of this bunch. They meant it when they said you tell them what to do, and they would do their best to get it done," Randy commented, for she had left her patients in the care of the hospital so she could attend the festivities.

"I was never without, maybe not the best available, however, never without what was needed. I can only imagine my feelings if in their shoes. They will not have less than I have if they work with me. I want them each to pick up a minimum of four pairs of jeans, six shirts, and underwear. Two hats are a must and gloves plus they need two pair of boots and a pair of shoes for church, with a decent pair of slacks and shirts for church or dresses if the females prefer. We will wait on the winter stuff as I think they might get a little stronger and heavier due to training. We will buy that stuff closer to time. Shandra, I do not know how to relate to this bunch. Please, will you help me out? I will watch and learn only please will you get them squared away?" asked Mara.

Shandra signaled for Cherry to take her place with Mara and moved to where the young women were.

"Would you be open to a few suggestions?" asked Shandra.

"Oh yes, we don't know what we are supposed to purchase," said one of the women.

Shandra gave them a list of what they should purchase and how many. She helped them make sure there were no skin-tight jeans, no sleeveless shirts, no fancy boots, and no bangles on the jeans, just standard working gear. They each got a jeans jacket for chilly nights or rainy days. Then she led them to another store, and they picked up a rain poncho for those days were coming soon. The guys followed along and purchased whatever the women did that they felt they might need. Gloves, hats, and boots came from that western wear store. Later they could get other items as needed.

Shandra continued making suggestions for the females to get everything they needed.

The men had Kennet to see that they, too, got what was required.

"Use the front basement as the back one has a rider." Shandra directed for she had put oxygen in for the man that was frozen.

Mara paid for the purchases, and it was time to head home.

"This new batch will be in the west wing. Don't know if we should put the guys and gals on two different floors or let them decide," commented Mara to her guard after asking for a silence bubble.

"The women will have the floor with us. The males will be on the floor with the men. We will have no discussion there. We have children living with us; let us not set a bad example," said Shandra sternly.

"Thank you," said Mara with a smile. That was her preference as well. She just wasn't sure how to address this bunch. She had never been that age, and whatever it was, she was not comfortable with the situation.

"I know, dear. However, it is alright. If I had a dime for every new troop I had to break in, I would be rich. Now I am the richest ever; you are my Mom," said Shandra with a smile, for she seriously meant it.

Mara hugged her Mom despite the cramped bus seats. When they reached home, the men escorted the boys/ men to their floor and told them to pick out rooms for now. The AI had spaces open according to the number of new persons on site.

Randy escorted the girls to their new quarters and got them settled.

When they reached home, each of the Thunder teams received a boxed .32 dated a long time ago. Each of those who held Master degrees found their notebooks on the coffee table in their front room.

"Now all I have to do is figure out how we are going to train this new bunch while flying to Switzerland or Ireland," said Mara to her guard.

"Do the same as with the rooms. You now have men that can fly; why not have them control the men's plane and use the usual pilots the women do for the flight?" offered Shandra, for she could understand what Mara must be going through.

To react to people her age and have no reference to use as she said, 'I have never been that age.'

Poor kid, Shandra thought, then she thought of the twenty years she had lost to keep up with this kid. Who was kidding, she wondered, yet kept it inside?

A soft bell sounded, and everyone headed for the dining room. New people learned that meant that Mara had called a meeting. It had allowed enough time for mothers to get their small ones in bed, and the bell was soft enough not to bother the little ones.

Mara had sent the students to their rooms while she got the under-five group ready for bed and told the others to do the same. Joy came with Joey and put him to bed. Kelly arrived with her Mom. Then the older kids were checked on, and it was time for the meeting. With hugs around, the children were all ready for bed and would most likely be asleep by the time she returned to her bed.

The adults made their way to the dining room from all directions. The Tutors would be there for the first part of the meeting; then they would be excused to prepare for the following day once they knew the schedule.

Mara was so looking forward to the trip overseas again. Then she realized they would have to delay a day to have the new group tested if they wanted to be adopted and part of the group.